A
of a
a race
against time.

SHADOWS of SALEM

JENNIFER J. FARRINGTON

I dedicate this book to my sister and two cousins, whose love and memories inspired this story.

A special thank you to my family (and the cat) for their unwavering love and support.

Follow your dreams and believe in Magic—it's all around us.

ONE

London to Salem - 1999

Sleep eluded me. Last night had confirmed what I'd already known: he would never stop hurting me, and he would never let me leave peacefully. I had no choice.

Tears trickled down my temples, soaking into my pillow. My swollen lip throbbed, a brutal reminder of what had happened at dinner. I brushed my fingers over the cut, the metallic taste of blood still lingering in my mouth. Squeezing my eyes shut, I tried to push away the stinging, but the ache in my chest wouldn't let up.

Above me, the glow-in-the-dark stars I had stuck to the ceiling when I was seven still shone brightly. I'd spent thirteen years looking up at them, and tonight would be the last.

I tried to calm my racing heart, listening to my sister's soft breathing across the room. Each inhale was a gentle whisper, each exhale a quiet sigh. Ava was turned toward the wall, her small frame curled beneath the duvet.

I glanced at the clock on my bedside table: 4:10 a.m. It was time.

Adrenaline jolted through me as I sat up, scanning the room one last time. The familiar chaos stared back at me—books stacked on my desk, framed photos on the shelf of Ava, our cousins Elisa and Salma, and me pulling silly faces, and our favorite VHS tapes leaning against the TV: *Scream*, *Practical Magic*, and *Titanic*.

My gaze landed on the *Titanic* poster on the door, Jack and Rose frozen in that iconic pose at the bow of the ship. Ava and I had seen the film five times at the cinema across the street. The memory made my chest ache. This room had been a sanctuary once, but now it felt like a prison.

I slipped out of bed, already dressed in the jeans and sweater I planned to leave in. Moving carefully to avoid the creaky spots in the floor, I crept to the window. A rare super blue moon hung low in the night sky, its silvery light pouring into the room. It cast the trees below in an otherworldly glow, their bare branches reaching like skeletal fingers toward the stars.

On the windowsill sat the amethyst crystal Julie had given me. I picked it up, cradling it in my palm.

"You'll need this one day," she'd said with a knowing smile. Julie was a regular at my dad's bakery, and the moment she'd mentioned Salem in Massachusetts, five months ago, it had captivated my imagination. She'd told me about the infamous witch trials, the museums, and the mystical charm of the town. "A place like that," she'd said, "is made for new beginnings."

I closed my eyes, clutching the crystal tightly. *Please*, I prayed silently. *Let us get out safely. Let us start over.*

A familiar image appeared into my mind—the large Queen Anne Victorian house, the charming cottage at the back bathed in sunlight, a dark-haired woman at the door saying, "Welcome to the Salem Guesthouse." The vision always left me feeling hopeful, and tonight was no different.

I tucked the crystal into my pocket and turned toward Ava, who was still fast asleep. I perched on the edge of her bed, touching her shoulder gently. "Ava," I whispered. "Wake up. We need to leave now."

She didn't stir. I leaned in closer.

"Ava," I tried again, my voice trembling. "Sis, wake up."

Her eyes fluttered open, unfocused and heavy with sleep. "What…?"

I winced as my lip throbbed, biting back a hiss of pain. "Shhh," I said, raising a finger to my mouth. "We have to go now."

She stared at me for a moment, still groggy, before nodding. Yawning, she peeled the duvet off of her and swung her legs over the edge of the bed, her bare feet brushing the cold floor.

We'd packed light: a change of clothes each, our passports, jewelry, some photos, and the money we'd saved from working at the family bakery. It wasn't much, but it was enough to start over.

I glanced at the notes I'd left on my dressing table, my throat tightening. I could already picture the shock on Mum's face when she found them. Our decision to leave hadn't been easy after years of conditioning, but something in me had finally snapped. I would not go along with his plans, and I definitely wasn't going to leave my sister behind.

Dear Dad,

We've decided to leave and follow our own path, not the one you're forcing on us. Don't look for us. We're never coming back.

Jenna & Ava

Dear Mum,

We're sorry. Please don't worry about us. You'll always be in our hearts. Thank you for everything. We love you.

Jenna & Ava xx

I swallowed the lump in my throat and motioned for Ava to follow me. We tiptoed past our parents' bedroom, my heart hammering. The hallway was pitch dark, the only sound the faint ticking of the clock in the living room.

I wrapped my hand around the front door handle, turning it as slowly as I could until I heard the soft click of the latch. I pulled the door open, holding my breath.

Once we stepped into the communal hallway, I let out a shaky exhale. The usual smell of disinfectant wafted up my nose, and the half-broken ceiling bulb flickered on and off. I looked over my shoulder and saw a tear roll down my sister's cheek. I grabbed her hand, leading her down the three flights of stairs.

The wind was cool against my face when we finally pushed through the building's main door, stepped out onto the street, and headed toward the Stratford tube station.

"Jenna," hissed my sister from behind me. I stopped and followed her gaze. The light in our parents' bedroom had flicked on, and I saw the curtain move. My stomach dropped as the hall light came on next.

"I'm too scared to move," Ava whimpered.

"We don't have a choice," I said, my voice fearful. "Look at me, Ava." I cupped her face, forcing her to meet my eyes. "We're so close. We can do this. Just keep moving."

Tears filled her fearful eyes, mirroring my feelings. She took a deep breath and nodded, and together we walked to the station.

The platform was cold, the wind biting through my jacket as I paced back and forth. The drizzle felt icy on my skin, typical of London; it was early August, and we still hadn't seen a sign of summer. I pulled my hood tighter, glancing anxiously at the tracks, waiting for the Tube to arrive. I kept expecting Dad to appear out of nowhere and drag us back home. The thought made my chest tighten.

When a train rumbled into the station, the screech of the brakes jarred me from my thoughts, and I nudged Ava forward. I scanned the half-empty carriage and quickly sank into the first available seat. As the Tube doors slid shut, I let out a sigh of relief, feeling the tension begin to drain from my shoulders.

"We made it, Jen," Ava said, her eyes bright as she placed her bag between her feet and leaned back in her seat. "Let's hope Elisa and Salma make it to Heathrow on time."

"They'll be there. I have no doubt. Elisa will make sure of it."

Elisa and Salma, our cousins on Dad's side, were just as keen to escape London as we were. We had all saved every penny we could and pooled our money together. Elisa and I were two weeks apart in age, and we had always been inseparable.

When I had first told Elisa about my plan to run away, she had panicked. "So I'll never see you again?"

"You can visit once I'm settled."

"You're the one thing that brings joy to my life. I can't see you only once in a blue moon. Plus, my dad is no different from yours. They live in this warped reality. The outdated rules, the abuse, the restrictions—it's suffocating. I'm coming with you,

Jen." Elisa had always been impulsive, leaping into action with abandon whether she was trying a new skill or diving headfirst into mischief. Her unpredictability added to her magnetic presence.

Salma, a year younger, had immediately insisted on joining us. Analytical by nature, she tended to observe more than she spoke, carefully thinking everything through, but in this case, she hadn't hesitated for a moment. We'd been planning our escape for months, waiting for Ava to turn eighteen. She was the baby of the group, and we all felt protective of her.

Finally I was leaving this depressing place behind. Crime and poverty shadowed every corner of our neighborhood, but my dad did well for himself. He owned a bustling bakery with a dining area in the shopping center just ten minutes from our flat. Since leaving school, I'd been working there, but only because I wasn't allowed to work anywhere else.

The bakery was a haven for weary customers, due to the cheap prices. I would constantly spray air fresheners as their odors of sweat and damp coats was unbearable at times. It also attracted leering men, their comments scraping against my skin.

"All right, gorgeous," or "Cheer up, love, might never happen," they'd say. I hated that phrase. What was there to be cheerful about?

I endured it all, keeping my head down, saving every penny for this escape. I couldn't let anything stop me—not the fear, not the uncertainty, not him.

Ava's voice broke through my thoughts. "Oh no! Your lip is bleeding," she exclaimed, her voice a bit too loud for the quiet of the train. She fumbled through her pockets, pulling out a tissue.

I wiped the blood away, trying to hide the sting.

"Sis, I'm so sorry," Ava whispered, her eyes welling with guilt. "I should've done something. I should've stopped Dad from punching you, but…I was too scared." She looked down, her hands twisting the end of her jacket nervously. Ava had strikingly delicate features and a slender, almost fragile frame. I was grateful that our dad rarely laid a hand on her; perhaps he saw how breakable she was. If he had hit her the way he hit me, I'm certain he would have caused her serious harm.

I forced a smile, placing a hand on her knee. "Don't worry. It doesn't hurt," I lied, trying to sound strong for her. As her older sister, I had to be.

She didn't look convinced, but she nodded, gracefully brushing back her long, straight, silky brown hair.

The memory of last night clawed its way back into my mind. My dad had arranged for me to marry his friend's son at the end of the month, someone I had never met. The plan was simple: get married, bring him from Turkey to the UK on a spousal visa, and build a life together—whether I wanted to or not.

"You'll fall in love after marriage," Dad had insisted. "It's worked for generations, and it will work for you."

When I had refused, he'd hit me. Every time I'd tried to reason with him, he had threatened me. And my mum had never objected. "Your dad knows best," she'd say, her voice hollow. "You can't have a boyfriend; you have to be a virgin on your wedding night or you'll bring shame to the family."

"How can anyone even tell?" I'd retorted once, bitterness creeping into my voice.

Her answer had made my skin crawl. "You have to provide the sheet with the virginity blood after intercourse." Apparently, family members waited outside until the husband handed the bedding over like some grotesque trophy.

"Mum, are you hearing yourself?" I had shouted. "Did you do that?"

"Well…no," she admitted, her voice sheepish. "It wasn't expected of me, since I'm not Turkish."

I couldn't understand her. She had married someone outside of these suffocating traditions, and yet she defended them. I resented her for it. And I hated my dad.

"It's different for men," he always said, a smug smile on his face.

Thinking about it now, anger burned in my chest. Not me. I would not conform. I would run forever if I had to.

If it hadn't been for Julie, though, I wouldn't have known where to start. She had been my guiding star through all of this, helping me plan every detail of the escape. She had arranged for us to stay at the same guesthouse she'd visited in Salem. She'd negotiated a good price, helped me buy one-way plane tickets, and even provided detailed directions from Boston to Salem.

"You won't find anywhere better," she had said, her eyes dreamy. "The view from the house is stunning. You can walk by the wharf, eat fresh fish…" She had chuckled then, a mischievous gleam in her eye. "It's not for the fainthearted, though. The house can be a bit spooky at times, with its creaky floorboards. And there might be occasional whispers. Not to mention the maze." This had only piqued my interest more.

Once we arrived at the airport, Ava scanned the crowd frantically. "Where are they?" she asked, her voice nervous as we headed toward the check-in desk.

"They'll be here," I said, trying to sound more confident than I felt. We stood in the queue patiently.

At the desk, a blond middle-aged woman with a flat expression glanced between our passports and our faces. Her eyes lingered a little too long on my swollen lip.

"Place your suitcase on the scale, miss," she said.

"We don't have suitcases," I replied with a forced smile. "We plan to shop there."

Her gaze didn't soften. She handed the passports back slowly, as if debating whether to say something. I grabbed them quickly and walked away.

I checked the departure board; the nine-fifteen flight from London to Boston was leaving on time from gate fifteen, and we'd start boarding in less than two hours. Ava was growing more anxious by the minute. She stared at the doors, tears glistening in her eyes. "They're not coming," she whispered. "I bet they changed their minds."

"They'll be here," I repeated, though doubt gnawed at me. "Let's wait for them at the gate. We can grab snacks while we wait."

A passenger hurried past, his bag brushing against my arm. I had to jump out of the way as another man rushed to keep up with him.

As we passed through security, memories of our holidays to my dad's village—the only holidays we ever took—came flooding back. There, time seemed frozen. Men ruled everything. Women weren't even allowed to go for coffee alone, and if a woman visited the supermarket twice in one day, people assumed she was out looking for men. If you weren't married by twenty, something was wrong with you. "Maybe she's not a virgin," people would whisper. My aunts often told me I was getting old and that soon no one would want me. The pressure to conform, to stay silent, was crushing, and everyone gossiped about everything.

It wasn't just me. Girls in the village ran away to big cities all the time, trying to escape lives they hadn't chosen. Some succeeded. Others didn't.

On the plane, Ava sat beside me. I glanced at the two empty seats in front of me, feeling a sinking sensation in my chest. It seemed less and less likely that Elisa and Salma would make it. I couldn't help but picture their future—they were likely to be married off this year or the next to misogynistic men. They would be expected to cook, clean, and care for babies while the men made all the decisions. Some men cheated, some were abusive, and some controlled all the finances. Though a few marriages of this sort appeared successful from the outside, most were unhappy unions full of regret and despair. The tiny village where Dad's family lived, remote and isolated, was notorious for domestic murders and suicides.

"I want the window seat!" Elisa's familiar voice called out from farther up the aisle. She looked down at her ticket, searching for the right seat number.

Relief crashed over me like a wave. I let out a laugh, tears blurring my vision. Ava clapped her hands, her excitement bubbling over. "They made it!" she shrieked, drawing disapproving glances from other passengers. "Salma, *over here*!" I hated when strangers looked at me, but my sister didn't care.

Elisa, standing tall at five feet seven, placed her bright yellow bag in the overhead compartment with ease, beaming as she closed the door. "We nearly didn't make it," she said with relief in her voice.

A pretty flight attendant with an American accent approached. "I need you to take a seat, miss."

Ava stood up and moved up a row to sit next to Salma, and they immediately dove into a conversation about how they had each made their escape. Elisa rolled her eyes, her back to the flight attendant, and mimicked, *"I need you to take a seat miss."* She then squeezed past me to sit by the window.

"We nearly didn't make it," she repeated, hugging me. "Dad wasn't home—probably at the casino again—but Mum was up all night, kept going to the—" She stopped mid-sentence, and her expression darkened, concern replacing her relief. "Your lip, Jen—did Uncle do that to you?" Her voice was filled with quiet anger. "I don't know if I hate your dad or mine more."

"It's fine," I said quickly, brushing it off. "It's nothing."

"Well, he won't be doing that again, that's for sure," she chuckled, leaning back into her seat. Elisa never took things too seriously and was always the life of the group. She effortlessly brought humor to even the most tense situations. Her sharp wit, playful banter, and slightly cynical outlook always makes us laugh when things get tough. Salma, on the other hand, is a calming presence, the quiet anchor. She is shy and reserved, but her kindness shines through in her actions; she is always ready to help and likes to keep the peace.

A flash of lightning illuminated the cabin, followed by the low, rumbling roar of thunder. The storm outside seemed to mirror the whirlwind of emotions within me.

"I don't like flying," Salma said in front of us, her voice shaky. She turned toward Elisa. "How many hours did you say it was?"

"Seven hours and forty minutes. Hopefully we'll take off on time. Boston is five hours behind, so if we land on schedule… let's see…" Elisa checked her watch, calculating. "We'll get there around midday."

Salma groaned and leaned back, letting her head thud softly against the seat. "This is going to be loooong. I need something to pass the time. I forgot to grab my book. I was just getting to the good part too—*Flowers in the Attic*."

"What's it about?" Ava asked, genuinely curious.

Salma's voice perked up. "Well, the mum locks her kids in the attic for four years, and the older brother and sister end up having sex."

Ava's voice rose, a mix of shock and disgust. "That's gross. I won't be reading that anytime soon." Her head disappeared farther down in her seat.

Salma just shrugged, unbothered. "It's based on a true story. I'm definitely getting another copy in Boston. I can't wait to finish it."

The engines roared to life, the deep rumble vibrating through the cabin. My seat shook slightly as the plane began to gain speed, the force pressing me back. I gripped the armrest tightly, my stomach flipping as the nose tilted upward and the ground disappeared beneath us.

For a moment, I felt weightless. The sensation filled me with a sense of freedom. I was finally leaving it all behind—Dad's anger, Mum's silence, the bakery, the flat. Everything that had chained me to London was falling away, shrinking and then disappearing below.

The plane levelled off, and the vibration eased. I closed my eyes, exhaustion settling in as I wrapped my jacket around me like a cocoon. My eyelids grew heavier with every passing second, and soon the familiar vision crept into my mind once again.

The house appeared first—that beautiful Queen Anne Victorian with a grand porch and tall windows gleaming in the sunlight. Then the dark-haired woman emerged, her green eyes piercing as she stepped toward me. She smiled, her voice soft and lilting as she said, "Welcome to the Salem Guesthouse."

Her words lingered in my ear as sleep finally claimed me.

TWO

The plane journey was uneventful, giving me plenty of time to second-guess my decision. Doubts crept in during those long hours over the Atlantic, but each time they did, I reminded myself of the miserable life I'd left behind—a life where I could never be myself. Halfway across the world was my chance to breathe. I was a bird being let out of its cage for the first time. I was free.

Salma and Ava passed the hours on the plane by chatting nonstop, their laughter a comforting background hum. I smiled at their silly jokes, I loved the way their energy fed off each other. Elisa, on the other hand, was quieter. She sat by the window, staring out at the clouds, occasionally tapping her pen against her lips. Every so often, she scribbled something in the small notebook she carried everywhere. I sensed that, like me, she was mapping out all the possibilities ahead. The plane touched down at Logan Airport with a jolt, the engines faded as the pilot welcomed us to Boston.

We felt a little lost in the busy airport, I kept asking for directions and we just about managed to get the two p.m. train to Salem. We stowed our bags in the overhead metal racks, settling into the train car. The seats, upholstered in shades of blue and gray fabric, were arranged in neat rows, some facing forward, others clustered around small tables. This time, I chose the large window seat, watching as the city blurred into the rocky coastline. The landscape shifted as we moved, the old colonial homes dotted the horizon. The hour-long train ride was mostly steady, though it occasionally jerked, swaying gently as the train tracked its way north.

When we finally stepped off the train in Salem, the warm salty breeze welcomed us. I took a deep breath, savoring its freshness. It felt surreal to be here, standing on foreign soil, but for the first time in years, I felt alive.

"We should head into town and buy some essentials," Elisa suggested, taking a sip from her bottled water. She handed it to me, and I took a swig, easing my dry throat.

I unfolded the map we'd picked up at the small station, squinting at the unfamiliar streets. "Okay, we go straight ahead," I said, pointing. "That should take us into the town center."

Elisa lit a cigarette, nodding as she blew out a plume of smoke. Salma's stomach growled loudly enough for all of us to hear it. "We should also grab something to eat while we're there," she said.

Ava, who'd been trailing behind, caught up to us, swinging her rucksack carelessly. It smacked into an old man's walking stick, and he stumbled. The man steadied himself, his face turning red. "Are you blind?!" he snapped. "Can't you see I'm walking? Damn tourists!"

Ava's mouth opened and closed like a fish before she burst into laughter. "Is he still looking at me?" she asked Salma.

Salma peeked over her shoulder and grinned. "Nah, he's moved on. And why was he so close to you in the first place?"

Elisa stubbed out her cigarette, glancing around the crowded street. "We really need to get moving. We look like total tourists standing here, blocking the entrance."

As we reached the center of Salem, I glanced around, feeling an eerie sense of familiarity. The old brick buildings, the narrow alleys, the distant sound of church bells tolling—it was as though I had walked these streets before. Turning a corner, I spotted a towering church steeple that tugged at the edges of my memory. The atmosphere was rich with history, and the timeless charm of the town felt like a promise, a whisper of inspiration and hope for a better future.

After picking up our essentials, we stopped in front of a weathered wooden house, its creaky sign swinging gently in the breeze. strega's coffee house, the sign read in creepy font. There were cakes displayed in the windows, each one adorned with spider webs and green ghouls. The door handle was shaped like a gnarled broomstick. As I stared inside the shop, a vision of Ava and Elisa working behind the counter came to me.

"We are going in here," I announced.

"Okay, boss," Salma teased, raising her eyebrows as Ava pushed the door open. The bell above it jingled softly, and we stepped inside. Elisa stumbled on the step and slammed into the doorframe with a loud bang. The café fell silent. Dozens of eyes turned toward her. Elisa's cheeks turned beet red, and she immediately looked down at the floor, pretending to find it fascinating.

Salma tried not to laugh but couldn't help herself. "No one noticed. You okay, sis?"

"Fine," Elisa muttered through gritted teeth, avoiding eye contact with all of us.

A young, pretty waitress approached us. She was pale with jet-black hair and thick eyeliner that made her dark eyes look even sharper. Her eyebrows were pierced, and a small black teardrop tattoo sat beneath her left eye. I thought I liked dressing in all black, but she loved it more it seemed, she was wearing black jeans and a tight black shirt that matched her jet-black hair and makeup.

"Hey there, welcome!" she chirped in a high-pitched American accent, handing four menus to Salma. Her nails were painted black, and her fingers were covered in silver rings. "Have a seat, and I'll be with you shortly." She gestured toward a red booth with a black table shaped like cauldron in the center.

The walls were covered in witch-themed paintings. A warm aroma of coffee filled the room, and the low murmur of conversations between customers wrapped around me like an echo from a dream. I couldn't shake the feeling that I'd been here before.

"Why does everything in this town look like it's Halloween?" Ava whispered, flipping through the menu. "This place looks like a witch's den, and the waitress looks like a witch, too."

I clasped my hands, leaning forward. "Well, in the late sixteen hundreds, this town was full of real witches. At least, that's what the townspeople believed. They were so scared of them that they hanged anyone suspected of witchcraft. They believed they were casting evil spells or something."

Ava's eyes widened. "What?! Is this a true story, or did you read it in one of your fantasy books?"

"No, I'm being serious." I said, smiling at her skepticism. "Julie told me. Twenty people were executed. We should check out the museums so you can read about it for yourself." I couldn't wait to learn and explore more, with or without the girls. Witches had fascinated me from a young age. I loved to read about how on Halloween Eve, witches would cast spells and invite the dead to walk among the living.

Ava leaned back in her seat. "If that's the case," she said, lowering her voice, "is this a safe place to start a new life?"

Before we could answer, the waitress returned, flashing a smile with too many teeth. "What would y'all like?"

"I'll have a strawberry milkshake and maple pancakes," Salma said, sliding the menu back toward the waitress.

"Make that two," Ava added, grinning at Salma.

"Pancakes and coffee, please," I said.

Elisa looked at me, smirking. "Same for me." We both loved coffee.

The waitress scribbled down our order on a notepad covered in doodles of stars and crescent moons. "Are y'all from England?" she asked, her accent thick and cheerful. "I love the accent."

"Yes, we are," Elisa said with a polite smile. "It's our first day here. Can you recommend some places for us to visit?"

"Depends on how long y'all are here for," the waitress replied, popping her gum obnoxiously. When none of us answered, she continued, "Well, you gotta see the witch museum, for starters. And if you come back during Halloween, you've gotta try the ghost tours and the trolley ride through town. Oh, and Gallows Hill—that's where the hangings happened. Super spooky."

I glanced at Ava smugly, raising an eyebrow as if to say, *See? I told you so.* Ava rolled her eyes and looked away, trying to hide her discomfort.

Leaning in closer, the waitress lowered her voice conspiratorially. "If you're lucky, you might even see the ghosts of some of the witches who were hanged. They like to linger, you know."

Salma snorted softly, unimpressed. Switching to Turkish, she said, "I don't believe any of that. Witches and ghosts are just old myths to scare people."

Also in Turkish, Elisa responded dismissively, "I don't believe her. She's just trying to get under your skin. Ignore her."

Ava whispered, "Yeah, she's just fishing for a reaction. Don't fall for it."

The waitress tilted her head slightly, her brows furrowing as she tried to decipher what we were saying. After a moment, she straightened up, shrugged, and said, "Well, anyway, my name's Megan. I'll be back with your drinks and pancakes soon. And by the way, the coffee's refillable."

Elisa and I exchanged excited looks, mouthing, "Refills!" at the same time.

Megan spun around and walked back toward the kitchen, her shoes clicking softly against the floor.

I turned to the girls with a triumphant grin. "See? The stories are real!"

Elisa yawned, brushing me off. "Just because she said it doesn't make it true. Even if the hangings actually happened, I still don't believe in ghosts." She rubbed her tired eyes and leaned back against the booth.

Ava nudged me gently under the table with her foot. "Sis, I think you're going to fit right in here. You're always going on about hearing things and seeing visions."

I shrugged but didn't respond. My sister thought I was strange, but I didn't blame her. There had been one night years ago when I'd woken up in a trance and told her that her best friend would be hit by a car on the way to school. I didn't remember saying it, but it had actually happened the following week. Whatever I pictured in my mind's eye—whatever I truly believed—always somehow came to pass. I didn't understand why, but I didn't question it anymore.

"I believe in all things supernatural," I said after a moment, my voice calm and steady. "The mysteries of life, the things we can't explain…there's more to this world than what we can see."

Ava shook her head, a faint smile tugging at her lips, but Salma didn't look convinced.

As the girls chatted, I turned away, letting their voices fade into the background. My gaze drifted to the bustling street outside the window, which hummed with life. A building across the road drew my attention: the Bluebell Lodge. The name rang a faint bell in my mind. Had Julie mentioned it? I couldn't remember.

Suddenly, an image flickered into my mind. Inside the lodge, I saw a young man sitting at a desk, staring at a computer. He had messy blond hair and an easy smile. A strange sensation bloomed in my chest, starting in my stomach and rising to my heart like a bubble about to pop. Butterflies. I didn't know who the man was, but something told me I needed to meet him. The vision was so vivid, so real, that I nearly stood up. I could go over there, ask for directions to the Salem Guesthouse, and see what happened. Maybe I could figure out what the vision meant.

"Jen, your pancakes are here," Elisa said, interrupting my thoughts. She handed me my cutlery, her brow furrowed slightly.

I blinked, shaking off the trance, and let out a long breath.

"What's wrong?" Elisa asked, studying me. "Why were you holding your breath?"

"I don't know," I admitted, fidgeting with my napkin. "I didn't realize I was."

She narrowed her eyes. "You didn't hear a word we said, did you?"

I smiled sheepishly, but before I could respond, Salma leaned toward Ava and whispered, "If this guesthouse even exists! We haven't even met this Julie she always goes on about."

I frowned, pouting slightly. The girls loved teasing me about my visions.

Salma stuffed a forkful of pancake into her mouth. "Mmm," she moaned. "These are the best pancakes I've ever had. No wonder Americans love them so much."

I cut into my pancakes and took a bite, letting the sweet buttery taste coat my tongue. "Of course the guesthouse exists," I said. "How could Julie book us a month's stay if it didn't?"

Ava, sipping her milkshake, raised an eyebrow. "Do we even have enough money for that?"

"Elisa and I did the math," I said confidently. "We have seven thousand pounds saved, and we exchanged a thousand at the airport, which is about fourteen hundred dollars. Altogether, we should have enough to last us a few months until we find work."

Megan returned to refill our coffee, her smile sharp. "Y'all are staying for a few months?" she asked casually. "Sorry, I didn't mean to eavesdrop." I didn't like Megan being so nosey, so I didn't answer her.

"That's all right," replied Elisa, wiping her mouth with a napkin and handing Megan her plate. "We plan to stay for good if we can find jobs here."

Megan's eyes lit up. "I can ask around if y'all want."

Ava sensed my uneasiness and cut in. "Er, can we get the bill, please? We need to be going."

I watched Megan as she took the plates away, then turned and glared at Elisa. "Not sure if we should be telling her our life story."

"Who said anything about our life story?" Elisa replied defensively. "How do you expect to make any friends or network if we make no effort?"

She had a point. "You're right," I said, rubbing my neck, which felt stiff. "I feel a bit tired. It's been a long day."

In truth, I didn't like small talk and rarely made an effort with anyone. People often told my sister that I was standoffish, whereas she was the friendlier one.

Megan returned with the bill and handed Elisa a note. "This is my cell number. Call me or pop back in, and I'll see what I can do about finding you some work. I can even ask my boss, Antonio, if there's a job for you here. I think he said he was looking for someone. Do you have any experience?"

"Yes, I used to run my dad's café in London," Elisa responded. "Shouldn't take me long to get used to things here." Like me, Elisa had only ever worked for her father.

"Well, come back tomorrow. Antonio's a bit busy now."

"Thank you," Elisa said with a smile.

We stepped outside, and Elisa tucked Megan's number into her bag, grinning. "See? If you don't make the effort, you miss opportunities."

I smiled faintly, conceding. "Fair enough."

"Cell number?" Salma asked. "Does she mean a mobile phone? Looks like everyone here has one."

"We should each get one, when we start working" Ava suggested.

"Not a bad idea," I said. "It would provide peace of mind when we need to get hold of each other." My dad hadn't allowed us to have phones back in London. He didn't want us talking to boys or making plans he couldn't control. But here in Salem, things were different.

Here, we could live.

THREE

I had to find the man from my vision. I gestured to the elegant building across the street and said, "I'm going to pop into the Bluebell Lodge and ask for directions to the Salem Guesthouse."

"Sure," Elisa replied, already pulling out a cigarette. "We'll wait here."

I walked up the path, noting the sign that read built in 1795. The building didn't show its age much. Its exterior featured white fluted pilasters, and the paint was only slightly weathered.

Pushing open the heavy door, I heard chimes announce my arrival. A young man sat behind the reception desk, his eyes glued to the computer in front of him. He didn't look up until I was only a few feet away. His bright blue eyes met mine, and for a moment, I was caught off guard.

He was in his early twenties, maybe a year or two older than me, with wavy golden hair that looked effortlessly glossy, as though it caught the sunlight even indoors. When he stood up, I noticed his athletic build; his shoulders were broad, and he was easily over six feet.

"Can I help you?" he asked, running a hand through his hair.

I hesitated, my thoughts momentarily scattered. His voice had a casual confidence to it, but there was also something guarded in his tone.

"I'm looking for the Salem Guesthouse," I finally said, working to keep my voice steady.

He blinked, his expression unreadable. "Well, clearly, this is the Bluebell Lodge," he said, gesturing to the sign above the desk with a touch of sarcasm.

"I can see that," I replied curtly. "I need directions."

He threw his hands up in mock exasperation. "What makes you think I know where it is?"

"Well, do you?" I said impatiently, tapping my fingers on the counter. My dad's strict rules about interacting with boys had left me awkward around them, unsure how to handle even the simplest conversations.

He exhaled sharply, clearly puzzled by my tone. His phone pinged, and he looked down at it, frowning as he read whatever message had come through. He began typing, his fingers pressing down hard on the buttons. Cell phones were indeed very popular here, it seemed. In London, not everyone had them.

After a moment, he set the phone back on the desk and slowly raised his eyes to mine again. This time, his gaze lingered, and something shifted in the space between us. He stared at me—really stared. My heart unexpectedly skipped a beat. Then his eyes dropped slightly, focusing on my lips. I stiffened, suddenly remembering the injury I'd tried to cover with makeup. A flush crept up my cheeks, though I doubted it was very noticeable on my olive skin. For reasons I couldn't explain, I felt drawn to him, but I quickly suppressed the feeling and straightened my posture.

"Well?" I prompted.

"Well, what?" he said, his full lips curling into a slight smirk. His bright white teeth flashed when he spoke. He didn't seem to have a single fault.

"Do you know where the Salem Guesthouse is or not?" I asked, shifting my weight nervously from one foot to the other.

He leaned back, rubbing the back of his neck. "*Please* would have been nice."

I ignored the comment, glancing toward the lobby TV as though distracted.

He sighed, shaking his head. "I'll let you off this once, since you're obviously not from around here," he said jovially. I looked down at my feet. "Take a left and walk toward the harbor. It's the largest house on the waterfront—you can't miss it." Then, without another word, he sat down at his computer and began typing again.

As I turned to leave, I felt his eyes on my back. "You're very welcome," he called after me, his voice laced with sarcasm.

I stopped briefly, a small smile tugging at my lips, though I didn't turn around. I stepped through the door and let it close behind me. Maybe I should have said thank you.

Back outside, the girls were waiting. Elisa had just finished her cigarette, and Ava leaned against a lamppost.

"You okay? You look flustered," Salma said, raising an eyebrow.

"The man at the desk was grumpy," I muttered. "I hope everyone here isn't as moody as him."

"Maybe he was upset because we're not staying at his lodge," Salma offered with a shrug.

"Maybe," I said absently. "But he was good-looking." My cheeks suddenly began to burn. "Did I say that out loud?" I laughed.

Elisa looked shocked. "I've never heard you comment on a random guy before!"

To change the subject, I said quickly, "He said the guesthouse is near the harbor, so we're not too far."

We began walking, and Ava looked back over her shoulder. "If that's him, he's looking at you," she whispered, nudging my arm excitedly.

"What?" I turned my head slightly, catching a glimpse of the lodge out of the corner of my eye.

"He's definitely looking," Ava said, almost squealing.

I held my breath and faced forward again, refusing to turn around.

After about ten minutes, the Salem Guesthouse came into view. It was breathtaking. The three-story Queen Anne Victorian mansion majestically overlooked the harbor and marina. Its white exterior and steep navy-blue roof, paired with the iconic navy turret in the center, gave it a magnetic, timeless charm. The balcony above the wraparound porch was the epitome of decorative appeal. A large sign at the entrance reading the salem guesthouse confirmed that we were in the right place.

The déjà vu was overwhelming. This was exactly how Julie had described the house—and just as I had seen it in my visions.

We stepped through the gate in the white picket fence and followed the curved stone walkway, flanked by low hedges. A vintage lamppost stood in the corner of the porch, glowing softly, that added to the house's historical appeal.

"This is it," I said softly, my voice tinged with awe. As I walked up the granite steps, the girls lingered behind, too enchanted to speak.

I pushed through the large oak door, chimes tinkling above me. For some reason, every door I had walked through in Salem so far had chimes, almost like it was a form of protection. Inside, the house felt warm and inviting, with hardwood floors that gleamed under the soft glow of the chandelier. Stained-glass windows splashed subtle colors across the foyer, and a handsome terra-cotta fireplace stood next to the grand staircase. The faint aroma of lavender and sandalwood incense lingered in the air.

The girls followed me in, and we waited by the reception desk opposite the grand staircase. It was covered in notes and a teacup that read salem guesthouse. I loved how the first few steps led up to an octagonal landing with leather seating under the window, providing an unobstructed view of the sea. I stared at the many portraits on the walls—previous owners, perhaps—along with oil paintings of landscapes.

"Good afternoon," a voice called from one of the side rooms. I turned toward the sound, and my breath caught in my throat.

A woman emerged—a woman I recognized instantly. I had visited this house many times in my visions, and I'd seen her here every time. Those piercing emerald-green eyes, her jet-black wavy hair, and the dimple in her left cheek—everything was the same. The wrinkles around her eyes didn't detract from her beauty. I could only imagine how exquisite she must have been when she was younger.

"Did you just say you've seen me before?" she asked, locking eyes with me.

My heart pounded. Had she just read my thoughts?

Elisa frowned, looking between us, twirling her long auburn curls around her finger. "I didn't hear Jenna say anything."

"I…" My voice faltered, and I smiled awkwardly. "No, we've never met. It's my—well, *our* first time in Salem."

The woman's lips curled into a knowing smile. "I see," she said softly. "Well, my name is Rosalie."

Rosalie's eyes skimmed over the cluttered desk in front of her. She seemed momentarily distracted as she scanned through a large appointment book, its edges slightly worn. Her movements were deliberate, her long fingers trailing over the pages.

"Do you have a reservation?" She asked without looking up, her voice smooth and warm, like honey drizzled into tea.

"Yes, it's under Julie," I replied quickly. "She called about two weeks ago."

Rosalie's expression remained calm as she flipped through the pages, her dark brows furrowing slightly. "Julie…" she murmured, then paused. "What's the last name?"

I rubbed my chin, trying to recall. "I think she said Violet—or maybe Varlett? Something like that."

Her fingers froze in the middle of turning a page. Slowly, she looked up at me, her emerald eyes narrowing slightly. "Did you say Varlett?"

"Yes, I think that's what she told me," I answered, suddenly unsure. "I hope I'm not pronouncing it wrong."

Rosalie straightened, her gaze sharpening. "Hmm…" She flipped through the pages again, but her expression remained unreadable. A long pause stretched between us.

"I'm afraid," she said finally, her voice quieter now, "that there's no booking under that name."

"What?" My stomach twisted. "There must be a mistake! Could you check again, please? Maybe it's under Jenna Aslan? She told me she'd arranged a month-long stay for the four of us."

Rosalie glanced at me, then at Elisa, who had stepped closer to the counter. "What's going on?" my cousin whispered in Turkish, nudging my arm.

I shrugged, feeling confused and uneasy. Julie had been so confident when she'd told me about the booking. "I've arranged everything for you," she'd assured me. "The owner is a lovely lady named Rosa—well, Rosalie. She's in her sixties but looks much younger. She'll take good care of you all. She treats her guests like family. I've always had a wonderful time there and felt right at home. All you have to do is turn up."

The last time I'd seen her before we left, Julie had given me a tight hug. "Life is too short, lovey," she'd said. "Live in the moment. Don't look back, and don't let fear stop you." In her embrace, I'd felt safer than I ever had with my own parents. Every time she'd walked into the bakery, the grey clouds that always hovered above my head had lifted. She had often sat by the window with a small cup of black coffee, her presence always a beacon of comfort.

Julie was in her early thirties but had wisdom far beyond her years. Once when my dad had shouted at me from the kitchen, she had looked at me with sadness in her eyes. When he wasn't around, I had confided in her.

Now, standing in front of Rosalie, I felt a wave of doubt and anxiety crash over me. What if I was wrong to trust Julie? What if there was no booking?

"Are you absolutely sure?" I asked, trying to keep the worry out of my voice.

Rosalie sighed, her fingers drumming lightly on the desk. "I can double-check…" She began clicking through her computer system, her brows furrowing once more.

Elisa, noticing my growing anxiety, stepped forward. "Maybe Julie booked us under a different name?" she suggested helpfully.

I nodded. "It's possible. Can you try one more time, try Jenna Aslan please?"

Rosalie scanned the screen carefully, but after what felt like an eternity, she shook her head. "I'm sorry, there's no booking here under that name either." Her voice was soft, almost regretful, as if she hated being the bearer of bad news.

My shoulders sagged. The gravity of everything—the long journey, the uncertainty, the sheer exhaustion—settled heavily on me.

Elisa, ever the optimist, took over. "Is there any chance we can still stay here, even if there's been a mix-up? We can pay. We just need somewhere to sleep."

Rosalie studied us for a moment, her piercing gaze landing on each of our faces in turn. Then, slowly, she nodded.

"Well, as it happens, you've arrived at the perfect time," she said. "I have a cottage at the back of the garden that's becoming available next week. My tenants are moving unexpectedly—they told me yesterday they have to leave for Orlando due to a family crisis. So…" She paused, as if considering something. "It seems fate may have brought you here."

Fate. The word sent a shiver through me. I instinctively touched the outline of the amethyst crystal in my pocket, the one Julie had given me for protection.

Rosalie's lips quirked into a small smile, as if she could sense what I was thinking. "Four hundred dollars a month is all I'd ask," she said. "My tenants paid through the end of the year, so I can offer it to you at a lower price than usual."

Elisa and I exchanged wide-eyed looks. We had budgeted for at least a thousand a month, so this was far better than we had hoped.

"That's…very generous," Elisa said, trying to sound calm, though her excitement was evident.

"In the meantime," Rosalie continued, "you can stay here in the guesthouse. I'll put you in room ten—it's one of my favorites. It overlooks the harbor." She reached for a set of keys, her movements slow and deliberate.

"Thank you," I said sincerely, relief washing over me.

Rosalie checked us in, making photocopies of our passports, and finally handed me the key labeled ten and a small card. "The front entrance code is seven-two-seven-four," she said. "I change it weekly for security. And here's my cell number, in case you need anything urgently." She gestured toward the staircase behind us. "Room ten is up the stairs and to the right. It has two queen beds and, as I said, a view of the harbor. Breakfast is served in the dining area down that hallway between seven and nine a.m." She pointed toward an archway on the first floor.

"Feel free to explore the gardens," she continued, her tone shifting slightly. "There's even a maze, though I wouldn't advise venturing into it tonight. Guests often come out disoriented; some even claim to have had peculiar experiences in there. Best to wait until you're more familiar with the grounds."

Elisa yawned, covering her mouth. "Right now, all I want to do is sleep," she said.

Salma followed with a yawn of her own. "Are we good to head up?"

"If you don't have any more questions, then yes, go ahead," Rosalie said kindly. "You all look like you could use a rest."

We climbed the wide staircase, the creak of the wooden steps echoing through the quiet house. As promised, room ten had a balcony overlooking the harbor. I unlocked the door and stepped out onto it, the metal railing cool against my palms. The warm evening breeze kissed my skin as I closed my eyes and inhaled deeply. The sound of gentle waves lapping against the boats in their slips in the marina soothed my soul. I had envisioned this moment many times, and finally, I was here.

I looked up at the sky, which was awash in orange as the golden sun had disappeared.

"Girls, come out here and see this!" I called.

Ava was the first to join me, looping her arm through mine. "It's beautiful," she whispered, her voice filled with wonder.

Elisa took my other arm, and Salma rested her hand on Ava's shoulder. Together, we stood in silence for what felt like hours, watching the day fading into twilight, its light shimmering on the water.

For a moment, everything felt perfect. But then a fleeting vision flashed before my eyes.

I saw the balcony again, this same view of the harbor. But in the vision, only three of us stood here.

FOUR

Every morning by eight a.m., we were ready for breakfast in the dining room. The smell of freshly baked bread and cinnamon muffins greeted us, making our mouths water in anticipation.

The buffet contained nothing short of a feast: toast, pancakes, rolls, muffins, powdered doughnuts, fruit, cheeses, and an array of jams and condiments. My favorite was the powdered blueberry doughnuts, which melted in my mouth. Freshly squeezed orange juice stood beside the coffee pot, and everything about the setup felt home like yet indulgent.

The kitchen itself was charming, with rustic wooden cabinets and wide countertops that gave the space a cozy, lived-in feel. A large vintage stove served as the centerpiece, its surface gleaming despite its age, with pots and pans hanging overhead. On the shelves, jars filled with dried herbs, teas, and spices were carefully labeled, while antique teapots and mismatched china added a touch of whimsy.

The long oak table in the center of the dining room, made to seat up to fourteen, encouraged guests to interact. A mother and her young son always sat at the far end of the table. Every morning, they waved to us politely but kept to themselves. I sensed that they didn't want to be disturbed during their meals. The room was bathed in soft natural light from the large windows that offered a view of the sprawling garden and the intricate maze we hadn't yet explored.

Maisie, the middle-aged maid who managed the house with practiced care, greeted us warmly each day. "Morning, beautiful young ladies," she'd say. "I've never met such sweet girls in all my life." Her exaggerated compliments always made us blush.

Maisie adored us because we stayed behind to help clear the table after breakfast and entertained her with exaggerated Cockney accents. "'Ello, sweet'art, 'ow are ya? Whatcha doin'?" I'd joke, and Maisie would throw back her head with laughter, her gold tooth gleaming. Elisa loved to play along, dropping into overly dramatic curtseys. In her poshest accent, she'd say, "I'll have Earl Grey tea and a scone with clotted cream, please." Maisie doubled over every time, wiping tears from her eyes.

Salma and Ava charmed her in their own way, greeting her each morning in Turkish with a bright "Günaydın" and saying goodbye with "Hoşçakal." Maisie tried to mimic them, always mixing up the words, much to our amusement.

A week into our stay, after the other guests had left, Ava and Salma swayed to "Dreams" by The Cranberries as it played on the radio, and Maisie joined in with surprising rhythm, especially considering her size. Elisa twirled and danced alongside them like a ballerina, her laughter ringing out like a bell. I watched from the table, unwilling to join in but warmed by their joy. Rosalie lingered in the background, keeping an eye on us from the patio doors that led to the conservatory on the left and a greenhouse on the right. She often seemed lost in thought, her expression unreadable as she observed us.

I loved the greenhouse. It was a sanctuary bursting with life. Its glass walls gleamed in the sunlight, creating an airy, almost magical space filled with lush greenery. Shelves and wooden tables overflowed with potted plants, vibrant flowers, and rows of glass jars. Herbs hung by the windows to dry, their scents mingling with the aromas of fresh soil and blooming jasmine. During the day, I often saw Rosalie there, crushing herbs with a mortar and pestle or mixing ingredients into small vials. She moved with purpose, sniffing or tasting her mixtures before pouring them into glass decanters. Was she making remedies? Potions? Maybe even spells?

I found myself drawn to the greenhouse at night, too. I'd sit among the plants, gazing up at the moonlight filtering through the glass panels. The mystical elements heightened my senses, and images flashed through in my mind unbidden. The man from the Bluebell Lodge often filled my thoughts, his piercing blue eyes locking with mine. The vision was so vivid that I swore I could hear his voice: *I want to know you.* Just thinking of him filled me with excitement.

But my visions weren't always pleasant. I often saw my mother screaming into the night: "My babies, where did you go? *Come back!*" Guilt gripped me when this happened, but I reminded myself of all the times she had stood by silently while my father had unleashed his rage on my body.

The worst vision, though, was always the same. The balcony of our room. The harbor in the distance. But only three of us standing there. The emptiness was agonizing, and I could never see who was missing.

"C'mon, Rosa, join us!" Salma called as Rosalie lingered by the patio doors, watching us with a mystified expression.

Rosalie shook her head gently, waving her hand. "I don't want to risk slipping and injuring myself," she said with a small smile. "But you girls carry on." Her eyes, though, remained distant, as if her mind was somewhere else entirely. Then they suddenly cleared. "Don't forget, before you head out, I need to show you the cottage."

Elisa nodded, munching on a piece of toast. "Once we've cleared up here, we'll be ready."

"No rush." Rosalie poured herself a cup of coffee, then walked over and sat beside me. She was wearing a wine-red top that matched her lipstick. "How's everything been with the room? Anything we could improve?"

"We're not used to hotels, so I don't have much to compare it to," I replied. "But we've been sleeping well, and the views—especially the sunrise—are breathtaking."

I left out the unsettling details—the strange feeling of being watched, the odd whispers, and the vivid images I'd been seeing, particularly in the greenhouse.

Rosalie reached into her pocket and placed a small pot of balm on the table in front of me. "Here, take this. I made it myself, all natural. It'll help with the cut on your lip, and you can use it on the scar by your left eye, too." She gently pointed to the spot.

I unscrewed the lid, and the scent of roses and tea tree oil wafted up to greet me. Dipping my pinkie into the balm, I spread it over my lip and the faint scar by my eye. It melted into my skin instantly.

"This texture is incredible," I said, stunned. "Thank you so much."

"You're welcome," Rosalie replied. "I make all my own remedies."

"I've seen you working in the greenhouse," I said. "Can you teach me about the plants someday?"

Her eyes softened, and she reached out to touch my hand. "I have a feeling we'll be doing a lot of things together."

The world around us seemed to fade, her touch grounding me even as an image flashed into my mind: an ancient book surrounded by candles and intricate symbols. The only sound was Rosalie's voice, quietly reciting something unfamiliar. A chill crept up my neck. I turned to meet her gaze, and in that moment, I knew—she was a witch.

Her voice, calm and steady, echoed in my head: *And so are you, my dear.*

I pulled my hand away. Had she just read my mind? Or had I read hers?

I looked away, and as quickly as it had faded, the noise of the house returned. Elisa and the girls were laughing at something Maisie had said, and music from the radio filled the kitchen once more. As if nothing had happened, Rosalie waved at the mother and her son as they popped their head through the doorway to say goodbye "Have a lovely day," she called after them. "Enjoy exploring the town."

I felt light-headed as I stood up, my stomach churning violently. Had I overeaten again, or was it my nerves? Bile rose to my throat as I ran out into the hallway, desperate to reach my room before I embarrassed myself. Beads of sweat dotted my forehead as I took the stairs two at a time and ran into the room, nearly tripping. I pushed open the bathroom door, slamming it into the wall.

Bent over the toilet, I closed my eyes and held my stomach. My body convulsed, and all the doughnuts and coffee came back up, burning my throat. My breath came in shallow, rapid gasps as I heaved again until nothing was left. It felt as if my body had released years of hurt, anxiety, and anger.

I flushed the toilet and splashed water on my red, blotchy face. I wiped the smudged black mascara from around my eyes and waited for my heart rate to slow down. This was the third day this had happened; the first two times, I forced myself by sticking my fingers down my throat. Despite the unpleasantness, I couldn't deny how light I felt. My stomach was flat underneath my hands. I could eat anything and never worry about gaining weight.

I reapplied lipstick with careful precision, mindful of the cut on my lip, but strangely, it seemed to have disappeared. I checked with the magnifying mirror. It couldn't be—the small scar next to my eye was no longer there either. The balm surely wasn't magic, was it? A flashback hit me of the argument three months ago that had led to that scar. My father's voice rang in my head, stern and unyielding, declaring that he had purchased the plane tickets and I would be married by the end of August. I had dared to disagree, to speak my mind. His response had been swift and brutal—his fist silencing me, making sure I knew his word was final.

That hadn't been the first time he'd interfered in my life. He had crushed my dreams of going to university the same way, forcing me to work in the family bakery instead, preparing me for the future he had mapped out for me—one I had no say in.

I had tried in vain to understand what had made him this way. He had come to the UK in the seventies, fleeing poverty, determined to build a better life. He had married my English mother, which I realized now must have been for the spousal visa. He had wanted to ensure that I didn't stray too far, didn't fall into what he considered the dangers of a Western lifestyle. But his vision for my life felt like a cage, locking me away from my own desires and dreams.

Now that we were gone, he would likely take his anger out on my mother. The thought made my stomach twist, but I pushed it away quickly, not allowing myself to linger in that pain.

The strange moment I'd just had with Rosalie had triggered my anxiety, which made me worry about everything. Was I really some sort of witch? How did someone become a witch? Were you born that way? Did that mean I was evil?

With a deep breath, I brushed my black hair into a neat ponytail, ruffling my fringe slightly to give it some volume. With one last glance at my reflection, I whispered, "Pull it together, Jenna."

And I headed back downstairs.

When I sat back down at the breakfast table, Elisa immediately noticed my red, glazed eyes. She didn't miss a thing.

"Why are your eyes like that?" she asked, putting the magazine down on the table and examining me.

"It must be hay fever," I said, avoiding her gaze and pouring myself another cup of coffee.

"Since when do you have hay fever?" she pressed, her tone skeptical.

"It might be an allergic reaction to something else. I don't know," I replied dismissively, pulling out my notepad to review the itinerary I had made.

Elisa sighed and pushed back her empty glass. She turned to face me, narrowing her honey-colored eyes. "Don't do that, Jen." Her voice was low but firm. "I'm not stupid. Tell me the truth."

I hesitated, keeping my eyes fixed on the notepad.

"Look," she said softly, "you know you can tell me anything, so why are you being cagey?"

I glanced over my shoulder. Ava and Salma were distracted, trying to teach Maisie how to say "I have a big bum" in Turkish. Their laughter filled the room. I leaned in closer to Elisa.

"Don't judge me, Els," I whispered, "but I've been making myself throw up and now it just happens on its own." I forced the words out before I lost my nerve. "Don't look so worried—it's not as bad as it sounds. I feel…happier after."

Her eyes widened in alarm. "Are you crazy?"

"Shh!" I hissed. "I don't want the others to know."

Before Elisa could respond, Salma plopped down next to me, grinning as she scanned the notepad. "What are you two whispering about?" she asked suspiciously.

"Nothing much," I said quickly, giving Elisa a pointed look. "Just going over today's plan."

Elisa took another bite of her toast, clearly annoyed but choosing not to push further.

"Where are we going today?" Salma asked.

"Boston," I replied, feigning enthusiasm.

Ava slumped into the chair opposite me, letting out an exaggerated sigh. "Jen, every day has been so jam-packed. Can we have a day to just…not?" She gestured dramatically at Elisa and Salma, waiting for them to back her up. "We're not tourists, sis. We're staying here. We can see things at a regular pace."

"Well, today's the last day of sightseeing anyway," I said. "Tomorrow, we'll move into the cottage and start looking for jobs."

As I thought of the places we'd already visited—the Witch Dungeon Museum, the Salem Maritime Historic Site, Max and Dani's house from *Hocus Pocus*—I couldn't help but feel a pang of nostalgia. We'd packed so much into the past six days: exploring the harbor, trying local food, shopping at the Witch City Mall. My favorite had been the Oyster Shack, though the other girls hadn't been as adventurous with seafood as I had. I could still taste the octopus drizzled with garlic and lemon. But now our carefree days were ending and reality was creeping in. Soon we had to start being adults and earning some money.

"I need to pop in and see Megan, I was meant to go the following day but I didn't get a chance," Elisa said suddenly, her voice filled with anticipation. "I wonder if she spoke to her boss about giving me a job."

"Great," I said distractedly, my mind elsewhere. I was thinking about the man at the Bluebell Lodge again. I'd hoped to see him around town, but he hadn't appeared. For a brief silly moment, I considered making an excuse to visit the lodge again, but I pushed the thought aside.

"Jen!" Elisa waved her hand in front of my face. "Are you even listening?"

I turned and looked at her, trying my best to guess what she'd just said. "Yes, Megan, job, got it," I said quickly.

Elisa rolled her eyes. "I said, let's skip Boston and go one day next week." She put emphasis on each word as if I were a slow learner.

Honestly, I didn't feel like trekking to Boston today either. "Fine," I said. "We'll do the Witch Trials Memorial and Ropes Mansion gardens instead. Then we'll go see Megan."

The girls nodded in agreement, and I marked the stops in my notepad.

Rosalie reappeared, jingling four sets of keys. "If you're all ready, let's go see the cottage," she said.

We followed her through the side door, stepping into the two-acre garden. The sun was bright and hot, reminding me of Turkey for a fleeting moment. If we hadn't escaped, I would have been flying out to get married next week. I pushed the thought deep down, determined never to think about it again.

As we walked past the maze, its towering hedges cast cool shadows over the path. The slender lighthouse rose in the distance, its white exterior weathered and gleaming in the sunlight. The lantern's beams had guided us back to the guesthouse when we'd gotten lost one night.

"You can enter the maze through this opening," Rosalie said, gesturing to an archway in the dense greenery. "There are four entrances, but if you go in from the front, you can walk straight through to the lighthouse."

Salma's eyes lit up. "Can we go into the lighthouse?"

"Of course," Rosalie replied with a smile. "The glass seating area at the top has a perfect view of the harbor. Just be careful on the narrow stairs."

"It's so romantic," Elisa said dreamily. "We should all watch the sunset from up there one evening."

"And I could sit up there and read my book," Salma added.

Rosalie's smile faded slightly as she stared up at the lighthouse. "Just don't try the maze after dark, especially if the lamp isn't on. People have gotten…lost."

Ava shuddered dramatically and shook her head. "You'd never catch me in there after dark, not for a million dollars!"

Opposite the maze, large trees dotted the lawn, their canopies casting dappled shadows on a pebbled path. Behind the trees was the cottage. It was even more enchanting than what I'd seen in my visions. Its white exterior and maroon door stood out against the greenery, and the porch was adorned with hanging flower baskets and whimsical fairy and angel ornaments. Rosalie searched through her pocket and pulled out a set of keys and unlocked the front door. Ava and Salma entered first, and Elisa and I followed close behind.

The foyer was square and quite spacious. An archway to the left opened up into the living room, which exuded warmth and comfort. Next to it was a bedroom with two single beds, ready for guests. Straight ahead was a bathroom, and the door next to it led to the master bedroom, boasting an en suite and two small double beds. Built-in closets lined one wall, and a dressing table with a stool sat beneath a window.

"Jenna and I will take this room," Elisa declared.

Finally, to the right of the front door, we found the kitchen. It featured white cupboards, wooden countertops, and a cozy corner table with bench seats, perfect for family meals and long conversations. A side door led out to the garden, completing the picturesque scene. The whole place felt homey and welcoming.

"It's perfect, thank you," I said.

Ava's voice rang out from the guest bedroom, her excitement palpable. "I'm sleeping on this side!"

"Fine, but this side of the wardrobe and these drawers are mine," Salma responded, her tone playful yet firm.

Rosalie led me to the kitchen table and gestured for me to sit. "I know you're looking for a job," she began, "so I wanted to ask if you'd like to work at the guesthouse a few days a week, or more, depending on your plans. We'll have a lot of visitors through the rest of the summer and into the autumn, especially with Halloween coming up."

"I would love to," I replied earnestly. It would help a lot if at least one of us started earning money right away. Yes, a lot of bizarre coincidences were happening, but I felt as if I belonged here. "What exactly would I be doing?"

"Well, you'd handle the phones and the internet bookings," Rosalie explained. "And you can assist Maisie in the mornings but it's not a must."

Unable to contain my excitement, I said, "I can start tomorrow, if you like."

"Perfect. Maisie can show you the ropes."

"That's great news, sis," Ava said, joining us with a smile. "If Elisa gets a job at Strega's, then it's just Sal and me who need to sort something out."

"I'll ask my friends in town," Rosalie offered kindly. "And the library has a bulletin board for job listings. You should pop in and check it out"

Salma clapped her hands together. "Perfect—let's go now!"

As we left the cottage, Rosalie handed me the keys. "Be careful in the maze after dark," she warned one last time.

I glanced at the towering hedges and the lighthouse beyond, unease settling in my chest. Something told me they held secrets that waited to be uncovered.

FIVE

When we stepped into Blue Ink Books & Candles on Essex Street, I was expecting a typical bookstore, but it quickly became clear that this was no WH Smith. This place was designed for the Wiccan community, not for casual readers. The shelves stretched from floor to ceiling on one side, crammed with books on green witchcraft, spell-casting, and self-healing, while the other side held rows of candles in every color imaginable. Each was labeled: love, awareness, spirituality, healing, money, luck.

The air was rich with scents, pine, strawberry, coffee, and rose blending together in a strange, heady harmony. I picked up a pine-scented candle and closed my eyes as the earthy aroma relaxed me. It was comforting. Without hesitation, I bought it.

By the counter, necklaces with birthstone crystals glinted in the dim light, and tucked in the back was a small alcove with velvet curtains marked psychic readings. It tugged at me, making my fingers itch to pull back the fabric and step inside. But not today. Another time.

We couldn't resist grabbing black witch hats. "If we're going to the Witch Trials Memorial and Ropes Mansion, we might as well do it in style," Elisa joked, adjusting the brim of hers.

The cashier offered directions to the Witch Trials Memorial. "It's about ten minutes away if you walk slowly," she said, her tone warm.

"We're heading there now—you're more than welcome to follow us," said a cheerful woman in a bright green, high-visibility vest. She handed the cashier money for a few crystals. "I'm Trudy, tour guide extraordinaire—and yes, this ridiculous vest is so my elderly group doesn't lose me." She laughed, her voice full of energy.

I smiled at her; the vest *was* ridiculous. We introduced ourselves and agreed to follow the group.

"Right, listen up, everyone," Trudy announced to her group of ten elderly tourists as we stepped outside. "We've got four lovely girls from England joining us." All eyes turned to us. I waved and said hello. Some people smiled warmly at us, while others just clutched bouquets to place at the foot of the memorial with quiet reverence.

After a short walk, we reached the memorial. "Gather round," Trudy instructed her group. Since we weren't officially part of the tour, we hung back, listening quietly.

The memorial's simplicity struck me immediately. It was a quiet, solemn space surrounded by a low stone wall. Twenty granite benches jutted out, each etched with the name and execution date of a victim of the 1692 Salem witch trials.

I walked slowly around the memorial, my fingers brushing the edges of the benches as I read the names. Rebecca Nurse, July 19, 1692; Sarah Good, July 19, 1692; Elizabeth Howe, July 19, 1692. Three women hanged on the same day. My chest tightened with sadness.

Flowers, letters, and small gifts had been left by visitors, tokens of remembrance for lives cut short by fear and hysteria. I suddenly wished I'd thought to bring flowers, too.

"This place is giving me the creeps," Elisa whispered, appearing at my side.

"It's okay," I replied softly. "There's nothing harmful here." I reached out and touched her arm, trying to reassure her.

Ava and Salma joined us, their faces unusually somber. "It's so heartbreaking," Ava murmured. "I can't imagine how scared they must have been."

"It's tragic," I said, my voice low. "And so unnecessary. It's hard to believe this actually happened."

We stood together in silence, the encumbrance of history settling over us.

We thanked Trudy, who gave us directions to our next stop, then headed to the Ropes Mansion a short walk away. Its white colonial exterior gleamed in the sunlight, and the lush gardens surrounding it felt like something out of a film.

Salma, camera in hand, darted ahead, snapping pictures of everything. "Okay, group photo!" she announced, waving us over.

We posed in front of the mansion in our new hats, pulling ridiculous faces and laughing until our sides ached. Other tourists smiled at us, and a kind stranger offered to take a photo of all four of us together.

"I hope these come out nice," Salma said.

"How many shots are left?" Elisa asked.

"Seven more," Salma replied, grinning mischievously. Without warning, she clicked a photo of us mid-laugh.

"Sal, stop wasting the film!" I protested, reaching for the camera, but she danced out of reach, giggling as she clicked one after another.

"Oops, all finished!" she teased, shaking the camera in front of me.

I rolled my eyes, half amused, half exasperated. "All right. Let's get them developed."

After dropping off the film, we headed to Strega's Coffee House , sliding into the same booth as last week. As we settled in, I couldn't help but glance toward the Bluebell Lodge. I felt that familiar pull again. Why couldn't I stop thinking about the blond man? When I thought of seeing him again, I got butterflies.

Megan appeared at our table, looking worn-out, like she hadn't slept in days. Her bright smile was dimmer, and dark circles shadowed her eyes. It was obvious something wasn't right.

"I wasn't sure if y'all had left town," she said to Elisa, her voice lacking the energy she'd had last time. "You never called."

Elisa hesitated. "I kept meaning to come in to speak to your boss directly, but I got sidetracked by sightseeing every day. Is he around today?"

Megan nodded. "Sure thing. Follow me." She led her toward the kitchen. My curiosity got the better of me, and I followed at a distance.

"Antonio," Megan called out. He didn't turn right away, focused on flipping pancakes and turning bacon on the grill. "I have someone here asking about the job."

"Sì, sì, come through," Antonio responded in a thick Italian accent, his voice booming. I watched from the doorway as Elisa and Megan stepped inside. Antonio appeared to be in his mid-forties, around six feet tall with a bit of a potbelly, likely from all the delicious pastries and pancakes. His hair was receding at the temples, and he carried himself with the easy confidence of someone who knew his way around the kitchen. Elisa and Megan looked small next to him.

"Do you have any experience?" he asked, glancing at Elisa briefly while flipping another pancake.

"Er…yes," Elisa replied, a bit flustered. "Back in London, I ran my father's café. I've been working there since I was fifteen."

"How long are you staying here?" Antonio asked. "Are you from London? You'll need a green card to work." He gave her a quick, impatient glance while tending to the sizzling food.

Elisa blinked, taken aback. She clearly hadn't expected the question. "Oh, of course, a green card," she said, letting out a nervous laugh. "I'll apply for one right away, since I'm here to stay." She hesitated, then added, "Maybe you could hire me on a trial basis and see what you think?"

"No, no, no!" Antonio responded firmly, waving his hands in the air. "I'm sorry, I can't."

Elisa's face fell. "I'll leave my number with Megan in case you change your mind," she said softly, her disappointment evident as she turned away and headed toward me. I felt bad for her. Antonio didn't have to be so abrupt, he clearly needed more staff if he was the manager and the cook.

I walked back to the booth and slid into my seat, then watched as Megan whispered something to Elisa. She listened intently, then smiled and nodded. A few seconds later she said, "Oh, and can we get four burgers with fries and cokes, please?" Megan nodded and Elisa approached the table and sat beside me.

"Well, that was a waste of time," she muttered, frustration clear in her voice. "The moody owner said no! Apparently I need some green card rubbish. Whatever! But Megan's boyfriend can help us get green cards. He knows someone in immigration. It'll cost four thousand dollars for all four of us. I know it's a lot, but it'll be worth it."

It sounded promising—a solution to the whole work issue. We hadn't known where to start with applying for work permits. We were hesitant to give out our London addresses, afraid our parents might track us down. Without anyone to sponsor us here, the whole process felt daunting. I picked at my nails, considering. "It does sound good, but I think we need more advice. We don't want to get caught up in something risky or illegal."

"I'm going to stay behind and wait for Megan to finish work, and then we'll talk about it some more," Elisa said, determined.

Salma nodded. "Ava and I will pick up the pictures from the photo place."

After we finished our burgers and fries, I wiped the grease from my fingers and lips with a napkin. "Right, I'm heading back home, then. I need to talk to Maisie about tomorrow."

I crossed the road to pass by the Lodge on my way back to the guesthouse, my eyes instinctively darting to the door, hoping to catch a glimpse of the blond man. But the place seemed empty. I forced myself to look ahead—and then I saw him walking toward me, a casual spring in his step. My stomach dropped. *Oh no.* Of course he'd seen me staring at the lodge like a fool.

I cringed inwardly but kept my face neutral, refusing to show how flustered I felt. As we got closer together, I dared to glance up, and our eyes met. My breath caught in my throat. His gaze was intense, and for a moment, everything else faded. He was more striking than I remembered, far more handsome than he'd been in my hazy visions. We passed one another, our eyes locked until our necks could twist no farther. My cheeks flushed with heat.

I kept walking, every instinct screaming at me not to look back, but the temptation was too strong. I caved. I turned my head, and—oh god, he was looking back, too. Our eyes locked again, and my heart thundered. I snapped my head forward, quickening my steps. Why did I do that?

Suddenly, I heard quick footsteps behind me, and then his voice—low, deep, and unmistakable. "Excuse me."

I pretended not to hear him and continued to walk, my stomach fluttering wildly with nerves, my mouth suddenly dry as sandpaper.

"Excuse me." His voice came again, closer this time.

I stopped in my tracks and slowly turned to face him. His golden wavy fringe hung just above his left eyebrow. He wore a fitted blue polo shirt that complemented his athletic physique. This close to him, my mind went blank; I couldn't speak.

"I remember you," he said, his blue eyes piercing. "You came into the lodge last week."

I furrowed my brow, pretending to think back. "Ah, yes," I stammered, brushing a strand of hair behind my ear. "I asked you for directions."

He inclined his head slightly, and a slow smile spread across his face. No doubt he was remembering our rather abrupt exchange.

"I assumed you'd left town by now," he said, clearing his throat. "I mean, most tourists only stay a few days." Was that a blush creeping onto his face? I couldn't quite tell.

His gaze was so intense as he waited for my response that I had to look away for a second to gather myself before meeting his bright blue eyes again. "I'm still here," I replied awkwardly. "I'm actually here for a while." I paused, not wanting to give too much away. "I'll see how it goes. If I like it, I might stay for good."

He inhaled and extended his hand. "I'm Troy. If you need anything, feel free to stop by the lodge. I'm there when I'm not in seminar."

I reached out to shake his hand, feeling the warmth of his skin as his slender fingers wrapped around mine. A rush of heat passed between us as our eyes locked again, and my heart raced. Neither of us seemed willing to let go. Did he feel it, too, or was it just me?

"I'm Jenna," I finally managed to say, "but you can call me Jen." Instantly I regretted it. Too casual too soon. I broke the eye contact and looked at my feet, blushing.

As we slowly pulled our hands apart, a tingling sensation lingered on my skin. I slipped my trembling hands into the back pockets of my jeans, trying to steady myself.

"Are you here in town with your boyfriend?" he asked casually, but his gaze was anything but.

My eyes widened in surprise. "Boyfriend?" I repeated, looking away as a shy giggle slipped out. I felt his gaze lingering on me as he waited for me to answer. I finally looked up and said, "No, I don't have a boyfriend." Was that a hint of relief in his sigh? "I'm here with my sister and cousins."

His face lit up as he beamed. "I've lived in Salem my whole life. Seriously, if you need anything, I can help."

My eyes moved to his hands as he rested them on his hips, muscles subtly tensing beneath his shirt.

"I'll keep that in mind. Thanks," I replied.

He brushed his hand through his hair and said, "Well, I won't hold you up. See you around, no doubt." His voice softened as he turned to leave.

I bit my bottom lip. "See you around," I echoed before turning and walking home.

SIX

When I arrived back at the guesthouse, just after five p.m. the stillness was striking. The usual sound of quiet conversation and soft clatter of plates was absent. My footsteps resonated faintly on the hardwood floors as I made my way toward the kitchen, hoping to find Maisie and discuss my schedule for tomorrow. But the kitchen was empty.

I moved toward the main room. The afternoon light from the bay windows splashed across the walls. And there, seated in her armchair, surrounded by a circle of flickering candles, was Rosalie. She looked serene, almost regal, a thin book resting on her lap and a steaming cup of tea by her side.

"Jenna," she said, her voice smooth and calm, as if she'd been expecting me.

I stopped in my tracks. "Hi," I managed, my voice breathless. My heart was still racing from my encounter with Troy, and something about Rosalie heightened it even more. "Have you been waiting for me?"

Her lips curled into a deliberate smile as she removed her reading glasses and set them delicately on the side table. "Yes, I have. Sit down." She gestured toward the plush sofa across from her, her eyes steady on me.

My curiosity flared. "How did you know when I'd be back?"

Her expression didn't falter. "Oh, I just had a feeling."

Hesitantly, I lowered myself onto the sofa, unsure why I suddenly felt so exposed. The room seemed larger than usual, the corners stretching out unnaturally. The portraits on the walls seemed alive, their painted eyes watching me. I looked back over at Rosalie, the faint sound of a lilting melody drifted from the record player, weaving a nostalgic soundtrack around her.

"I was actually looking for Maisie," I said, trying to fill the awkward silence. "I wanted to talk about tomorrow."

"Maisie's off this afternoon," Rosalie replied gently, leaning back in her chair with a thoughtful expression. "You'll see her in the morning. I thought it might be nice for us to talk."

"All right," I said softly, sitting up straighter. I felt slightly on edge, remembering how she'd read my thoughts that morning.

"Let me make you some tea," she said suddenly, rising from her chair with grace.

"No, I can—" I started, desperate to burn off the restless energy swirling inside me. I needed to do something, anything, but she raised a hand to stop me.

"Sit," she said with a warm smile. "I'll make one of my special teas. You'all like it." Her eyes gleamed mischievously as she disappeared into the kitchen. After her strange magic balm that had healed my scars, I didn't argue. I'd try anything she made.

Left alone, I sank deeper into the cushions, leaning my head back. My mind wandered to Troy—his piercing blue eyes, the way his hand had felt in mine, the softness in his voice. Every detail replayed in my head like a loop, and I didn't want it to stop. My fingers tingled at the memory of his touch. I wasn't used to feeling this way—so vulnerable, so captivated, so unsure what to make of these emotions. I wondered if he felt the same.

I let out a slow breath, but I couldn't relax. It felt like someone was watching me.

Suddenly, I was very sure that I wasn't alone. Even though the room was warm, a chill crept over me, my senses spiked. I glanced to my left, then to my right, but the room remained empty. No one was there. And yet I could feel it—something, someone.

My gaze fell on the largest portrait hanging above the fireplace. A young woman stared back at me from the canvas, her features strong and striking. She wore a black dress and a wide-brimmed hat and held a scepter adorned with stars. Her eyes were deep, piercing, and hauntingly familiar.

I stood up and walked closer to examine it. Then it hit me. I inhaled sharply. No—it couldn't be. But the resemblance was undeniable.

The woman in the portrait…it was Julie. I knew it without a doubt. I stepped back in shock, nearly tripping over a cat that had appeared from nowhere, brushing against my leg. A flurry of whispers filled the room.

I gasped, chills crawling down my back. I spun wildly, trying to trace where the whispers were coming from.

"Are you okay?" Rosalie's voice cut through my thoughts, making me jump. I turned sharply to see her walking toward me, a tray balanced in her hands. Her lips quirked into an amused smile as she set the tray on the coffee table.

"Sorry," I stammered, my pulse pounding in my ears. "The portrait just...caught my eye."

Rosalie followed my gaze, her expression softening. "That's Aurelia," she said quietly.

I blinked. "Aurelia?"

"My sister," Rosalie explained, settling back into her chair and pouring tea into two delicate china cups. "She left for London decades ago. She..." She sighed heavily. "She never returned. Years later, I found out that she had passed away." Her voice cracked with emotion.

I felt the blood drain from my face. I sat back down and turned to face Rosalie. "I—I know this sounds strange, but..." I hesitated, but then my words tumbled out before I could stop them. "That's Julie."

Rosalie's hand paused mid-pour. For a fraction of a second, something flickered across her face—surprise, or perhaps recognition—but she quickly composed herself.

"As I said, my sister's name was Aurelia." Her tone was measured. "I don't know this Julie you keep referring to."

"I'm sure I'm not mistaken," I pressed, my voice uneven. "Julie—she helped me. She told me all about Salem and this house. She'as the reason I'm here."

Rosalie's gaze lingered on me for a moment too long before she turned back to the tea and handed me a cup. "Drink," she said softly. "It'll calm you." Her eyes fell on the cat. "And this is Luna. She's the sweetest cat. I can tell she likes you. One blustery day during a fierce blizzard two years ago, she appeared in the back garden, and she's been here ever since."

As if on cue, Luna leapt gracefully onto the sofa beside me, curling up against my leg. Her fur was soft and white as snow, and when I stroked her, it felt like warm silk beneath my fingers. One of her eyes was a deep green, the other a piercing blue, and she began to purr softly, contentedly, as she licked her paw.

I picked up the tea from the tray and inhaled. The scent was floral and earthy with a hint of lemon. I took a sip, the warmth spreading through me instantly, soothing my nerves. "What's in this?" I asked.

"It's a special blend," Rosalie replied. "China black tea, yarrow root, moonwort, rose hip…and a little intuition."

I smiled weakly, taking another sip. The tension in my chest began to ease, but my mind still spun with questions about the portrait.

Rosalie leaned forward, her eyes locking onto mine. "When you finish, I'll read your leaves."

I stared at her. "You can read tea leaves?"

"Among other things," she said cryptically.

Curiosity overcame my hesitation, and I quickly finished the tea, savoring its unusual but calming flavor. As instructed, I flipped the cup upside down onto the saucer, excitement surging through me. "Okay," I said, pushing the saucer toward her.

Rosalie's hand hovered over the cup for a few seconds before she picked it up and turned it slowly. Her brows furrowed as she studied the patterns in the tea leaves, her expression growing more intense with every passing second.

"What do you see?" I asked, my voice barely above a whisper. I started picking at my nails in anticipation.

Rosalie said nothing, her gaze fixed on the cup, though she nodded from time to time. Anxiety started to gnaw at me. Did she see something bad? Was that why she wasn't speaking?

"I went into a shop today," I added anxiously, "and I was tempted to get a psychic reading."

Still she said nothing. I glanced at my watch, wondering if the girls would come back soon and thinking about how I still needed to pack for the move to the cottage. Just as I was about to speak again, Rosalie broke the silence.

"Jenna," she said, her voice soft but firm.

I looked up, leaning forward instinctively.

"What is your mother's name?" she asked.

"Sally," I replied, confused.

"And your grandmother? On your mother's side?"

"I…I'm not sure. My mum never talks about her. She grew up in foster homes."

Rosalie's face was pensive as she studied me. "She's not Turkish?"

"No, she's English," I said quickly, feeling a bit defensive.

"The cup disagrees," Rosalie said, her voice firm yet calm. "She's not English either."

I forced a smile, trying to brush it off. *Well, the cup obviously doesn't know everything*, I thought.

As if reading my mind, Rosalie looked directly at me and said, "The cup doesn't lie." Her words startled me, and I blushed, looking away. I'd forgotten she could read my thoughts.

Her expression softened slightly as she leaned closer. "You are more connected to Salem, and this house, than you realize." She hesitated, then added, "Your gifts are awakening, Jenna. You can sense it, can't you? The visions, the feelings—they're not coincidences. You've inherited something extraordinary."

I shook my head as her words sank in. "You think I'm... gifted? What else do you see?"

Rosalie's emerald eyes shot to mine, and her voice grew more serious. "Your father is a violent man. I can see here that he has hurt you many times."

My heart skipped a beat. I nodded, unable to meet her gaze, my hands shaking slightly in my lap.

"He has a temper he can't control," she continued, her voice a little quieter, as if walking through my memories. I nodded again, shame creeping up my cheeks as I focused on my hands, trying to keep my old wounds from reopening.

Rosalie leaned in closer, her voice low. "Are you ready?"

I blinked. "Ready for what?"

"Look into the saucer," she instructed, handing it to me.

I hesitated but took the saucer, my hands shaking. As I looked into the small pool of tea, the leaves began to swirl. The liquid darkened, and suddenly it wasn't just tea anymore—it was a portal. I gasped as an image started to form.

My mother appeared in front of me, sitting in my bedroom, crying. She clutched my father's arm, begging him to stop. My father loomed over her, his face twisted with rage. He slapped her face, and the sound echoed in my ears. I couldn't move, I couldn't breathe. "How dare they dishonor me like this!" he roared. He ripped up our family photos, smashing everything in sight. "I'll kill them with my bare hands!"

I snapped out of the vision, gasping for air, unable to bear it any longer. "I don't want to see any more," I whispered, my voice shaking. I handed the saucer back to Rosalie. My legs felt weak as I stood up, trembling uncontrollably. "Rosalie, I…I need to be alone."

She nodded as if she understood and said nothing more.

I rushed out into the hallway, taking the stairs two at a time until I reached my room. My body felt cold and drained. Crawling under the covers, hot tears spilled from my eyes. My poor mum. *Please, God, don't let him hurt her. Please don't let him find us.* I squeezed my eyes shut, desperate for the thoughts to stop.

The tea's calming effects finally took hold, and I drifted into a deep, dreamless sleep.

SEVEN

I woke up the next morning to an empty room. The other bed was still neatly made, Elisa and the girls were nowhere to be seen. Their belongings were gone, too. A strange emptiness settled in my stomach. Where was everyone?

As I sat up, fragments of yesterday flickered through my mind—Troy's piercing gaze, the peculiar whispers in the guesthouse, the haunting tea leaf reading, the portrait of Julie, and that terrifying vision of my father. It all swirled in my head, disjointed and unnerving. Yet beneath the weight of those memories, I felt oddly…lighter. Freer.

I glanced at the clock—seven fifteen. I had been asleep for nearly thirteen hours. That was a first. Must have been the tea. I stretched, my muscles loosening as I reached upward and leaned to the side, feeling the stiffness of deep sleep dissipating.

Then I noticed the note on the nightstand.

Hey Jen,

Couldn't wake you from your deep sleep. We're at the cottage.

See you in the morning.

Els xx

I smiled. How had I not heard them come and go? I usually woke at the slightest noise. Maybe I'd been more exhausted than I'd realized.

Pushing the covers back, I walked over to the balcony and stepped outside. The crisp, salty breeze hit me like a cool wave, sharpening my senses and waking me fully. Below, the sea stretched out, glittering and calm and endless under the morning sun. A dog walker strolled by, their golden retriever trotting happily alongside them, followed by a couple of early joggers. This was my kind of morning: peaceful, quiet, and full of possibilities.

My thoughts drifted unbidden to Troy. I wondered what he was doing right then. Was he thinking about me? Almost immediately, the answer came to me in a vivid flash, clear and certain: *Yes. He hasn't stopped thinking about you all night.* Warmth spread through my chest, and I couldn't help but smile. I felt…happy.

After a long, hot shower, I packed up my things and made my way downstairs. The smell of cinnamon wafted through the hall, mingling with the faint hum of activity in the kitchen.

Time to start the day.

With brisk efficiency, Maisie explained the basics of running the guesthouse. "On my days off, breakfast needs to be prepared before the guests are up, and we cater to all dietary preferences," she said, her tone serious. "It's important to create a warm, welcoming atmosphere. That's key. The cleaner arrives at eleven and is responsible for making sure all the rooms are tidy, comfortable, and well-stocked with essentials like linens and toiletries."

Rosalie chimed in, "When new guests arrive, give them a brief tour, and make sure to offer recommendations—local attractions, restaurants, events, all that good stuff." She showed me the booking system on the computer. "We mostly take reservations by phone, but some come through on here," she said, tapping the screen. "In a few years, I think everything will be online."

I nodded, taking notes.

"The reception desk isn't staffed after six p.m. Guests come and go on their own using the code. Give them all my cell number so they can reach me if anything urgent comes up."

I scribbled down details, codes, and safety protocols. The idea of handling so much on my own felt daunting, but Rosalie and Maisie reassured me that I'd pick it up quickly.

"Don't worry about the garden, maze, or lighthouse," Rosalie reassured me. "Roman and his grandmother Betty take care of it. Betty's an old family friend, and she comes over every day to work in the garden. She gets lonely, so we have coffee and a chat afterward."

In the afternoon, I met Betty, who was tending the garden with careful precision. She was a petite woman with kind warm brown eyes, eyes that had seen it all. I found her presence soothing. "Gardening keeps me busy," she said, brushing dirt from her gloves and taking off her straw hat. "It gets lonely at home, so I come here to help out. It's good for the soul. Always good to have a chat with Rosalie." Her voice was soft and gentle.

I admired her handiwork—the vibrant flower beds, the neat rows of herbs. "I don't know anything about gardening," I admitted. "Maybe I could learn from you."

Betty chuckled, her laugh soft and musical. "Of course, dear. There's no rush—plants grow in their own time, and so do we. Plus, I really can't take the credit for these lovely gardens," she said with a touch of pride in her voice. "My grandson, Roman, designed them all. He's the artist, not me. He's here three times a week. I just come along for my own sanity. I can't sit at home and watch TV all day."

I liked Betty immediately; at eighty-five, she was going strong, and I wanted to spend time with her. "If you ever need help with anything, let me know," I said, smiling.

She nodded, picking up the watering can and moving toward the shrubs.

Later, the girls insisted that we visit the lighthouse. I grabbed the keys from reception, and we made our way to the maze, using the front entrance taking us straight to the lighthouse.

"Wait, there's no lift?" Ava groaned, looking at the towering lighthouse with an exaggerated pout.

"Nope," I replied with a grin. "It's old. Spiral stairs all the way up."

We started to climb, the narrow iron staircase winding tightly through the walls. The air inside was cool, and every few steps, we paused at small windows offering glimpses of the maze and gardens below.

By the time we reached the top, our legs were burning, but Rosalie was right: the view was worth it. The glass room provided a stunning 360-degree panorama of the landscape. The gardens and maze were laid out below us like a living map, the shimmering sea stretched to the horizon, and the town sprawled in charming clusters of buildings. Even the rooftop of our cottage was visible. The room had cushioned benches at the base of the windows with a small table in the center. It was a cozy place to sit with a hot drink and read a book.

We lingered there for a while, catching up, whilst Salma snapped photos of the sun casting a golden glow over everything as it dipped lower. "I haven't seen the photos from the other day, are they any good?" I asked.

"You're not going to be happy about the ones I took of you." Her amber eyes glittered as she giggled mischievously.

"Well, if they're that bad, I'll be tearing them up," I joked back. "Next time, I'll take the photos."

"We should head down before it gets dark," Elisa said, her gaze fixed on the window, her hands resting on her slim waist. Something was clearly on her mind. I figured she was still preoccupied with Antonio's refusal to give her a chance at Strega's until she had a work permit.

Reluctantly, we made our way back down. By the time we reached the maze, the last rays of sunlight were fading, and the dense hedges cast long, foreboding shadows. We had to navigate the maze to reach the exit that led directly across from the cottage, using it as a shortcut.

Elisa led the way.

"I'm not going in last," Ava muttered, biting her lip nervously as she darted ahead.

"I'll stay at the back," I said, trying to sound confident.

The moment I stepped into the maze, an unsettling feeling took hold of me. The scent of damp earth filled my nose as I made my way through the towering, neatly trimmed hedges. I sped up to get closer to Ava just before she disappeared around a corner. I turned right, but no one was there. I glanced back to see the lighthouse, but it had vanished behind a wall of green.

"Ava!" I called out, as I wandered deeper, feeling the hedges closing in on me. I peeked through a small opening between the leaves, but I couldn't see or hear the girls.

"Salma!" I shouted. I stopped to listen for footsteps, but the only sound was my heartbeat drumming in my ears.

I turned right and then left, but each path led to a dead end.

"Elisaaaaaaa!" I screamed as loud as possible, but my voice vanished into the maze's chilling corridors. Again, no response. I turned back, trying to retrace my steps, but the path ahead forked, each way leading to a dead end. Panic began to bubble in my chest as the daylight faded completely, replaced by a cold, inky darkness. My breaths came faster and shallower as the passages seemed to lengthen, taunting me.

"Elisa! Can you hear me?" I called desperately. How long had I been in here? I needed to get out. I didn't want to spend the night in the maze. My legs felt like lead, and my heart pounded wildly as I stumbled around and around in circles.

"Salma!" I shouted desperately, my voice shaking. But it was no use. No one could hear me.

Then I saw it: a tall, dark figure loomed at the end of the path. My feet froze, my body stiffening with fear. I strained to see its face, but it remained shrouded in shadow.

A primal urge to flee overwhelmed me. I spun around, sprinting away. I veered left, only to find myself at another dead end. Desperation fueled my frantic steps as I turned right. The hedges seemed to conspire against me, their branches reaching out to trip me. I crashed to the ground, my hands and knees stinging. The crunch of twigs announced the approach of footsteps. I turned my head back, as the figure drew closer. My throat constricted and my eyes widened. The blood drained from my face and turned to ice as recognition washed over me.

I knew him. My head spun. This couldn't be real.

"Dad?" I breathed, terror tightening my chest. I scrambled backward, pressing against the unyielding green wall.

He leaned over me, his face twisted with rage, his eyes searing into my soul. Then he crouched until his face was inches from mine. "You thought you could escape me, did you?" his voice thundered. "You'll never get away from me."

I shrank back, instinctively covering my head, bracing for a blow. "Nooooooooo!" I screamed, the sound tearing from my throat until my voice gave out.

"Hey, hey, hey, it's okay." Firm hands gripped my shoulders. I flinched, protecting my head and keeping my eyes closed. "Don't be scared, I'm not going to hurt you. It's all right."

Confused, I lifted my head and blinked several times, scanning the maze. "Where…where did he go?"

"It's just me," a man said gently. "My name's Roman. I look after the gardens and the maze."

Relief washed over me like a cold wave, but I couldn't make sense of what had just happened. My dad had been here—or at least it felt like he had. His face, his voice had been so vivid, so real.

"I heard screaming," Roman continued. "I ran in to see what was going on, and I found you." His hand was steady on my arm, grounding me as I struggled to catch my breath.

The lighthouse lamp turned on, its beam slowly rotating and illuminating the maze in shifting patches of light and shadow.

"I know this maze inside and out," Roman said, his tone calm and even. "I trim the hedges and take care of it. That's why

I found you so quickly. I practically grew up here, helping my grandma, Betty."

Quickly? It felt like I had been lost for hours, wandering in circles. My throat was raw from screaming, and my chest heaved as I tried to steady my breathing.

I nodded silently, hugging my knees to my chest. The dampness of the ground seeped through my jeans, but I barely noticed. Painful memories of my dad's voice, his rage, clawed at me, threatening to pull me under again. My stomach churned violently.

No. Not here. Not now. Not in front of him. But it was too late.

I turned my head away from Roman, bile rising uncontrollably. My body convulsed, and the contents of my stomach hit the ground. My throat burned as I coughed, gasping for air.

"This happens often," Roman said. "Not the vomiting part, thankfully." He chuckled, his voice warm and unbothered, as if trying to ease the tension.

Despite my embarrassment, his laughter felt oddly comforting—a small piece of normalcy in this nightmare.

"What I mean is," he continued, "guests wander into the maze all the time, especially at night, and they all say the same thing. They get disoriented, swear they've seen or heard things that aren't real." He paused thoughtfully. "God knows why anyone comes in here after dark. I'm going to ask Rosalie if I can put up arrows inside the maze."

Had it never occurred to him that the guests' claims might be *real*? I wanted to tell him it wasn't just my imagination, but I bit my tongue. Instead, I focused on steadying my breath.

"I'm sorry about this," I finally managed to whisper, my voice hoarse.

"Nah, don't be sorry," he replied easily, his tone reassuring. "I'm just glad I was here. I only work three days a week."

"I wasn't alone," I said shakily, clearing my throat. "I was with sister and my cousins, but they disappeared. I was right behind them, and then…every turn I took was a dead end. I couldn't find a way out."

Roman nodded knowingly. "Yeah, it happens. This maze plays tricks on people, especially at night. Don't worry, I'll get you out of here. Which exit do you need?"

"The one across from the cottage," I said, slowly rising to my feet and brushing the mud from my jeans. My legs felt unsteady, and I wobbled slightly.

Roman stood with a swift, fluid motion, towering over me. He was tall—about six feet—with a strong, athletic build. In the dim light, his chiseled features stood out sharply, though I couldn't make out the color of his hair or eyes.

"Oh right, I remember now. My grandma mentioned new tenants were moving into the cottage. That must be you, right?" Before I could answer, he switched on a torch pointed straight at my face. The beam of light made me flinch.

"Ah man, I'm so clumsy sometimes. Sorry about that!" he said quickly, lowering the torch. "Didn't mean to blind you."

I squinted and muttered, "It's fine."

He gestured ahead with the light. "C'mon. Stick close to me. We don't want you getting lost again," he said jovially.

I kept pace with him, jogging a bit to keep up with his long strides. I didn't want to get lost again either.

"How long are you staying for?" Before I could answer, he fired off another question. "Are you from England? Let me guess—London?"

I exhaled a little too loudly. He talked too much. Too many questions. But he had found me and offered to help; the least I could do was be polite. "We haven't decided how long we'll stay," I said flatly, then added, "Yes, London."

As we neared the exit, a familiar voice called out, "Jenna! Jenna!"

Roman stopped, shining his torch toward the opening of the maze. "Is someone calling you?"

I nodded. Relief washed over me as I saw Ava standing just outside, waving frantically.

"I should've introduced myself earlier. Yes, my name is Jenna. That's my sister."

"Nice to meet you, Jenna." Roman smiled.

When we stepped out, the girls rushed toward me, their voices overlapping.

"Where did you disappear to?"

"What happened?!"

"Are you okay? We were getting really worried about you!"

Elisa's sharp gaze landed on Roman, her tone instantly turning defensive. "Who the hell is he?" she demanded.

Roman offered a calm smile, extending his hand. "I'm Roman."

Elisa didn't take his hand. Instead, her eyes narrowed. "And what were you doing in the maze at night?"

"I heard Jenna screaming and went in to help," Roman said evenly. "I work here in the gardens on Mondays, Wednesdays, and Fridays."

"Today is Tuesday," Elisa pointed out, her voice sharp with suspicion. The girls exchanged wary glances, then looked at me for an explanation.

"Yes, that's right," Roman replied calmly. "I'm here to pick up my grandma. It's getting late, and I don't want her walking home alone. We live just ten minutes from here, but I'd rather she not be out at night, especially with the recent murders."

My stomach tightened. "Murders?" I asked, my voice edged with worry.

Roman softened his tone. "It's late, and I don't want to scare any of you, especially if it's your first night in the cottage."

Ava chimed in, "It's our second night, actually."

"Well, I'll be here tomorrow," Roman said. "If I see any of you, I can tell you what I've heard then."

I nodded, grateful he wasn't going into detail right now. The last thing we needed was the other girls panicking. "That sounds good," I replied, trying to keep my tone light. "I've just started working at the guesthouse, so I'll probably see you around."

"Sure thing. I'll be here around noon." Roman smiled warmly before turning to the girls. "Lovely to meet you all. I know you're new in town, and I'd love for you all to meet my friends. We can show you around."

Ava's face lit up. "Yes, I'd like that."

Salma nodded enthusiastically. "That would be cool."

Elisa forced a smile, saying nothing before turning and walking toward the cottage. Salma and Ava followed, waving goodbye to Roman.

I hung back for a moment, then blurted out, "Thank you for not mentioning the state you found me in."

He grinned. "What state?"

I smiled faintly. "Good night, Roman."

"See you tomorrow," he said warmly before disappearing into the shadows.

Once Elisa and I were alone in our room, I closed the door so the girls wouldn't overhear us. "Els, some freaky stuff has been happening to me," I said, my voice low and urgent.

She put down the magazine she was flipping through and sat next to me on my bed. "What do you mean? What kind of stuff?"

"I've been hearing and seeing things," I whispered, glancing at the door.

She leaned in closer, concern etched across her face. "Like what?"

I took a deep breath. "Yesterday, I heard whispers in the guesthouse, but no one was there."

"Okay…" she said slowly, her expression blank, as if she wasn't sure whether to believe me.

"And in the maze…" I hesitated before continuing. "I saw a shadow, and when it came toward me…it was my dad."

Elisa frowned, tilting her head. "Your dad? Here? If that's true, then where is he now?" Her voice held a hint of sarcasm.

"It was him, I swear. I was terrified. I was screaming, and that's when Roman found me."

"Yeah, that's suspicious. How convenient that only he heard you and we didn't," Elisa shot back.

"Els, you're not getting it."

"I'm trying to understand!"

"And I can't stop thinking about the man in the lodge," I confessed, switching gears, hoping she'd take this more seriously.

"You mean Grumpy Boots you always look for when we pass by Bluebell Lodge?" she asked with a smirk.

I laughed despite everything. "Yeah, him. Turns out he's not grumpy at all. I ran into him yesterday on the street…"

I felt my cheeks heat up as I trailed off, and Elisa's eyes lit up. "Go on. Tell me more."

"His name is Troy, he has these…these intense eyes," I said, feeling a little silly.

"Aw, it's cute hearing you gush like this." She got up and started putting on her yellow pajamas.

I smiled but sobered up. "There's just been a lot going on. Maybe I am imagining things," I admitted, trying to make sense of the strangeness I'd experienced and the new feelings stirring inside me.

"On a different subject entirely…" Elisa pointed to the double bed closest to the en suite. "This side is mine."

"Hey! I wanted that side," I protested. The bed I was on was near the door. "I don't like being stuck over here."

She chuckled, clearly amused. "Well, you know what they say, Jen—you snooze, you lose.

EIGHT

A week flew by as I settled into my routine at the guesthouse, working Thursdays through Mondays. The days blended together as I took on more responsibilities, lightening Maisie's load and giving her more time to bake. The sweet smell of her cakes constantly filled the house, tempting the guests. She left them out on the kitchen counter so people could help themselves throughout the day. Whenever I could, I grabbed a few slices for the girls.

Ava and Salma had started attending hip-hop dance classes twice a week with their new friend Carmen. They always came back breathless and glowing, excitedly recounting their progress, making us watch them as they practiced in the living room. I had to admit, they were flexible and learned the moves with ease.

Elisa, on the other hand, spent most of her time hanging out with Megan and the rest of it in the library, her nose buried in business books. She'd become obsessed with owning a coffee shop, and her enthusiasm was infectious. She hadn't been able to enroll in a course but was determined to educate herself.

"I'm going to do it one day, Jen," she said with a fire in her voice, her eyes bright with determination. "You'll see—my coffee house will be the best in town. It'll have a section that sells books, too."

I could already picture it: a warm, cozy atmosphere, the scent of fresh coffee mingling with the crisp smell of new books. Elisa behind the counter, chatting with customers, making them feel special.

"But Elisa, you'll need a lot of money to get something like that off the ground. And you don't even have a job yet."

"I know, I know," she sighed, rolling her eyes, though her enthusiasm didn't wane. "I'm not saying it's going to happen tomorrow, am I?"

What I didn't tell her—what I couldn't tell her—was that I'd seen it in a vision. Her coffee shop would be exactly as she imagined. But I didn't want to risk saying it out loud, as she might lose her drive, thinking it would just happen on its own.

"Keep looking, Els," I encouraged her. "You'll find a job soon. In the meantime, keep reading. Learn everything you can about coffee, the best machines, what kind of seating you should get. Think about themes and colors for the decor. Oh, and look up distributors for coffee and pastries, and find out where bookstores get their stock."

Elisa nodded enthusiastically, jotting everything down in her notebook.

"You'll also need to learn how to write a business plan," I added, "and figure out the legal stuff. That way, when the time comes, you'll be ready."

She let out a frustrated breath, crossing her arms. "I've responded to every job ad I find, but as soon as they hear I don't have a work permit, it's game over."

"Just keep going," I said, wrapping an arm around her shoulders. "You've got this, Els. The girls and I will help however we can."

Working with Roman was fun; the energy in the guesthouse completely shifted when he was around. His cheerful talk could fill even the quietest spaces, making the place buzz with life. At first, I wondered how he got any work done, what with all his chatter, but he was surprisingly efficient. Sometimes, though, I wished he would stop talking. He had warm brown eyes framed by thick lashes, skin bronzed from working outdoors in the garden, and a natural ease about him. He wasn't arrogant, despite his Hollywood-worthy looks, though I couldn't help but notice how he occasionally glanced around to see if anyone was watching him. He liked attention and being admired, I realized.

Wherever Roman was, Ava and Salma were close behind. They'd become fast friends, spending most of their time together, helping him in the garden and meeting up with his group of friends to play board games, hang out at the beach, or drink and watch films at Carmen's house. One night, they came back late, which sent Elisa and me into a panic. The next day, we all decided to buy cell phones, finally putting my mind at ease when they were out.

Having a cell phone felt like a game-changer. No more pay phones, it felt like freedom in my pocket. No wonder everyone here had them.

Despite working with Roman, it was impossible to get him alone, I really wanted to talk to him about the murders he had mentioned. It kept nagging at me, and I couldn't relax until I knew more. Finally one afternoon, the girls went to their dance class, Elisa was at the library or with Megan, Maisie was baking an apple tart, and Rosalie was tending to her herbs in the greenhouse. The house felt unusually quiet, and I finally had my chance. I spotted him in the garden, putting away his tools in the shed, and went out to meet him.

"Roman," I called out.

He turned with a bright smile. "Hey, Jenna! How's it going? You done for the day?"

I opened my mouth to answer, but he kept talking. "I'm just packing up and then picking up Ava and Salma. We're meeting Isaac and Carmen to see *The Sixth Sense*."

"That's nice," I said, quickly adding, "Elisa and I are planning to go tomorrow night, so don't give anything away okay?"

Roman grinned, then mimed zipping his lips.

"Actually, can we talk for a second?" I said, cutting in before he could switch topics again.

He raised an eyebrow, his curiosity piqued. "Sure. Am I in trouble?"

I led him to the porch of the cottage, wanting privacy. The soft creak of the boards under our feet broke the stillness. I gestured for him to sit in one of the wooden chairs while I went inside to grab us a couple of Cokes.

Through the open window, I heard him muttering to himself. "These plants need a drink," he said, eyeing the swaying hanging baskets. "And these pots…" I caught a glimpse of him testing the dry soil in the flower pots by the window seat.

When I returned, I handed him a glass and sat across from him. My stomach twisted slightly now that I had to bring up the reason I'd pulled him aside. "I've been dying to ask you about the murders you mentioned the other day," I said, keeping my voice low.

The nightmares I'd been having were so vivid; every night, I was overwhelmed with images of strangled bodies. I woke up drenched in sweat, my hands clutching at my throat as if trying to free myself from invisible hands. Even now I could feel the phantom pressure. I couldn't switch the feeling off.

Roman set his drink back on the table, the glass wobbled slightly in his hand. His expression darkened, the carefree energy that usually radiated from him suddenly gone. The wind picked up, setting the chimes tinkling softly above us, and he took a deep breath like he was trying to collect his thoughts.

"It was in the local paper," he began quietly. "Two months ago, a waitress named Melinda was strangled up by Gallows Woods. Last month, another waitress, Selena, was found in the same woods. She'd been strangled, too."

I felt the color drain from my face. Strangled, like in my dream. My throat tightened, and I instinctively began rubbing my neck.

Roman continued, his voice quieter now. "Selena was Carmen's classmate. She used to work weekends with Melinda at the Moonlit Diner. She was so full of life, you know? I keep thinking, what if I had been there that night? Maybe I could have done something." His voice was tinged with guilt, and he exhaled before continuing, "It hit her family really hard, and everyone else in town. It's supposed to be a safe place and all. The police think it's the same person who murdered both of them. The Salem Slayer, they're calling him." For the first time since I'd met him, he looked vulnerable.

A chill ran through me. "I'm sorry if I upset you by bringing it up. Do they have any leads?"

He shook his head. "Not that I know of. But the whole town's on edge. It's like everyone is waiting for something else to happen."

We sat in silence, the chimes tinkling loudly as a sudden gust of wind came out of nowhere.

"I know my grandma doesn't fit his pattern," Roman said, his voice a little quieter now, "but I still hate it when she leaves here late in the evening." The tension in his brow matched the intensity of his words. He took the last sip of his Coke and set the empty glass down on the table with a soft clink. "I'd never let Ava or Salma walk home alone. Not a chance."

Before I could respond, he added, "Or you. If you ever need a ride, call me. Doesn't matter what time, Jenna. Just call me." His gaze was steady and serious. "Here, let me give you my number."

I nodded. "Thank you, Roman. I mean it."

As he typed it into my phone, a deep sense of unease settled in my chest. The killer was still out there, and I felt like I was connected to what was happening somehow.

"Be careful," Roman said, standing up. "Enjoy your evening. And don't forget to water those flowers."

"Okay, I won't." I smiled. "And you enjoy the film."

As I watched him vanish into the trees, a tremor crept down my back. Roman's words left a seed of fear in me. Someone was out there, watching and waiting, I couldn't ignore it, not with my visions and dreams.

As I walked into the cottage with the two empty glasses, I remembered Elisa's skepticism that Roman had just *happened* to be nearby when I'd gotten lost in the maze. I shook my head, dismissing the thought. Roman had been nothing but helpful. But still, something about our conversation left me uneasy.

NINE

The following day, Elisa and I planned to visit Strega Coffee House. Knowing I'd be walking past the Bluebell Lodge, I made an extra effort with my hair and makeup, adding a plum-toned blush to highlight my cheekbones. I'd traded my usual black jeans and shirt for a white crop top and blue jeans; I wanted to be prepared in case I bumped into Troy.

"Megan hasn't responded to any of my messages," Elisa said worriedly as I locked the cottage door behind us. Ava and Salma were still sleeping, having come home late from the movie.

"Maybe she's out of credit?" I suggested, slipping the keys into my black bag and zipping it shut.

"I called her a couple of times. Nothing," Elisa replied, lighting a cigarette. She took a long drag and passed it to me. I inhaled deeply, hoping to settle the unease growing in my chest. Something felt off. I exhaled and handed it back to her.

"Well, she can explain when we see her," I said, trying to sound reassuring.

We walked toward town, the morning sun soft against the sleepy streets. As we passed the Bluebell Lodge, I glanced at the windows, hoping to catch a glimpse of Troy. But the curtains were drawn, and there was no sign of him. I tried to hide my disappointment.

The bell above the door jingled as we stepped into Strega Coffee House, but the usual warm, cozy atmosphere was nowhere to be found. Elisa and I exchanged wide-eyed looks. The café was a disaster—tables cluttered with dirty plates and cups, bits of scrambled eggs and sausages scattered across the floor. Customers shouted over one another, complaining that they'd been waiting more than an hour for their orders.

I slid into our usual booth, pushing aside a sticky fork. "Where's Megan? This place is a wreck," Elisa muttered, grimacing as she wiped up spilled tea with a napkin. She began drumming her fingers uneasily on the table, a quick, sharp rhythm that grated on my nerves.

"Els, can you stop that? It's driving me mad," I snapped.

She frowned at me but stopped. A few customers stormed out, muttering complaints as they went.

"I don't think she's here. Should we go talk to Antonio?" Elisa asked, her voice tight with worry.

I nodded. "If you don't know where she lives, maybe he does."

Elisa hesitated, then said, "I don't," avoiding my gaze.

Something about her tone didn't sit right with me—she was obviously hiding something—but I didn't say anything as I followed her through the swinging kitchen doors.

Antonio was a whirlwind, muttering curses in rapid-fire Italian as he juggled flipping pancakes, frying bacon, and scrambling eggs. The sink was piled high with dirty dishes, and empty tins littered the countertops, adding to the chaos. His hair stuck up in frizzy tufts, and his flushed face betrayed his growing exhaustion.

Elisa stepped closer. "Er…Mr. Antonio?" she called hesitantly. He turned, startled, his wild eyes locking with hers.

"Sorry to bother you," she said, "but we've been trying to get hold of Megan. Do you know where she is?"

Antonio slammed a spatula down on the grill with a force that made me flinch. "Megan! L'idiota! She's been gone for two days—no call, niente! I try calling, she doesn't answer! I go to her place, she's not there. She's gone!"

"Gone? Where?" Elisa sounded truly alarmed.

"I don't know!" Antonio snapped, his anger spilling over as he slammed a pancake onto a plate, making me jump. "She left me in merda! Look at this mess!"

"Els, calm down," I said, placing a hand on her arm. I could understand Antonio's fury, but her reaction seemed disproportionate, and it only deepened my unease.

Elisa blinked, her face pale. "I am calm," she replied, her voice softer now.

Antonio's eyes darted between us. "You ask me for a job, sì? Can you help me today, per favore?"

Elisa's face lit up. "Yes, of course!" She shrugged off her jacket and began rolling up her sleeves.

I had no plans for the day and decided to pitch in. "I'll help, too. I can start by serving the customers who are waiting."

"And I'll handle the dishes and help Antonio with food preparation," Elisa added, her energy renewed.

Antonio's shoulders sagged with relief. "Grazie, grazie! The clean aprons are in the back," he said pointing toward the storage room.

I went out front and started handing out orders. Some customers had already left, which wasn't the worst thing. With fewer people, I could get things back under control. I quickly got the hang of the coffee machine—it wasn't too different from the ones I'd used back in London. Soon I was whipping up drinks, and a few customers even complimented my frothy cappuccinos. Most of the customers were understanding and kind, but a few stared at me pointedly, which made me feel a little uncomfortable. I brushed it off and focused on my tasks, pretending I didn't notice.

Between customers, I cleared the dirty tables, wiped them down, and cleaned up the food on the floor. Once I figured out the table numbers, serving became easier. Antonio popped out occasionally to handle large orders and take payments, and his frantic energy began to settle. Takeaway orders were the simplest—just wrapping pastries and making drinks.

By midday, the café was running more smoothly, but eventually it got so busy that Elisa came out to help take orders. We mixed up a few here and there, but Antonio didn't complain once, even when he had to remake the order.

I was halfway through making a cappuccino when Troy walked in. My stomach flipped, and the milk pitcher nearly overflowed in my quivering hands. Panicking, I dashed into the kitchen. "Els, he's here!" I hissed, barely able to catch my breath.

"Who's here?" she asked, not looking up from the cucumbers she was slicing.

"Troy," I whispered, peeking through the swinging doors.

"Well, go serve him," she replied flatly, clearly unimpressed.

"But I feel nauseated! And my hands are shaking."

Elisa sighed in annoyance. "Jen, I'm busy making this salad. Just go out there and stop being so childish."

Antonio looked over, concerned. "Is something wrong out front?"

"No, no, everything's fine," I lied, taking a deep breath. I exhaled slowly and forced myself to go back out front, trying to calm the adrenaline rushing through me.

Troy stood near the counter, scanning the chaotic café. When his eyes landed on me, they softened, and a small smile tugged at his lips. A warm, familiar tension hung in the air between us, thickening with each passing second. His gaze fixed on mine, and for a moment, it felt like the world around us faded into the background. Conversations hummed softly, cups clinked, but all I could focus on was him. He was wearing a fitted grey shirt and smart trousers, clearly dressed for work at the lodge. His cologne hit me, a fresh, refined, woody scent.

My favorite song, "Fade into You" by Mazzy Star, started playing on the radio.

"Oh, hi, Jen," Troy greeted me, running a hand through his hair. His gaze dropped briefly to my apron. "When did you start working here?"

"Just today," I stammered. "Well, only for today." My voice cracked, and I cringed inwardly. Why did I always get like this around him?

His eyes flicked toward the kitchen. "Where's Megan?"

I hesitated. "Erm. She didn't show up, so my cousin and I are helping Antonio."

"That's lucky for Antonio," Troy said, smiling as our eyes locked again.

"Is my cappuccino coming?" The sharp voice of a waiting customer jolted me back to reality. I flushed with embarrassment, poured the milk into the coffee, and handed it over, apologizing profusely before returning to Troy. "What can I get you?" I asked, hoping he hadn't noticed that my hands were shaking.

"Just a coffee with cream and a croissant, to go."

He fumbled for his change, dropping a few coins onto the floor. People nearby glanced over, but I pretended not to notice, quickly bagging up the croissant and pouring his drink. As I handed him the coffee, our fingers brushed for a split second, sending a wave of tingles through my hand. His eyes lingered on mine, and my breath caught in my throat.

"Thank you," he murmured, his voice soft, almost unsure as he handed me the correct change.

I smiled, feeling my cheeks warm again. "I hope you like my coffee."

"I'm sure I will," he said, winking at me, making my heart skip a beat.

He hesitated, as if wanting to say something more, but instead he gave me a small smile and turned to leave. I watched him walk out the door, feeling a swirl of emotions I wasn't quite sure how to unravel. I had been expecting Troy to ask me to hang out—I'd seen it happen so many times in my visions. As he walked out the door, I couldn't help but wonder why he hadn't. It was clear that he liked me, so what was holding him back?

The sharp ring of the bell snapped me out of my thoughts—Antonio signaling that someone's food was ready. I shook my head slightly, trying to refocus. As I carried the food to a customer, I found myself humming along to the song still playing softly in the background: *"Smiles cover your heart, fade into you…"*

By three p.m., the rush of customers had slowed. Antonio, grateful for our help, made us Strega house specials: Angus steak burgers with five cheeses and fries, along with Cokes. As we ate, he sat down beside us, wiping his hands on his apron.

"Grazie," he said, sighing. "I would've had to shut the café today if you hadn't stepped in."

His expression darkened. "Megan's never done this before," he said grimly. "For six months, she's been reliable. I don't understand why she'd disappear without notice. Her boyfriend isn't answering either. Before she got her cell phone, I used to reach her through her boyfriend."

Elisa lowered her head, rubbing her temples, then started tapping on the table again, her fingers drumming in that familiar nervous rhythm. She looked up at Antonio and then at me, taking a deep breath.

"I think I know what happened," she said, her voice quieter than usual. When she turned toward me, my stomach twisted. I had a feeling she was about to say something really bad.

She took a deep breath and looked down, avoiding my gaze. "I gave her four thousand dollars and our passports." She covered her face with her hands and mumbled through them, "She said her boyfriend could get us green cards."

The words hit me like a slap. "You did *what?*" I shouted, rising from my chair.

Antonio let out a sarcastic laugh. He turned to Elisa, "Did you even meet the boyfriend? The guy looks like a crackhead, and you trusted him?"

Elisa looked up at me, "I'm sorry!" she cried. "I thought I was helping—I was fed up with getting rejected from all the jobs I have been applying for." Her shoulders slumped, the sadness clear in her eyes.

"Yes, but we're talking about *four thousand dollars and our passports*, Elisa! How could you fall for that?" I threw my hands in the air, anger surging through me. I shook my head, feeling bile rise in my throat.

Antonio interrupted before I could say more. "We should report this to the police, see if they can help," he said. He pulled out his phone and started dialing.

I gave Elisa a hard side-eye. "I need the bathroom," I muttered, walking away quickly.

As soon as I reached the bathroom, I put my finger down my throat and everything I'd just eaten came rushing back up, splashing into the toilet. The urge to vomit wasn't from the food—it was from the shock of nearly all our savings being gone. Feeling a little better, I stayed there for several minutes, letting the cool air settle my nerves.

When I finally returned to the table, Antonio had returned to the kitchen. I sat back down without saying a word to Elisa, avoiding her gaze altogether. The silence between us was deafening, so I picked up the daily paper and pretended to read.

Twenty minutes later, two uniformed officers arrived. The taller one removed his hat and shook hands with Antonio, exchanging pleasantries in a mix of Italian and English. His black hair was neatly cropped and combed to the side, his dark, soulful eyes framed by sun-kissed skin. He introduced himself as Officer Marco Luca. His partner, Officer Owen Mitchell, stood beside him—a bit heavier, with a round face and a hint of a double chin. His uniform strained slightly around his midsection. He appeared a bit older than Officer Luca, maybe around thirty.

Officer Luca sat down with a reassuring smile and kind eyes that instantly put us somewhat at ease. Elisa, her voice shaky with regret, explained that she had handed over the money and passports in exchange for four green cards.

Officer Mitchell jotted down all our details in a small leather-bound notebook, occasionally nodding or asking clarifying questions. Antonio, ever the host, busied himself at the coffee machine, preparing cappuccinos for the officers.

Officer Luca turned to Antonio, his expression serious. "Do you have Megan's address and phone number? We'll head over there and check things out. If missing shifts is out of character for her, we could be looking at a welfare issue. But if it looks like she and the boyfriend have taken off, I'll file a report for theft, and we'll do everything we can to find and arrest them." He handed his card to Elisa with a reference number jotted on the back.

When the officers stood to leave, Elisa turned to me. "He's gorgeous," she whispered.

I shook my head and grinned. "You've got your priorities straight, at least."

"I will contact you with an update later," Officer Luca called from the door, and Elisa nodded, her eyes following him out onto the street. I nudged her, raising an eyebrow and teasing, "Stop staring at him like that, it's so obvious."

Elisa blushed, her cheeks warming. "I mean, look at him! He's friendly, tall, dark, and handsome."

Antonio approached our table, rubbed his temples like he had a headache. "Elisa, if you still want a job here, you can start right away." Then he added, "Jenna, how about you? I can help you both get green cards."

I shook my head, smiling. "I'm already working at the guesthouse, but my sister Ava would be interested."

"Sì, sì, please," Antonio said hastily. "I need reliable and hardworking people. I'm very impressed with both of you. If your sister is anything like you, I'd be happy to have her start right away, too." He smiled warmly, clearly relieved at the prospect of extra help.

TEN

The following evening, I vented to Rosalie about how upset I was that Elisa had given our money to Megan. "The only upside is that she and Ava have been offered jobs at the café," I added, my voice thick with frustration.

"Everything happens for a reason," Rosalie replied in her usual wise tone, her calm presence soothing me. "What seems bad now might turn out to be a blessing in disguise."

"That money was our safety net, though," I said, sadly picking at my nails. "What if something goes wrong again?"

Before Rosalie could respond, the front door burst open, and Salma and Ava stomped in, mid-argument.

"I saw you flirting with him," Salma accused, her amber eyes flashing with anger.

"I was just being friendly!" Ava shot back, throwing her bag onto the table. "Besides, it's not like he's asked you out. Why are you acting so territorial?"

Salma's voice wavered, hurt rising to the surface. "You know I like him, but you're always jumping into our conversations, trying to steal his attention. You never let us have a moment alone!"

Ava smirked, clearly enjoying pushing her cousin's buttons and riling her up. "He likes me, Sal. Deep down, you know it."

"Whoa, whoa! Easy, you two!" I interjected, stepping between them. "What's going on here? Who are you even fighting about?"

"Roman," they answered in unison, then exchanged a glance and half smiled, trying not to laugh despite the rising tension.

Rosalie, who had been watching quietly from her chair, set down her tea and raised an eyebrow. "Hmm, I hope he's not playing with both your feelings and turning you against each other. Be careful," she said gently. "I've known Roman for a long time. He's a sweet boy, but he craves attention."

They both sat down at the kitchen table, arms crossed, glaring at each other in silence. I let out a quiet sigh, relieved the argument seemed to be cooling off, at least for now.

After a few moments of awkward quiet, Salma turned to Rosalie. "So, what did you want to talk to me about?" she asked, her tone still laced with irritation but her curiosity winning out.

Rosalie smiled at her warmly. "I have some exciting news. My friend owns a print shop downtown, and she's looking for help designing cards for birthdays, Halloween, engagements—all kinds of things. She also prints photos and promotional materials. I showed her the sketch you did of the garden the other day, and she was really impressed."

Salma's expression brightened instantly, her annoyance melting away. "Oh my god, really?"

"She thinks you'd be perfect for the job. And if you're interested, I bet you could design cards and posters to help advertise the guesthouse, too," Rosalie added with a wink.

"Yes! I'd love to!" Salma said, nearly jumping out of her seat with excitement.

Rosalie chuckled. "Tricilla's shop is just a short walk from Strega's—it's called Salem's Crafty Arts and Print Store. She's expecting you tomorrow morning around ten."

Salma squealed, clapping her hands. "We've been there before! I know exactly where it is!"

Rosalie suddenly stood and looked toward the hallway, her expression tense. "We have company," she said in a worried tone. "Jenna, please go get Elisa."

Confused, I followed her out of the room, Salma and Ava right behind me. "There's no one here, Rosalie."

Just then, the sound of the front door chimes echoed through the house. Salma and Ava exchanged puzzled glances.

In walked Officer Luca and Officer Mitchell, both standing tall with their hats in their hands, their expressions grave. A cold knot tightened in my stomach. Something bad had happened.

"Hello again," Officer Luca said to me, his tone professional but soft. "We have some updates, but I'd like Elisa to be present, as she filed the initial report."

"She's at the cottage," I said quickly, my throat dry. "I'll go get her."

Rosalie ushered them into the living room. "Please, have a seat. Can I offer you some homemade tonic tea?"

I bolted out of the guesthouse, cut through the greenhouse, and raced past the garden, my pulse pounding not just from the officers' sudden arrival but also from the unease of approaching the maze. I sprinted past it without looking at the dark entrance. The cottage lights blazed, and I fumbled with my keys before finally bursting through the door. "Elisa?! *Elisa*, where are you?" I called out, breathless.

"What? I'm right here," she answered, looking up from the couch. "I'm not deaf! What's with all the shouting?"

"Officer Luca wants to talk to you," I panted. "It's about Megan."

Elisa shot up from the sofa. "He's here? Outside?"

"No, he's at the guesthouse."

"Oh my god. Do I look okay? I can't go like this!" She pointed to her frizzy curls and Minnie Mouse pajamas.

"Elisa," I groaned, rolling my eyes. "He's not here to ask you out!"

Still, she darted into our room, emerging minutes later in fitted jeans and a hoodie, her hair pulled back into a neat bun. She dabbed some gloss on her full lips, smacking them together and pouting. "How do I look now?"

"Beautiful, as always. Now hurry, I'm dying to know what he has to say!"

I left the porch light on and closed the door behind us, and we rushed back to the guesthouse. Elisa greeted the officers and sat across from Officer Luca, and I took the seat beside her. Salma and Ava hovered near the doorway, their faces etched with concern.

Officer Luca inhaled and sat up straight, his neck muscles tensing. "I have some bad news," he began, his voice low. "This may be hard to hear—I don't know how close you all were to Megan." He paused and lowered his gaze, twisting his hat t as if bracing himself for his next words. "We, ah…we were forced to break into Megan's apartment. We found her body. I can't share too many details right now, but we are treating this as a homicide."

A chill spread through my body, I stared at him in disbelief. The other three girls gasped, their hands flying to their mouths. "Oh my god," Elisa whispered.

"We suspect that her boyfriend, Orion, is responsible," said Officer Mitchell, his tone strained. "He's missing, along with the money, but we recovered your passports."

Elisa's face crumpled. "If I hadn't given her the money…"

"This isn't your fault," Officer Luca said firmly, leaning forward. "We believe Orion is connected to a series of murders we're investigating. Megan was already in danger, even before she met you."

Salma, pale and weak, muttered, "I need some fresh air," heading for the garden. Ava followed close behind her. She seemed to have shrunk into herself.

Officer Mitchell continued, "We think Orion may be the Salem Slayer, as the modus operandi matches."

Elisa's head shot up, her brow furrowed in confusion. "The what?"

"We believe he's a serial killer," Officer Mitchell explained. "Three women have been strangled, one at the end of each month. Megan's murder fits the pattern."

The room fell silent, the impact of his words pressing down on all of us. Elisa's face was ashen as she clutched her head, struggling to process the horrifying details.

"There's a forensic team at Megan's flat," Officer Luca continued. "They're collecting DNA, fingerprints, fibers—anything we can use. We already have a warrant out for his arrest."

I sank back into the sofa, my stomach churning. This was far more serious than I had imagined. My mind whirred, and I closed my eyes for a brief moment, trying to make sense of everything I'd just learned. I wanted to ask a dozen questions but found myself unable to speak at all.

Officer Luca broke the silence, his voice softer now. "We'll need a full statement from you, Elisa. You may have been one of the last people to see or speak with Megan. Can you recall anything unusual?"

Elisa shook her head slowly, and when she spoke, her voice was barely above a whisper. "I never met her boyfriend. She only mentioned his name. That's all I know." Her voice cracked as she lowered her head. "I feel terrible. If I hadn't given her the money, maybe they wouldn't have fought…maybe he wouldn't have killed her."

Officer Luca leaned in slightly, placing a reassuring hand on her shoulder. His tone was steady but kind. "Elisa, you shouldn't blame yourself for this. There was nothing you could've done to change the outcome. This wasn't just about the money."

Rosalie entered the room just then, balancing a tray with two cups of tea. She moved with quiet composure, handing one to each officer before settling into the armchair. But her eyes were watchful as she listened to every word.

Officer Luca took a sip of tea and continued, "We've contacted Megan's mother. She's flying in from Oregon tomorrow. She may want to speak with you, Elisa, if you're willing, just to understand more about her daughter's last days."

The room fell silent, broken only by the static crackle of the officers' radios. Officer Mitchell spoke briefly into his before turning to his partner. "The sheriff's asking for an update. We should head back to the station."

Both officers stood, preparing to leave. Officer Luca turned to Elisa. "Can you come by the station tomorrow at ten a.m.?" His voice was gentle.

Elisa nodded, trying hard to hold back her tears. "I'll be there," she said softly.

"I know this is difficult," Officer Luca added, his dark eyes steady. "But we're going to do everything we can to find him."

I leaned closer to Elisa and whispered, "Do you want me to go with you?"

She shrugged, her expression tired and defeated, but she nodded slightly. "Maybe."

As the officers headed toward the door, Officer Luca turned to Rosalie with a small polite smile. "Thank you for the tea, ma'am."

"You're very welcome," Rosalie replied warmly. She let them out and locked the door behind them.

Elisa let out a long breath, then stood abruptly. "I need a cigarette," she muttered, dazed.

I followed her through the kitchen and toward the garden, where Salma and Ava were already sitting, deep in hushed conversation.

"I'm here if you need to talk, girls," Rosalie called gently from the hallway.

I nodded, offering her a small smile of gratitude before stepping outside with Elisa.

Salma and Ava looked up as we joined them, their faces still pale and worried. Without a word, they walked toward us. Elisa lit a cigarette, took a drag, and then silently passed it to me and lit another for Salma and Ava to share. None of us spoke as we began the slow, quiet walk back to the cottage. The lighthouse's lamp flicked on in the distance, casting long, pale beams of light that danced through the trees. Our footsteps crunching over the gravel was the only sound breaking the silence.

As the cottage came into view through the trees, my breath caught in my throat. Every single light inside the house was on. I slowed my pace, staring at the glow spilling from the windows. I was certain I'd left only the porch light on. My pulse accelerated, a creeping sense of unease taking hold of me. I glanced at Elisa, but she didn't seem to notice anything unusual. Deciding not to alarm anyone, I kept quiet.

My fingers quivered slightly as I unlocked the front door. I stepped inside quickly, scanning the hallway, my eyes darting from corner to corner. Everything seemed normal, though I still felt uneasy. I made my way to the kitchen door and checked the lock. It was secure.

The others filed in behind me, their voices low as they talked about the officers' visit. I turned on the TV, hoping the familiar hum of background noise would ease my nerves. It didn't.

Salma and Ava excused themselves early, heading to their room. "I'm exhausted," Ava mumbled. Salma just nodded, her face still drawn.

"Els, you want to talk?" I asked as Elisa lingered near the living room doorway.

"I think I'll shower first, try to relax," she replied, shaking out her curls. She disappeared into the bedroom.

I sank into the sofa, flipping through channels absentmindedly until I landed on MTV. Ricky Martin's "Livin' la Vida Loca" burst through the speakers, the upbeat melody a sharp contrast to the gloomy mood pressing down on me. I forced myself to murmur along, hoping to lift my spirits.

But after a few minutes, something still felt…off.

A creeping sensation climbed up my spine, cold and deliberate, inching toward my neck. My breath stalled. It felt as though someone were sitting right beside me, watching, their presence creepy and oppressive.

I turned my head slowly, dread pooling in my stomach.

No one was there.

My jaw clenched. I forced myself to take a few deep breaths, whispering, "It's okay, Jen. There's nothing there. Just get up and walk to the bedroom. You can do this."

My hands shook as I switched off the TV and turned out the light. Not looking back, I dashed out of the living room. Only the faint glow of the hall lamp remained. The feeling of being watched stayed with me as I walked to my bedroom, shutting the door firmly behind me.

Elisa sat at the dressing table, drying her hair. She flinched when she noticed me in the doorway. "God, you scared me," she said, catching her breath as she switched off the hair dryer.

I crossed the room to close the curtains. The sensation of unseen eyes lingered, the darkness outside pressing against the glass.

ELEVEN

I glanced at my watch—I was already five minutes late. I had agreed to meet the girls at Strega's Coffee House at four. The exhaustion from a restless night weighed heavily on me. I had hardly slept at all. At some point, I'd heard the creaking of wood, like footsteps on the porch, followed by faint whispers outside the bedroom door. These sounds were familiar at the guesthouse, but not in the cottage.

I'd taken the long route to Strega's, wandering through the cobbled streets lined with historic buildings painted deep hues of red, orange, and brown. Their rustic charm always made me feel like I'd stepped into a postcard. I dreamed of owning one someday. The town was alive with a quiet hum as locals and tourists browsed the quaint shops selling handmade candles, tarot cards, and vintage books.

I stopped at Blue Ink Books & Candles to pick up some sage and candles. I'd seen Rosalie cleanse spaces many times before, and after last night, I felt like I needed to clear whatever was lingering around me.

Crossing the street, I spotted Salma waving at me from our usual booth in Strega's. As I pushed open the door, the comforting aroma of roasted coffee beans wrapped around me, but my breath caught. Behind the counter, I saw Megan. My pulse quickened, but then I blinked, and the illusion vanished.

It was Ava.

"Jen, how do I look?" she asked, grinning as she walked toward me.

For a moment, I was speechless. Ava had dark eyeliner smudged around her eyes, and her hair was pulled back into a sleek ponytail, defining her petite diamond-shaped face. She was dressed from head to toe in black.

"This is how Megan used to dress," she explained, spinning around to show off her new look. "The café has a witch theme, so I have to look the part."

"It worked—I actually thought you were Megan for a second," I admitted, sliding into the booth next to Salma.

"Everyone—and I mean *everyone*—has been saying the same thing!" Ava said, clearly pleased with herself.

"Oh, and before I forget," she added, lowering her voice, "someone was asking about you."

I took my jacket off and placed it beside me. "Who?"

She leaned in toward me. "Goldie!" she teased, giggling.

"Goldie?" I glanced at Salma, checking to see if she knew who Ava was referring to.

"You know…Troy from the Bluebell Lodge." Ava sat opposite me.

My cheeks flushed. "He was here?" I looked around the café excitedly, hoping he might still be nearby.

"He asked where you were, and I told him you're my sister. He got all flustered, then asked which of us was older. And guess what? He said he thinks you're stunning and he wants to take you out!"

I tossed a napkin at her, laughing. "You're making that up!"

"Okay, maybe he didn't say all that," Ava admitted with a grin. "But he did ask if you were working today. I definitely think he likes you."

Salma burst into laughter. "I've got to meet this guy and see what all the fuss is about."

Ava stood up. "Anyway, let me check on Elisa in the kitchen. And before I switch off the coffee machine, I'll make you both my decorative hot chocolates with cream. I've perfected them."

Salma and I raised our eyebrows, nodding.

As Ava disappeared into the back, Salma leaned forward, telling me about her day at Salem's Crafty Arts and Print Store. "Triscilla is such a perfectionist, but honestly, I don't mind it. I'm the same way," she said with a shrug.

She described the shop with an excited glimmer in her eyes. "It's tucked between a witchy apothecary and a tiny café. The smell of fresh espresso and pastries wafts in, and I know you'd love the apothecary. The shop itself has these vintage printing presses, and the smell of ink and paper hits you as soon as you walk in. We had so many customers today dropping off film. You're holding people's memories in your hands."

Salma's enthusiasm was infectious. The shop was the perfect place for her to work. It was as if Rosalie had known that she would thrive there.

A few minutes later, Antonio dimmed the kitchen lights and reminded Elisa to lock up when we were done. She finally joined us, sliding into the booth with a long sigh.

"Make room—I'm exhausted," she muttered, yawning. "I spent hours at the station this morning waiting to give a brief statement. Luca is really dedicated to the case and ever so hot." She blushed. "I could sit there and watch him all day."

"More importantly, sis, are they any closer to catching him?" Salma said, her tone anxious. "I don't feel safe knowing he's still out there. I'm always checking over my shoulder."

"They're close," Elisa assured her. "They know where Orion lives and are tracking down friends and family. It's just a matter of time."

Salma turned to me, studying my face. "What's up, Jen? You've been quiet. Everything okay?"

"I don't know." I shrugged. "I have this peculiar feeling, like Megan is here with us. When I first walked in, I actually thought Ava was her."

Ava glanced up, "I think it's just the makeup—you're not used to seeing me like this."

"Yeah, maybe," I said, absentmindedly picking the pumpkin sweet off the top of my hot chocolate and stirring in the cream.

Elisa spoke up, her tone serious. "I asked Megan's mum to meet me here. She has a few questions for me."

The door chimed just then, and a short middle-aged woman walked in. She wore a long grey coat over blue leggings and a V-neck top, her bright pink handbag bulging at the seams. Her eyes were swollen and red, and her bobbed hair clung flatly to her face.

Elisa stood up and took a few steps toward her. "Hi, are you Mary?"

"Yes. You must be Elisa," the woman replied softly.

Elisa nodded, extending her hand to shake Mary's. "Would you mind if my sister and cousins joined us?"

"Of course not," Mary said, taking off her jacket and following Elisa to the table. I shuffled over to make room. Mary sat next to me and placed her jacket on her lap.

"I didn't know Megan very well, but I'm so sorry for your loss," I said, my voice gentle.

Tears welled in Mary's eyes, spilling down her cheeks as her body shuddered. "We had an argument." She wiped her eyes before she continued. "Megan said she wanted to move out. I tried to stop her, begged her to stay, but she wouldn't listen. When she set her mind on something, there was no stopping her." Mary paused and looked at me. I nodded for her to continue.

"I got so angry…I told her I never wanted to see her again. I didn't mean it—of course I didn't. And now she's gone forever. I'll never forgive myself." Mary bowed her head and sat in silence, closing her eyes tightly.

Elisa shot me an awkward *what do I do* look. I shrugged. Salma and Ava just sat there awkwardly, not knowing what to say.

Elisa finally said, "Mary, I'll get you some water."

My cousin got up, and I slowly reached for Mary's hand, trying to offer what little comfort I could. The moment our skin touched, a vision hit me, vivid and sharp.

Megan stood at the door, suitcase in hand, her face twisted with anger.

"You never believed me when I told you over and over that Andy molested me!" she screamed. Her voice was raw, filled with betrayal.

Mary slapped her, eyes blazing. "You've always wanted to ruin my marriage. You're just like your father—always lying. I never want to see you again!" She pushed her daughter out into the cold.

"*I hate you!*" screamed Megan.

Elisa returned with a glass of water for Mary, and the vision faded, leaving me breathless. My chest felt tight as I looked at Mary. "Where is Megan's biological father?"

Mary's eyes widened in shock. "How did you—?" She hesitated, then lowered her gaze. "We haven't spoken in years."

"He needs to know she's gone," I urged gently. "Tell him for Megan. She wants him there at the funeral."

Mary's face crumpled as fresh tears spilled down her cheeks.

Tell her she mustn't punish herself for not believing me, Megan's voice whispered in my mind. *Or for letting me go.*

I exhaled slowly, gripping Mary's hand. "Megan forgives you."

At my words, Mary broke down completely, her raw anguish filling the café. Elisa passed her tissues, resting a hand on her arm, as the rest of us sat in solemn silence. Salma and Ava wiped their eyes, the pain of shared grief pulling us closer together. We, just like Megan, had left an unhappy home.

I thought of my mum and felt a sudden ache of longing. How must she feel now, or if she were in Mary's place? I decided then and there that I'd call her. She deserved to know we were safe.

"I'm so sorry," Elisa said softly, breaking the silence. "Megan and I talked every day. Most of the time, she seemed happy. She took me out, made me laugh—she was always so funny. But the last couple of times I saw her, she seemed…off. She looked thinner, and she had shadows under her eyes. She didn't talk much about Orion. If she'd given me any hint that she was suffering, I would've reported him to the police in a heartbeat."

Mary wiped her face with a tissue Elisa had given her. "I wish I'd known what was going on," she said, coughing. "She was always so stubborn, so headstrong. She kept everything bottled up." She looked down at her lap, smoothing the creases in her jacket. "We'll be burying her in Astoria, Oregon, where she grew up. She absolutely loved Cannon Beach. We had so many happy memories there, and I think it's best for her to be buried close to home."

"Oh yeah, she mentioned Cannon Beach once," Elisa said, her voice soft. "She wanted me to do a scenic drive to Seattle with her."

Mary's lip quivered as she let out a deep sigh. "A mother shouldn't have to bury her child." Her tears returned, spilling over as her voice cracked. "I don't know when they'll release her body or when the funeral will be, but you're all invited, if you can make it."

"We'll be there," I said gently, my hand resting on Mary's arm. Elisa nodded in agreement, her eyes glassy.

Mary had booked a room at a nearby bed and breakfast, but before she left, I insisted that she stay at the guesthouse from tomorrow onward. I knew Rosalie would make her feel at home with her calming teas and herbal remedies. The guesthouse, with its earthy warmth and quiet charm, felt like a good place for someone who was grieving.

Before we parted, Elisa gave Mary her cell number, telling her to call if she needed anything. We walked her to the door, the town felt quieter than usual as we watched Mary disappear around the corner.

TWELVE

Later that night, Ava abruptly shook me awake.

"Jenna, Jenna, wake up," she whispered urgently, her voice laced with fear as she jostled my arm. Disoriented, I blinked, momentarily confused, thinking I was in London before reality settled in. Ava's panicked face hovered above me, illuminated by the soft glow from the hallway. To my right, Elisa was fast asleep, her breathing steady and undisturbed.

"What's up, sis?" I whispered, sitting up quickly.

"I just saw a ghost," she replied, her voice cracking as she gripped the blanket with trembling hands.

A jolt of unease shot through me. "Where?" I asked, scanning the room, my voice hushed but alert. I reached for the bedside lamp. The soft amber light revealed the clock—it was just past midnight.

"In the living room," Ava said, her voice barely above a whisper. "I couldn't sleep, so I was sitting on the sofa, thinking about Megan and Mary and how upset she was…and then I saw it."

I swung my legs over the side of the bed and tugged her down to sit next to me. "Go on," I urged gently, trying to keep her calm even as my heart began to racing rapidly.

Ava took a deep, shaky breath. "I was staring at the blank TV screen, just, you know, zoning out. It was off, completely black. Then, suddenly, I saw a white shape reflected in the screen… standing right next to me."

I held my breath as my throat tightened. The fear in her eyes told me she hadn't imagined this.

Her voice wavered. "I didn't dare turn my head or look back at the TV screen. I just ran straight here. It scared me to death."

I squeezed her hand gently. "It's okay," I whispered, pulling her into a hug. The truth was, I believed her. I had felt something the other night, too—that unnerving sensation of not being alone.

"I'll go check," I said, standing up. My body tensed, but I didn't want Ava to see my fear.

She followed me as I tiptoed down the hallway. The cottage felt colder than usual, the air heavier. When we reached the living room, it was still. Quiet. The sofa looked undisturbed, and the TV screen reflected only the faint glow of the hallway light. But the chill lingered, crawling along my skin.

Then, suddenly—*thud*.

We both jumped, our eyes snapping to the ceiling.

The sound came again, faint but unmistakable—footsteps, slow and deliberate, coming from the attic.

Salma shuffled into the room, rubbing her eyes and yawning. "What's all that noise?" she muttered groggily.

I glanced at her, my teeth chattering. "I think it's coming from the attic."

Salma looked up just as another thud reverberated above us. Her eyes widened. "What the hell was that?"

Determined to stay rational, I turned on every light in the house as I made my way to the kitchen. I grabbed the long metal hook for opening the attic hatch.

Salma grabbed my arm. "Are you out of your mind? You're not seriously going up there!"

"It's probably a bat or something," I said, trying to make it sound logical even though I knew it wasn't.

With Ava and Salma huddled behind me, I reached up and pulled down the hatch. The door creaked on its hinges, sending a shower of dust down into the kitchen. The wooden ladder unfolded, groaning as it extended to the floor.

Elisa strolled into the kitchen, casually lighting a cigarette. "What's going on in here?" she asked, tying her robe tighter around her waist. Her expression shifted to annoyance as she took in the three of us standing frozen beneath the attic hatch. "Why is every light in the house on? And who's making all that noise?"

"It's not us," I whispered, my eyes fixed on the pitch-black opening above.

Elisa exhaled a long stream of smoke, her disbelief palpable. "Jen, don't start with your creepy haunted house nonsense. I'm really not in the mood for it tonight." She put on her slippers and plopped down on a breakfast bar stool. "You've been acting weird all day, including with Mary earlier."

"Shh!" I hissed, cutting her off. A deep thud echoed from the attic.

Elisa's face paled, her bravado faltering. She stared up at the hatch. "What on earth was that sound?" she said, her voice suddenly hushed.

"It started right after I saw a ghost," Ava whispered. She moved closer to Elisa as if proximity would protect her. "I saw it reflected in the blank TV screen—it was standing right next to me in the living room."

Elisa blinked, clearly unsure whether to take her seriously. "If you're trying to scare me, you're gonna have to do better than that."

Salma, now looking more serious, took Elisa's cigarette from her fingers and inhaled deeply before passing it to Ava. "I believe them," she said, glancing toward the ceiling. "I've been hearing noises, too. I'm freaking out."

Ava took a shaky drag and passed the cigarette to me. I took a few pulls, but the nicotine barely steadied my nerves. When I handed it back to Elisa, she muttered, "You lot need to buy your own packs," irritably crushing it into the ashtray. Sighing, she lit another. The air around her seemed to calm as she exhaled slowly, even though the rest of us were still on edge.

The attic remained eerily silent, but the stillness was just as unnerving as the noise had been. We all stared at the black void, unsure what to do next.

Elisa walked over to a cabinet, yanked open a drawer, and pulled out a torch. She flicked it on and off, testing the battery. Then, after a deep breath, she grabbed a rolling pin and handed it to me.

"All right, Jenna," she said, pointing the torch toward the hatch. "Time to find out who or what, or what is up there. We're going up. I'm not dealing with this nonsense alone." Her voice was firm, but I could see the unease in her eyes. She glanced at Ava and Salma, who were still huddled together near the doorway. "And you two, if anything goes sideways, call Rosalie."

With fluttering hands, I gripped the rolling pin and followed Elisa as she tested the ladder, its creak cutting through the silence. Each step sent a shiver up my spine.

The space grew colder as we climbed, carrying with it the musty scent of aged wood and decay. My heart thrummed, and I had to force myself to keep moving.

At the top, Elisa hesitated, then climbed fully into the attic. She turned to me. "Don't just stand there—get up here."

I pulled myself up behind her, wincing as my hands touched the dusty floor. I hated spiders and had no doubt there were plenty lurking in the corners. The attic stretched out in front of us, its wooden rafters draped in thick cobwebs, swaying in the shadows like ghostly veils. Old trunks and crates were scattered around, their cracked surfaces betraying years of neglect. It felt like stepping into a forgotten world.

I stood and reached for the string hanging to my right. When I pulled it, the overhead bulb fluttered weakly, barely casting light into the far corners of the attic.

The temperature dropped even further, and a prickle of unease swept over me. The attic felt stuffy, as if the air itself was holding its breath.

Elisa and I exchanged looks, silently acknowledging our fear. She took my hand, squeezing it for reassurance before stepping forward cautiously.

The floorboards groaned beneath our weight, each creak magnified in the eerie silence. Then, to our left, something shifted—a faint sound of something falling close by.

My stomach twisted with dread as we turned toward the noise. We moved slowly, hesitantly, until we reached a tarnished mirror leaning against the wall beside an old brown chest. My breath stopped as a shadowy silhouette flickered in the reflection, there for a split second before vanishing into the dark. I whirled around, searching for the source of the shadow, but there was nothing behind us.

"Elisa," I whispered. "Did you see that?" I pointed at the mirror.

"No," she muttered, shaking her head, her grip on the torch unsteady. "Let's just look around quickly and get the hell out of here." She swept the beam across the room, the light cutting through the dust and shadows.

I crouched by the chest, drawn to it by some unexplainable pull. I handed Elisa the rolling pin. "Here, hold this for me." The lid was difficult to lift, the hinges protesting as I pried it open, using all my strength. Inside were masks, sculptures, old books—relics of another time. Then something caught my eye—something flat and wooden sticking out from beneath the clutter.

You found it, said a whisper in my ear, so faint I wasn't sure if I had imagined it.

I froze, glancing up at Elisa. "Did you hear that?"

She shook her head. "No. The only thing I can hear is my heart pounding in my ears, and I like it that way."

Ignoring the unease clawing at me, I tugged the wooden board free, brushing off decades of dust with my sleeve. The word *Ouija* stared back at me.

Elisa crouched beside me, her voice sharp. "Leave that there, Jen. I've seen enough horror movies to know messing with that is a bad idea. Put it back."

I shook my head, the pull to take it irresistible. "No. I'm bringing it downstairs."

Elisa groaned, exasperated. "You're so stubborn! Fine. I'm not going to argue, but don't come complaining to me when something bad happens."

We waited a few more minutes, listening intently. The attic was silent now—no more footsteps or thuds.

Elisa swept the torch across the space one last time. "The noise we heard was probably just rats or something. Let's go." I nodded, closing the chest.

As we descended the ladder, the hair on the back of my neck bristled like I could feel unseen eyes lingering on me. Before pulling the attic hatch shut, I looked up at the dark, empty space above me one last time.

Then I saw it—eerie, molten green eyes flashing at me like a torch, before I closed the hatch, plunging the attic into darkness.

THIRTEEN

Salma set steaming mugs of hot chocolate on the kitchen table. The warm aroma of cocoa filled the room. "This will help us relax and go back to sleep," she said, attempting to sound calm. But as she moved to sit, her gaze landed on the object I was holding. Her brow furrowed. "What's that?" she asked, her tone uncertain.

I glanced down. "It's a Ouija board."

"A what board?" Salma asked, puzzled, sitting down slowly.

"Ouija," I repeated, placing it carefully on the table. The wood felt heavier and colder than it had when I'd picked it up. I wiped away the dust with a damp cloth, revealing a triangular planchette resting in the middle as if fixed in place. The board was engraved with the alphabet, numbers from zero to nine, and the words *yes*, *no*, and *goodbye*.

Ava leaned closer, her curiosity overcoming her fear. "What's it for?"

"More creepy crap," Elisa interjected sarcastically, crossing her arms as she leaned back in her chair. "I saw one of those in a horror movie once. People tried to talk to spirits, and everything went to shit."

"That's just a movie," I replied. "This is a legitimate divination tool meant to communicate with the spirit world. We could use it to connect with a friendly spirit and ask questions."

"We are doing nothing of the sort," Elisa replied flatly, lifting her mug. "We're drinking hot chocolate and going to bed. That's what we're doing."

Before I could argue, the cat flap snapped shut with a loud bang. We all screamed.

"Oh, it's just Luna!" Ava exhaled in relief as the cat leapt gracefully onto the table, purring as if she hadn't just scared the life out of us. One by one, we stroked her soft fur, her presence grounding us.

"Please, please, please can we try the Ouija board?" I begged after a few moments. "Let's just see if it works. We'll be careful, I promise."

Elisa groaned, rubbing her temples. "Fine. But if something weird happens, it's on you."

Encouraged, I grabbed a container of salt from the pantry and sprinkled it in a protective circle around the board. "This is for safety," I explained. Then I searched the kitchen drawers where I had stored blessed candles I bought from one of the witchy looking shops downtown. I handed each of them a candle—black for protection for Elisa, white for positive energy for Salma, and blue for communication for Ava. I lit a purple one in the center to enhance psychic abilities, its flame dancing in the ambience.

We sat around the table, placing our fingers lightly on the planchette. The energy felt heavier now, the warmth of the hot chocolate fading as an icy stillness crept into the room.

I began, my voice steady despite the knot of anxiety in my chest. "We call upon the spirit world."

Elisa snickered, mimicking me in a deep, theatrical voice. "We call upon the spirit world!"

Ava and Salma looked at each other and burst into laughter, and even I cracked a smile.

"Come on, stop messing around and take this seriously," I said, suppressing my grin. After they stopped laughing, I asked, "Does anyone else want to lead?"

They all silently shook their heads.

I cleared my throat and started again, my voice firm. "We are gathered here tonight to speak to friendly spirits. Spirits, we call to you. If you are good and kind, please communicate with us."

The room fell into an ominous silence, broken only by the soft crackle of the candles. Shadows danced across the walls, their shapes shifting as the flames swayed. We held our breath, staring at the planchette, waiting for any sign of movement.

"I don't think it's working," Ava whispered, breaking the silence.

"Maybe too many of us have our fingers on it," Salma suggested.

"These things aren't real," Elisa muttered, leaning back in her chair. "That's why nothing's happening."

"Let's try with just two people," I suggested, and Salma removed her hands. Ava and I kept our fingers lightly on the planchette.

"Kind spirit, if you're here, please move the planchette to yes," I said, my voice wavering slightly.

For a moment, nothing happened. Then, slowly, the planchette began to vibrate, shifting back and forth before sliding to yes.

We all gasped.

"Ava, did you move that?" I asked, my voice barely above a whisper.

"No! Did you?"

"No," I replied, my heart pounding. "It moved by itself."

"Sure it did," Elisa scoffed, leaning forward. "Let's see if it moves again. Ask another question."

Salma nodded, wide-eyed. "Go ahead—ask."

I took a deep breath. "Can you hear us?"

The planchette stayed on yes.

"Can you see us?" I asked.

There was no movement.

"Have you ever lived in this cottage?"

Slowly, it slid to no.

Elisa narrowed her eyes, scrutinizing us. "Okay, which one of you is messing around? Which one of you moved it?"

"Neither of us!" Ava protested, her voice fearful. "Our fingers are barely touching it."

I ignored Elisa's skepticism and asked another question. "Are you a spirit from the Salem witch trials?"

The planchette stayed on no.

"Were you making the noise in the attic earlier?"

Yes.

The room became creepier as we exchanged nervous glances.

"What do you want?" I asked cautiously.

The planchette began to move, spelling out: W-A-R-N-Y-O-U.

A cold rush surged through my body. "Warn us about what?" I whispered, my voice barely audible.

The planchette didn't move.

"Have we met you before?" Ava asked, her voice shaky.

Y-E-S.

"When did you die?" I ventured.

The planchette returned to the starting position.

"How did you die?" I asked, my breath catching in my throat. M-U-R-D-E-R.

Ava and I recoiled, yanking our fingers off the planchette as if it had burned us. Salma's face turned ghostly pale. "Should we stop? This feels wrong. I don't like it."

"One more question," I insisted, unable to resist the pull of curiosity. I laid my fingers on the planchette, and Ava reluctantly did the same. "What is your name?"

The planchette moved, slowly spelling out: M-E-G-A-N.

Ava shrieked, stumbling back from the table. "I can't do this anymore," she said, her voice breaking.

My chest tightened, fear rising inside me, but something stronger pushed me to continue. My fingers unsteady as I pressed them lightly to the planchette and whispered, "Who killed you?"

As I stared down at the Ouija board, I felt the mood around me shift, haunting and macabre. A knot twisted in my chest, but I couldn't tear my fingers away from the planchette.

Everything around me began to fade—the soft glow of the candles, the anxious murmurs of my sister and cousins. Even the flickering shadows on the walls dimmed into darkness. Suddenly, the Ouija board disappeared beneath my hands, replaced by an abyss of swirling black-and-violet mist. The world tilted, and I felt myself being pulled forward as if invisible hands had gripped me, yanking me into the void.

"I can't move!" I gasped, but the room had vanished, and with it, my sister and cousins. I twisted and turned, trying to find something to hold on to, anything, but there was nothing to grasp. I could still see myself seated at the table with the others, my body slack, my head lolling to the side like I was unconscious.

Panic surged through me. I was trapped in this disembodied state, untethered and helpless.

Then, through the swirling mist, she appeared.

Megan.

She was shadowy at first, but as she came closer, her features sharpened, illuminated by a soft ethereal glow. Her neck was bruised, the dark purple marks stark against her pale skin. Her eyes, brimming with sorrow, locked onto mine, and I felt a chill deeper than anything the attic could conjure. She was dressed in black, and her movements were slow and deliberate, as though she was wading through water.

She extended a hand toward me, her expression unreadable, her gaze piercing. Beckoning.

I hesitated, fear tightening its grip on my chest, but an invisible force urged me forward. Weightless, I floated toward her, no longer able to control my movements. My mind screamed for me to stop, to resist, but my body obeyed her silent command. I reached out reluctantly, my hand shaking, and when my fingers brushed hers, a jolt of icy energy shot through me, pulling me even deeper into her realm.

The mist cleared suddenly, and a room took shape around us. I was no longer floating but standing on solid ground. A sterile, suffocating coldness filled the space around me, and the faint hum of fluorescent lights buzzed overhead. Rows of metal tables lined the room, each one draped with a white sheet. The metallic scent of disinfectant mixed with something sharper, something foul, invaded my senses. The walls were a dull, lifeless grey, and the only sound was that of footsteps—heavy and deliberate—growing louder as they approached.

I was in a morgue.

The double doors at the end of the room creaked open, and Officer Luca appeared, his expression grave. He was out of place here, his uniform too sharp, his presence too vivid against the washed-out surroundings. He didn't look at me.

I tried to speak. "Why am I here, Officer?" My voice came out fragmented, distorted, as though it were coming from someone—or something—else. The words vibrated unnaturally, like a broken recording played over and over.

Officer Luca didn't answer. He walked to the nearest metal table, his boots clicking against the tile, the sound unnervingly loud in the otherwise silent room. He paused beside it, his hand hesitating over the edge of the white sheet. Finally, he looked at me, his dark eyes filled with something I couldn't quite place. Pity? Regret? Dread?

"Are you ready?" he asked, his voice robotic, glitching as though it was coming from a faulty speaker.

A knot formed deep in my stomach, but I couldn't stop myself from drifting closer to table, couldn't move my gaze away.

"Ready for what?" I asked, the word barely audible.

But Officer Luca ignored me. Slowly, he peeled back the sheet, revealing a body.

I struggled to breathe. The room tilted, and the world around me seemed to collapse inward as my mind rejected what I was seeing. For a moment, I couldn't think. And then it hit me—raw, consuming pain. I doubled over.

On the table was my sister.

Ava's face was pale and lifeless, her eyes closed, her features frozen in eternal stillness. Her hair was tangled, matted with twigs and orange-brown leaves, as though she had been dragged through the woods. Deep bruises circled her swollen neck, I saw a flash back of the rope that had stolen her last breath. Dried blood crusted where her left earring had been torn away, leaving her earlobe jagged and raw.

A sound clawed its way out of my throat—a primal, anguished scream that echoed in the sterile room.

"NOOOOOOOOO, NOOOO! It can't be! Avaaaaaa!" I wailed, falling to my knees. My body convulsed, my chest heaving with sobs so violent they stole the air from my lungs. "She can't be dead. She can't be dead. This is a dream."

My vision blurred with tears as I clawed at my hair, tidal waves of grief crashing over me again and again. I wanted to die, too. Officer Luca tried to help me to my feet as I shivered in agony, but I yanked myself from his grip, shouting, "LET GO OF ME!"

My hands shook uncontrollably as I touched my sister's cold, stiff skin. I pressed my forehead against hers, my tears dripping onto her lifeless face. "I'm so sorry, sis," I whispered. "I couldn't protect you. How did I let this happen?"

Officer Luca's voice cut through the haze, sharp and clinical. "She was found at Gallows Woods, strangled with a rope, between ten p.m. and midnight. The Salem Slayer's mark was carved into her back, just like Megan, Selena, and Melinda. We think she was killed around a quarter to midnight."

My stomach churned violently, and I convulsed, vomiting the hot chocolate I'd drunk earlier onto the pristine floor. But when I looked down, there was no mess, only a clean, shiny surface.

I was trapped in a nightmare that refused to end. This couldn't be happening, this couldn't be real.

And then Officer Luca spoke again, his voice glitching. "October thirty first."

I froze. "What did you say?" My voice was hoarse, and it hurt with every word I spoke.

"October thirty first. That's when she was killed," he repeated, his tone mechanical.

A flicker of hope jolted through me, cutting through the fog of despair. "But that's weeks away."

The realization struck me like a lightning bolt. This wasn't the present. This was a warning.

I had time.

Time to save her.

But before I could grab hold of that fragile thread of hope, the world around me began to disintegrate. The walls of the morgue cracked and crumbled, the floor beneath me falling away into endless darkness. I tried to scream, but no sound came. My body felt immobilized, pulled down by an invisible force.

Suddenly, Megan was there again, her hand outstretched. Her lips didn't move, but her voice repeated in my mind. *You've seen enough. Go back. Save her.*

The swirling mist returned, enveloping us both. Megan's presence faded, her figure dissolving into the shadows as the portal reappeared in the distance. I struggled to move toward it, my limbs stiff, my vision narrowing as blackness crept in.

From far away, I heard faint voices. Familiar voices.

"Jenna! Jenna!"

It was Salma.

"She's not breathing!" Ava shouted, her voice high-pitched with panic.

"What's happening to her?" Salma shouted. "Quick, call Rosalie or an ambulance, she's not moving!"

I wanted to respond, to tell them I was here, but the darkness was relentless. It pulled me under, suffocating and cold.

Megan's words resounded in my mind: *Save her.*

I had four weeks to stop the Salem Slayer.

Four weeks to save my sister.

"Jenna, wake up!" Elisa's voice was frantic. But their voices drifted farther away until all I heard was silence, and then—nothing.

FOURTEEN

The first thing I heard was the steady, rhythmic beeping of a machine. It was distant at first, like I was dreaming, but as I drifted toward awareness, it grew sharper, more insistent. Then came the smell—sharp and sterile, antiseptics and disinfectants stinging my nostrils.

I tried to move, but my body felt impossibly heavy. It was like I was pinned down by some invisible force. I tried to open my eyes, but my eyelids wouldn't budge, sealed shut like someone had glued them closed. When I finally forced them open, the overhead lights blinded me, and a stabbing pain shot through my temples.

Then it hit me—not the light, not the pain, but the fear. Raw and frayed, it surged up from the pit of my stomach, clawing its way into my chest and filling me with a suffocating sense of loss.

"Ava!" The name ripped out of me, jagged and desperate. My voice cracked, my emotions spilling out unchecked. *She's dead. Ava is dead.* The image came in a rush: her lifeless body, strangled by the Salem Slayer.

I tried to sit up, but a sharp tug at my left arm made me wince. A thin IV tube stretched to a bag of fluid hanging beside me. I looked around, disoriented. Why was I in a hospital bed?

"It's okay, Jenna." The voice was soft and familiar.

I turned my head slowly to the right, my neck stiff and aching. Rosalie stood beside me, her hand curling gently over mine. Her touch was warm against my clammy, cold skin.

"It's okay," she repeated, her voice steady and soothing, like she was trying to hold me together.

But it wasn't okay. The monitor beside me beeped steadily, indifferent to the fresh tears spilling down my cheeks. I couldn't stop them, the pain too sharp, too overwhelming for me to bear.

"My sister," I managed between shallow breaths. "Ava is dead."

Rosalie's grip tightened slightly, her brow furrowing, but her voice remained calm. "No, Jenna. She's fine. She left for work this morning."

Her words didn't make sense. How could Ava be fine? My mind rejected the possibility, but Rosalie's steady gaze stayed fixed on me.

Slowly, hazily, my memories began to filter back in. Disjointed fragments: the Ouija board, Megan at the morgue, Ava's face, pale and still. A chill ran through me, and my mouth watered as nausea churned in my stomach.

"You fainted last night," Rosalie said softly. "It happened after the séance. The girls called me in a panic. You remember, don't you? The Ouija board?"

The mention of it made my breath catch. I squeezed my eyes shut, trying to force my mind to clear. My chest rose and fell unevenly, but I managed to gasp out, "The portal…Rosalie, does what it reveals always come true?"

Her hand slipped from mine, and she looked away, suddenly unable to meet my gaze. A tear welled in the corner of her eye, betraying her calm façade.

"Yes," she finally said, her voice cracking. "Yes, Jenna. In my experience, it does."

A sob broke free from my chest, raw and uncontrollable. I felt helpless and empty. I wanted to go back to sleep and never wake up.

Rosalie reached into her bag and pulled out a small bottle, unscrewing the cap with practiced ease. She rolled the liquid behind my ears and under my nose. The soft, calming scents of lavender, bergamot, and something else I didn't recognize infused the air. Straightaway, it soothed my jittery nerves and stopped my tears.

"Breathe," Rosalie murmured, passing me a tissue. "I'll explain everything when we get home. But first, let's get you discharged."

I nodded weakly, my head pounding as I tried to piece my thoughts together. "What day is it?" My voice was barely more than a whisper.

"It's October second, 1999," she said, her tone steady.

The door creaked open, and Elisa strode in, holding a flimsy plastic cup of coffee. Her curly hair was in a loose bun, and worry lined her face.

"Jen!" she exclaimed, her voice full of relief. She hurried over and wrapped me in a tight hug, careful not to jostle the IV in my arm. "Thank god you're awake. You scared the hell out of us. What happened to you?!"

Rosalie stepped back, murmuring, "I'll get the nurse," before slipping out of the room.

Elisa placed the cup on the bedside table and helped me sit up. "Here, take a sip of this, it'll fix you right up," she said, blowing on the coffee. "It's not like Strega's, but it'll do."

The warm, creamy liquid soothed my dry throat, the familiar aroma felt comforting. "Thanks, Els," I muttered.

Before I could go into detail about what I'd seen, the door opened again, admitting Rosalie and a young man in green scrubs. His short black hair was neatly gelled, and his striking green eyes darted toward the heart monitor before settling on me.

"Good to see you awake, Jenna," he said, his voice soft and melodic. "I'm Edward Proctor—Ed for short. I'm your nurse, and I've been taking care of you today."

I offered him a faint smile, too tired to do much else. I took in his handsome features: straight nose, narrow forehead, prominent jawline. He was young, maybe twenty-four.

Ed began to check my vitals. "Heart rate stable and temperature back to normal," he said. Elisa stood back, sipping her coffee. I noticed her watching him out of the corner of her eye, a faint smile playing on her lips as he scribbled notes onto my chart.

"Good. Now I have a series of questions for you. What is your full name?"

"Jenna Aslan."

"Your date of birth?" he asked.

"February twenty-fifth, 1979."

"Do you know today's date?"

"October second, 1999," I replied, glancing at the clock behind him. "It's one fifty-five p.m."

"Good." Ed nodded approvingly, but then his expression turned more serious. "Jenna, what's the last thing you remember?"

My throat tightened. Elisa tensed visibly, cutting in sharply in Turkish, "Don't you dare tell him. He'll think you're mental."

Ed blinked, clearly taken aback. "Miss, could you step aside, please?" His voice was polite but firm.

Elisa eyeballed me from behind him. My thoughts scattered as I met Ed's gaze, trying to decide how much to reveal.

"I…well, my sister and my cousins and I were having hot chocolate," I said finally, forcing calm into my voice. "And the last thing I remember is feeling light-headed, and I must have passed out. That's it, that's all I can remember."

Ed glanced at Elisa, then back at me, his brow furrowed. "You were very emotional when you came in," he said carefully. "You kept calling for Ava."

"I don't remember that," I replied flatly, staring past him.

"Are you having thoughts of self-harm?" Ed's tone was gentle but direct.

The question made me want to cry, the resonance of everything crashing down on me again. My sister was going to die. What was the point of living if I couldn't stop it? I might as well die with her.

I swallowed hard, forcing down the lump in my throat. "No, of course not," I lied. "I just have a terrible headache."

Ed studied me for a moment, his expression unreadable, before nodding. "I'll speak to the doctor about prescribing you something for the pain."

Elisa interrupted, "She hasn't been eating properly. She keeps throwing up. Like, all the time!"

"Have you been throwing up on purpose?" I refused to meet his gaze. He sighed as he scribbled something in the notes, "I will refer you to a therapist who specializes in eating disorders," he said. The words made me uncomfortable even though they were delivered gently.

I glared at Elisa. She quickly looked away, staring intently at the coffee cup in her hands.

"All your tests are clear," Ed continued, moving toward the drip attached to my arm. "If the doctor agrees with my assessment, you'll be discharged."

I gritted my teeth as he carefully removed my IV, his gloved hands efficient but gentle. It stung for a minute, followed by the cool press of a bandage over the puncture.

"Do you work at Strega Coffee House?" Ed asked suddenly, his gaze shifting to Elisa. "I think I saw you there yesterday."

Elisa blinked in surprise before recovering and smiling softly. "I do, yeah. I thought you looked familiar. You had blueberry pancakes, right?"

Ed chuckled, glancing down at his feet like a shy schoolboy. "Yeah, that's right. You have a good memory." He looked back up at Elisa. "Antonio makes the best pancakes in town. I'm in there more often than I should probably admit."

"You look different in scrubs," Elisa teased, twisting a loose curl around her finger as she stared at him attentively.

A faint blush crept across Ed's face as he rubbed the back of his neck awkwardly. "Right, uh…let me go talk to the doctor about getting you discharged." He gave us a quick, polite nod, then walked out the door, his footsteps light. The door clicked closed behind him.

Elisa sank into the chair beside me with a long sigh, finally setting down her coffee. "Jenna, I'm so glad you didn't say anything," she muttered, leaning in close. "I heard them talking about you having mental health issues. If you'd told Ed about the Ouija board, the noises in the attic, they probably would've kept you here. Maybe even in the psych ward."

Her words heightened my anxiety. I reached for her hand and gripped it tightly, forcing her to look at me. "Ava is going to die," I whispered, my voice breaking. Hot tears spilled down my cheeks as the words escaped. "That's what I saw. The Salem Slayer is going to strangle her."

Elisa's face drained of color, the horror behind her wide eyes clear. "Jenna…" she breathed, her voice barely audible.

Rosalie stepped closer, placing a steadying hand on my shoulder. "We need to take you home," she said firmly. "You can tell us everything there."

Elisa's hand shook as she squeezed mine; I could feel her racing pulse in her fingers. "Ava's worried about you. Please don't say this to her," she pleaded. "You'll freak her out, Jen. Just…just keep it between us for now, okay?"

I swallowed hard, the lump in my throat impossible to ignore. "I won't say anything," I promised shakily. "But you have to believe me, Elisa. I saw her. Megan took me to the morgue. I saw Officer Luca there, too." I paused, my voice raspy. "Ava… she was lying there, cold and stiff. Her ear was torn, and her neck was black and blue."

Elisa gently stroked my arm. "Okay, okay," she said, her voice strained. "Don't get yourself worked up, Jen. I believe you."

Before I could say anything else, the door opened and Ed returned, clipboard in hand. His gaze darted between Rosalie, Elisa, and me. I forced myself to sit up straighter, brushing away my tears.

"Well," he said, "Dr. Wong has signed off on your discharge. You're free to go, Jenna."

"Thanks," I murmured, avoiding his eyes.

Ed stepped forward, handing me a blue plastic bag containing my clothes. "Bathroom's right there," he said, nodding to the door on my right. "Take your time."

Elisa handed me a small rucksack. "Wear these," she said, "You were wearing your pajamas when they brought you in."

I pulled the covers back and swung my legs to the side. I cringed as I realized I was wearing a white hospital gown with nothing underneath. Who had changed my clothes? Had it been Ed?

My legs wobbled when I stood, I felt weak and unsteady, but I managed to shuffle toward the bathroom without help. Once inside, I locked the door and leaned heavily against it, exhaling a shaky breath.

The fluorescent lights were harsh, illuminating every blemish and flaw on my face. My reflection in the mirror didn't even look like me. My olive skin was ghostly, almost translucent, and my dark hair hung limp, my fringe matted against my forehead. Dark circles bloomed under my bloodshot eyes, and my lips were cracked and colorless. I looked like I was grieving, but my sister wasn't dead…yet. I stared at myself for a long moment, then splashed some water on my face, I desperately needed a shower.

Pulling off the hospital gown, I caught sight of a faint handprint on my upper arm. My breath hitched. The mark was light pink, barely visible, but unmistakable—long, spindly fingers curved around my bicep like someone had gripped me hard. The memory surfaced without warning: Officer Luca holding my arm. The whisper of Megan's voice in the morgue.

I shivered and looked away from the mark, quickly pulling on the clothes Elisa had packed—a simple black T-shirt and a pair of faded jeans. I felt more like myself once I was dressed, but the sadness remained, a knot in my stomach that wouldn't loosen.

When I emerged from the bathroom, I heard Elisa talking to Ed outside in the hallway. "Thank you for looking after my cousin. If you come by one day, I'll make you a coffee on the house."

"How could I say no to free coffee?" Ed laughed, his voice warm.

"You ready?" Rosalie asked me, her voice kind and cautious. I nodded. "Yeah. Let's go."

Ed escorted us to the exit and held the door open as we stepped out into the sunlight.

"All right," he said. "You're all set. Take care, Jenna. And if you ever need anything"—he paused, his gaze flicking to Elisa for a brief moment before settling on me—"don't hesitate to reach out."

I nodded, mumbling a quiet, "Thank you."

"Don't forget to stop by for that coffee." Elisa flashed him a smile and waved, and Ed looked away shyly.

Rosalie's car was parked close by, and she helped me into the back seat, tucking a blanket over my legs. As the car pulled away, I leaned my head against the window, watching the hospital recede into the distance.

The memories from the séance began to resurface again—Megan's ghostly presence, Officer Luca's words, and Ava's battered body. The sun disappeared behind the thick clouds as rain hammered down on the roof, loud and unyielding, like the universe itself was grieving my sister's murder before it even happened.

Each drop struck the windscreen like a warning, amplifying the brutal finality of what I'd seen.

I swallowed hard, closing my eyes, wishing it had been me instead of Ava lying on the morgue table.

FIFTEEN

Later that evening, Ava burst into the lounge, where I was lying on the sofa, snuggled under a blanket. Her energy filled the quiet room, and before I could react, she threw her arms around me, squeezing me tight. "Sis! You're back! I was so worried about you."

The warmth of her hug crushed me deep in my soul. The terrible feeling of loss crept back into my chest, suffocating me. How could I live without her? I swallowed, fighting the sting of tears, and gently pulled away. "I'm fine, honestly," I said, my voice tight. "Everything's just…piling up." I sat up straight, making room for Ava to sit down next to me, then cleared my throat and picked at my nails. "I miss Mum."

Ava's expression softened, her usual fire dimming for a moment. "I know how you feel, sis. I miss Mum, too," she admitted quietly. "You should call her—let her know we're okay. Maybe that'll make you feel better."

I hesitated, carefully choosing my next words. "I've been thinking…" I paused, coughing up the emotion building in my chest. "I think we made a mistake coming here." I looked up at her dark eyes. "I want to leave. I think we should go back home."

Her eyes widened in disbelief. "What? Are you serious?" She stood up, her hands flying into the air. "We spent months planning this, Jenna—months gathering the courage to make the hardest decision of our lives! And now you want to throw it all away?" Her voice rose with exasperation, and tears welled in her eyes.

I looked away, unable to meet her gaze. The image of her lying cold and lifeless in the morgue flashed through my mind, stealing my breath. I didn't want to leave Salem either, but the thought of staying and losing her was unbearable. There is no way I could live without her.

"What is wrong with you?" Ava snapped, pacing now. "It took everything we had to get here. You haven't even tried! You haven't gone out, met anyone, given this life a chance."

She wasn't wrong. I'd kept to myself, busying myself at the guesthouse while Ava and Salma embraced their new lives.

Ava's voice dropped, sharp and accusing now. "Dad will kill us if we go back. You know that, right? He's been threatening us for years. You think he's going to let us just waltz back in? He'll marry you off first, then me. Is that what you want?"

"No," I said quickly, trying to redirect her. "Not back *home*. I just mean we should go somewhere else. Let's leave Salem. Florida, maybe? Somewhere sunny, where it's warm all year."

Ava crossed her arms, her posture rigid. "I'm not going anywhere," she said firmly, her tone brooking no argument.

Before I could respond, Salma entered the room, balancing a tray of teacups. Elisa followed behind her, carrying slices of our favorite Belgian chocolate cake from the Chocolate Coven. The sweet smell of dark chocolate and raspberries filled the room.

"We couldn't help but overhear," Salma said gently, setting the tray on the coffee table. "Sounds like we need to talk this over."

Ava jumped in, sounding frustrated. "I don't know why Jenna's acting so weird. I'm not leaving Salem. I've barely settled in here, and now she wants to uproot everything again. Everything's not all about you, Jenna."

Salma shot me a sympathetic look before raising her hands to calm Ava. "Okay, let's all take a breath." She turned to me. "What's really going on, Jen? Coming here was your idea. We followed you here, and we love it. And now you're ready to throw in the towel? I'm with Ava on this one—I'm staying in Salem. If you really want to leave, we can't stop you. But I'm not going anywhere."

I absorbed what she said, clearly realizing there was nothing I could say to change their minds. Or, I could tell them the truth. I wanted to explain, to tell them everything—the vision, the portal, the cold certainty of Ava's death. I opened my mouth, but Elisa must have sensed what I was about to say, because she jumped in quickly.

"I know last night scared you," she said. "The noises, the Ouija board—it rattled all of us. But Rosalie burned sage around the cottage, and it's been fine ever since. Right, girls?"

Ava glanced at Salma, and they both shrugged.

"Yeah, nothing weird has happened," Ava said. "Probably just a one-off. It's a lesson that we shouldn't mess with things we don't understand."

Salma nodded. "Exactly."

I nodded too and picked at the slice of cake in front of me, but I barely tasted it. My mind was elsewhere, replaying the memory of Ava's pale bruised neck, her stiff lifeless body.

Suddenly, Julie's voice cut through the haze—calm, warm, and unmistakable. *Sweetheart, you can stop him. You know the date and location. Find him.*

Julie was right. I could try to uncover the Slayer's identity first. If that didn't work, I could wait at the location and confront him on the night of the thirty first.

Salma's voice brought me back to the present. "Look, tomorrow there's a meeting at the town hall about the Halloween celebration. We should volunteer for decorations or face painting or serving drinks or something. It'll be fun. Jenna, you'll get to meet Roman's friends—Carmen, her brother Isaac, a few others. We can grab some food after the meeting and hang out."

Ava grinned. "You love all this hocus-pocus stuff. So come on, get your witch on!"

I couldn't help the small smile tugging at my lips. The thought of Halloween—the glow of jack-o'-lanterns, the crisp autumn air, the sense of community—sparked something warm and familiar inside me.

"Okay," I said quietly. "Let's do it."

Later, when it was just Elisa and me in our room, she said, "Thank god you didn't say anything about the vision to Ava."

I paused in the middle of brushing my hair and turned to face her. "I wanted to," I whispered. "If we leave now, she won't die."

Elisa frowned but kept her voice calm. "Orion's not coming back to Salem. He'd be stupid to try. The police would arrest him in a heartbeat."

"And if they don't?" I asked softly.

Elisa leaned back into her pillows, crossed her arms, and furrowed her brow in thought. "According to your vision it's gonna happen on Halloween night. There's no way the girls going to stay inside. But we'll stick together at all times. Nothing can happen to her if we're all there with her."

Slowly, I nodded, my anxiety easing just slightly. "Yeah," I murmured. "That could work."

Elisa relaxed, pulling up the bedcovers.

After a moment, I said, "I'll go see Officer Luca in a few days time and tell him what I know. Maybe he can help, and…"

I trailed off as I noticed Elisa raising a hand, signaling for me to stop. Her face twisted in disbelief. "No, no, no, no," she said emphatically. "He'll think you've lost your mind for sure!"

I sighed, putting the brush down and getting into bed. The familiar feeling of defeat settled over me, increasing the tension I already felt. Elisa wasn't wrong—Officer Luca wouldn't believe me, not without proof.

"Look," she continued, softening her tone slightly, "I'll go with you one day next week before work. Maybe Officer Luca will give us an update on the investigation. For all we know, they've already found Megan's boyfriend and arrested him."

I hesitated, doubt gnawing at me. "Maybe," I said finally, though the idea didn't ease the tightness in my chest.

Elisa gave me a quick reassuring smile before and turning onto her side, away from me.

After a moment of silence, I glanced over at her. "Can I ask you something, Els?"

"Go on," she replied, turning to face me again.

"Would you ever go back to London?"

She didn't even pause to think. "Not a chance," she said sharply. "This is our home now, Jen. I can't go back to how things were before. I know we're adults, but with our culture and our families…"

Her voice trailed off, and I could hear her frustration building as she added, "Going back means being trapped again. You know that."

I flipped off the lamp and let the room sink into darkness. But her words lingered, stirring up memories I wished I could forget.

"Have you forgotten what it was like?" she asked softly, her voice breaking the stillness. "They wouldn't even let us find jobs we actually wanted. It was all about controlling us."

The past came rushing back, sharp and bitter. I could still hear my father's booming voice the day my mum dared to ask him if I could go to college.

"No, she's not going to college to hang around with boys!" he'd thundered, his face dark with rage. "She'll work in the family business. Then I'll help her and the boy she marries set up their own business. That's how she'll have a stable future, not by mingling with English boys in some college!"

My mother had tried to reason with him, her voice nervous as she'd reminded him that she wasn't Turkish and he had still married her. His response had been colder than anything I'd ever heard.

"It's different for a man," he'd sneered. "A man can marry whoever he wants. But not my daughters. If you bring this up again, I'll make sure you both regret it."

The memory made my stomach turn, and I sighed heavily. "You're right, Els," I said finally, my voice barely audible in the dark. "Going back is not an option. Ever."

Elisa shifted in her bed, and the room grew quiet again. But my mind refused to settle, thoughts of Ava and what I'd seen in the portal replaying endlessly. My resolve hardened with each passing moment. We couldn't go back. But staying in Salem wasn't safe either—not for Ava, not for any of us.

SIXTEEN

Elisa stood as Officer Luca entered the small, brightly lit office at the Salem police station. "Thank you for seeing us," she said, extending her hand elegantly to shake his. I didn't miss the long flirty look she gave him.

I stayed seated, offering a polite smile but keeping quiet. Officer Luca's presence filled the room as he sank into the creaky chair across from us, his sturdy shoulders hunched slightly as he set a thick manila file on the cluttered desk. Its frayed edges spoke of constant handling. The room felt oppressive, its single grimy window letting in a thin trickle of daylight through rusted metal bars. The door behind us was heavy, more appropriate for a cell than an office, and the walls were plastered with faded missing persons posters and pamphlets about addiction recovery. The faint scent of sweat and stale feet hung in the air, mixing with the mustiness of old paper. This was a place where hope came to die.

My stomach churned as Officer Luca opened the file and pulled out a clear plastic evidence bag. "I've been meaning to return your passports," he said, his voice even. He slid the crinkly bag across the desk to Elisa.

"Thank you," she said, flashing him a brief smile. She opened the bag, inspecting the contents quickly before slipping the passports into her handbag.

"We have reason to believe Orion is hiding out in Connecticut," Officer Luca continued, a slight undercurrent of tension in his deep, steady voice. "He has family there, and officers are investigating a few addresses as we speak. If he isn't there, we have other locations to check."

The knot in my chest twisted. The air in the room felt stifling, as if the walls were closing in. Before I could stop myself, the words burst out of me. "My sister is next."

Officer Luca's head snapped toward me. For a moment, the room seemed to freeze, and I realized I was gripping the edge of my chair so tightly that my knuckles had gone white. His gaze was sharp, unrelenting, and I couldn't look away.

"She's next," I repeated, my voice shaking. "He's going to kill my sister."

Elisa stiffened beside me, shooting me a warning look. Her eyes widened, silently pleading for me to stop, but I couldn't. My throat felt raw, my mind was reeling of what I desperately wanted to say.

I leaned forward, my words tumbling out faster now. "I saw you, Officer Luca. In a vision I had. You were at the morgue. You showed me my sister's dead body."

His brow furrowed, confusion flickering across his face. "That's not possible," he muttered.

"It is," I said, my voice breaking. "You told me she'd been strangled with a rope. Her earring was torn out, and there was a mark on her back. You said that was the Salem Slayer's signature."

His hand froze in the middle of reaching for his pen. The disbelief on his face deepened into something darker. Slowly, he rubbed his jaw, his eyes narrowing as if searching for something hidden in my words.

"No information about the state of the victims' bodies has been made public," he finally said, his tone sharper now, laced with suspicion. "Where did you get those details?"

I forced myself to meet his eyes. "I saw it. In a vision. Like I said."

Officer Luca stared at me, his expression unreadable. The tension in the room thickened, wrapping around my body like a vise. Then he leaned back in his chair, exhaling slowly as he picked up his pen and began jotting notes in the file.

"I've seen some unusual things in my time here in Salem," he said after a moment, his voice quieter now. "Especially around Halloween. But I've never had someone come to me with confidential details of an active investigation like this. It's...unusual."

Elisa sighed, her shoulders rigid as she handed me a tissue. I didn't realize I was crying, but now I felt the tears streaking down my cheeks.

"It's going to happen on Halloween, October thirty first," I said, my voice trembling. "At Gallows Woods, between ten p.m. and midnight."

A tear splashed onto the desk between us, and I quickly wiped it away with the tissue, but more followed. "Please," I begged. "Have someone watch over my sister? If he tries to take her, you can catch him before it's too late." My voice cracked with desperation, my eyes searching his for any sign of hope. "I can't let her die."

Officer Luca didn't answer right away. He let out a long sigh, rubbing the back of his neck as he leaned forward, elbows resting on the desk. "Jenna, it's not that simple," he said, his voice gentler now. "We need solid evidence to authorize surveillance—something concrete I can take to my superiors. They won't approve it based on…visions."

I swallowed hard, my chest sinking. But Officer Luca's expression softened as he added, "I believe you. I do. But convincing them is another matter."

His words were like a lifeline, even if they couldn't fix everything. He believed me.

"Thank you," I whispered.

He nodded and scribbled something onto a card before sliding it across the desk. "I'm committed to this case, Jenna. I want to catch this guy as badly as you do. Please trust me, I won't let anything happen to your sister. Take my direct number. If anything changes—anything at all—call me immediately."

I took the card, clutching it tightly. "Thank you," I repeated, this time louder, more certain.

As Elisa and I stepped out into the crisp autumn air, she sighed and adjusted her bag over her shoulder. "Well, that went better than I expected," she admitted, glancing over at me.

"Sorry, Els. I know you were cringing, but I had to say something."

"It's gonna be all right, Jen." Elisa leaned in to give me a tight hug. "I've got to run, but I'll call you on my breaks."

I nodded.

After Elisa headed off to work, waving as she disappeared around the corner, I lingered on the sidewalk, restless. I let out a long breath. Rosalie had given me the day off, but the thought of returning to the cottage and sitting in silence with negative thoughts looping through my mind was unbearable. I let my feet carry me aimlessly through the streets of Salem, hoping a walk might clear my mind. The air smelled of fallen leaves and distant woodsmoke, and the chatter of tourists occupied the gaps between my thoughts.

About five minutes into my walk, something caught my eye: a small, peculiar shop nestled between two larger modern buildings. Its sign read the bewitched cauldron, the letters curling like tendrils of smoke. Something about it tugged at me, though I couldn't say why. I hesitated on the sidewalk, peering through the tinted windows. Shelves of books lined the walls inside, and one in particular caught my eye: *Forbidden Shadows: A Guide to Dark Magic*. The title seemed to whisper to me, pulling me closer.

Behind the counter, a woman stood, staring directly at me through the window. Her eyes were piercing, almost as if she was expecting me. A dark thought came to me, along with a mix of curiosity and apprehension: *Maybe I can use dark magic to find Orion and kill him before he can kill Ava.*

Then another part of my brain told me to keep walking. *You don't need this. You don't need black magic. Stay away.*

The air seemed to thrum with unseen energy, and my feet betrayed me. Before I even realized it, my hand was on the door. I mustered a burst of courage, then pushed it open and stepped inside.

The wooden door creaked on its hinges, and a delicate tinkle of bells announced my arrival. The scent of sage and incense wrapped around me, earthy and potent, instantly overpowering my senses. The shop was small but overflowing with books—some new, others ancient, their cracked spines barely holding together. Every surface seemed crowded with items: jars stuffed with herbs I had never heard of before. There were so many crystal balls shimmering under the dim light, and candles of every color. It was like stepping into another world.

A spark of fascination ignited within me as I took it all in. This was a place I didn't belong—a place I shouldn't belong.

And yet.

My eyes darted over the rows of books: *Grimoire of the Damned. Hexes and the Abyss. The Cursed Code*. I brushed my fingers along the spines until they stopped on one that seemed to whir beneath my touch: *The Witch's Black Book*.

The leather cover was warm. My hand felt clammy as I opened it, the brittle pages crackling softly. The ink inside was faded, its deep-red hue disturbingly reminiscent of dried blood. Symbols and diagrams filled the pages, incomprehensible yet oddly familiar, like echoes of something I'd forgotten. I flipped through it, excitement coursing through my veins—the same excitement that had kept me up late reading about the Salem witch trials as a kid, the part that had insisted on trying the séance despite Elisa's warnings. I couldn't look away. There was something in this book that could help me; I could feel it in my bones.

A voice broke the silence. "Can I help you with anything in particular?"

I startled, snapping the book shut. The woman behind the counter was watching me, her expression unreadable. My cheeks flushed, and I dropped my eyes to the book's cover, trying to regain some semblance of composure.

"No, I'm just looking," I mumbled, not meeting her gaze.

It was always awkward when you were the only customer in a small shop. The pressure to buy something felt almost palpable.

But even as I said it, I knew I wasn't just looking. I was searching—though for what, I didn't know yet.

I moved to another section, desperate to escape the woman's gaze. The shelf I stopped at was packed with books about witches, their titles both fascinating and intimidating: *Gray Witch*, *Eclectic Witch*, *Folk Witch*, *Sea Witch*. One book in particular caught my attention: a guide to solitary witchcraft. I flipped it open, scanning a passage: *A solitary witch performs spell work and rituals alone, drawing power from within rather than from a coven.*

The words sank into me. I read them again, and for a moment, I let myself imagine what it would feel like to live that kind of life. To pull strength from within myself instead of from the people around me.

"So, you don't know what kind of witch you are?"

The voice came again, this time startlingly close. I turned, clutching the book to my chest, and found the woman standing directly behind me. I hadn't heard her move. Her blue eyes sparkled with an almost catlike quality, their intensity impossible to look away from. She was incredibly striking, her sharp features framed by long gray hair swept behind her ear, her neck adorned with layers of colorful beaded necklaces. Silver rings glinted on her long, elegant fingers, each one set with stones that seemed to change color in the light.

"I'm not a witch," I said quickly—too quickly. My voice sounded defensive.

She tilted her head, her lips curling into a faint smile. "Then why did you come in?" she asked, her tone teasing but kind. "Places like this don't call to just anyone."

I bristled, her words stirring something I didn't want to name. "I'm just browsing," I muttered, setting the book back on the shelf. But my heart betrayed me.

"There's nothing wrong with admitting what you are," she said, low and soothing, as though she could sense the storm inside me. "Salem embraces it now. This is a town where our history runs deep. You may be more connected to it than you realize."

Her words startled me, Rosalie had said the exact same thing. I wanted to brush her off, to laugh and tell her she was mistaken. But I couldn't. Her words came too close to confirming what I had been suspecting for a long time.

"I'm just…not interested," I said, stepping back. But even as the words left my mouth, I felt the pull of *The Witch's Black Book* again. It was stronger now, like a whisper in my ear, urging me to pick it up.

The woman tilted her head, her necklaces clinking softly as she moved. "I can help you understand," she said, her voice almost hypnotic. "Help you find yourself, if you'll let me."

Her words caught me like a net, tightening with every breath I took. I didn't want to understand. I didn't want to "find myself." I wanted things to go back to normal. I wanted to stop thinking about portals and spirits and serial killers. My mind still felt raw, and I had no energy left for whatever she was offering.

"I—I need to go," I stammered. I fumbled for the door handle, my hand slick with nervous sweat.

The woman didn't move to stop me, but her voice followed me, soft and certain. "You'll be back," she said. "I'll see you soon."

The bells tinkled softly as I stumbled out onto the street. As I hurried away, the air outside felt different, as if I had crossed some invisible threshold. The woman's voice resounded in my mind, and I couldn't shake the feeling that she was right—I would be back.

SEVENTEEN

As I walked past the Old Burying Point, I paused to take in the scene around me. Halloween was transforming Salem into something magical and macabre. Skeletons dangled from lampposts, their bony fingers swaying in the breeze. Plastic pumpkins grinned wickedly from windowsills, their faces illuminated by flickering candles, and cobwebs stretched artfully over doorways. Tourists crowded around the graves in the cemetery, some snapping photos, others tracing the worn inscriptions on tombstones with quiet reverence. I pulled my coat tighter, trying to shake off the distressing thoughts that had dominated my mind since the séance. I had to find something to distract me.

I decided to treat myself to lunch at my favorite fish restaurant, the Oyster Shack, a cozy harborside restaurant that always calmed me. It smelled of the sea and freshly cooked fish, and the rustic wooden beams and weathered fishing nets draped along the walls added a nautical charm.

I chose a table by the window, a good spot to gather my thoughts. I had a perfect view of the harbor, where boats bobbed gently in the water and the lighthouse stood watch, stoic against the horizon. I picked up the menu, though I already knew what I wanted—prawn salad and sparkling water, simple but fresh.

Just as I placed the menu down, I saw something that made my stomach knot. Walking through the entrance was Troy—tall, broad-shouldered, and every bit as magnetic as I remembered him. His presence hit me like a wave, pulling me back into the memory of his easy smile, his voice.

But he wasn't alone.

The blond girl at his side was effortlessly beautiful, radiating a sun-kissed glow. They looked perfect together, like something out of a magazine, and as she touched his arm, she let out the kind of laugh that turned heads. I inhaled deeply, and I snatched the menu back up, using it as a shield.

Of course he had a girlfriend. Why wouldn't he? A bitter thought crept in: *What made you think you were his type?* He clearly liked girls like her—blond, radiant, everything I wasn't. Now it made sense why he hadn't asked me to hang out.

I pretended to be engrossed in the menu, but my mind was spinning. My pulse intensified, and the lump in my throat grew harder to swallow.

"Hey, I'm Jade. What would you like today?"

I barely glanced at the waitress. Keeping the menu in front of my face, I mumbled, "Prawn salad, please. And sparkling water."

Jade hesitated. "I can take the menu now, miss."

Reluctantly, I lowered it, offering her a tight smile. And then I froze. Of all the tables in the restaurant, Troy and his blond companion were seated directly across from me.

My stomach twisted painfully. I lifted a hand to my forehead, pretending to block the sun, desperate to hide my face. But I could smell his scent, woodsy and warm, even from where I was sitting. And then Troy's intense blue eyes locked onto mine.

Time slowed, every sound around me fading as we stared at each other, neither of us willing to look away. His girlfriend hadn't noticed yet, still engrossed in her menu. When she finally waved a hand in front of his face, the spell broke, and it felt like an invisible cord had snapped. She must have sensed something, because she slowly turned her head, elegant and curious, to see who had captured Troy's attention.

Panic flared inside me. I turned sharply toward the window, avoiding her eyes, pretending to be fascinated by the harbor. An elderly man struggled with a black plastic bag, trying to pick up after his dog, and I put my full focus on him, acting like I didn't even notice Troy.

"You never pay attention to what I say!" the blond girl snapped, her resentment sharp and loud. "I'm fed up with putting in all this effort and getting nothing back." I tried not to listen, but her words carried across the small space, impossible to ignore.

Troy's voice was strained. "I've been busy. The lodge and college…it's a lot right now."

"You've been distant for months, Troy," she countered. "I can't keep doing this."

The tension was unbearable. To spare him the embarrassment, I stood, intending to switch tables. But as I did, Troy's eyes found mine again and lingered. I couldn't look away.

"Are you kidding me?" the blond said, her voice rising. "You're checking out some girl right in front of me?" She stood up and threw her napkin down on the table. Heat rushed to my face as she turned toward me, her grey eyes locked onto mine, her glare cutting like a knife. "What are you looking at?" she hissed, her button nose flaring in anger.

Caught off guard, I stepped back and blurted out the first thing that came to mind, my voice high and broken. "Sorry, no understand…no speak English."

Her disgusted scoff was enough to make me want to disappear. She rolled her eyes and turned to Troy. Seeing my chance, I rushed toward the bathroom, desperate to escape the growing tension.

I leaned against the sink, staring at my reflection. "Why did I have to look at him?" I muttered to myself, guilt and embarrassment creeping in. "Why couldn't I just keep my head down and ignore them?"

I splashed cold water on my face and stared at my reflection again. My cheeks were flushed, and my chest rose and fell unevenly.

"Get it together," I whispered. But no matter how much I tried to calm down, all I could think about was Troy—his gaze, the undeniable connection between us, the blond girl's pointed, angry words.

I debated how long I could stay in here without it seeming strange. Maybe if I waited long enough, Troy and his companion would leave, and I could return to my table without the intensity of their eyes on me. But they were most likely still out there, waiting for me to reappear. The thought sent a flurry of butterflies through my stomach, equal parts panic and anticipation.

"You'll look even weirder if you don't go back. You're being childish," I muttered to myself, ruffling my fringe with trembling fingers. I grabbed a tissue to dab at my face and applied a fresh layer of lip gloss.

With a deep breath, I straightened my shoulders and pushed the door open.

The moment I cautiously stepped back into the dining area, my eyes darted to his table. My heart plummeted at first, then soared.

Troy was still sitting there. Alone.

The blond girl was gone, her chair pushed back, her untouched drink abandoned. My prawn salad waited for me on my table, and with her gone, there was no need to switch seats anymore.

Troy's gaze found me immediately, and I shoved my hands into my back pockets. My legs felt like lead as I forced myself to move toward my seat.

I avoided looking directly at him, pulled my chair out slowly, and sat down. I had just started to pick up my fork when I heard his chair scrape against the floor. I glanced up to see him walking toward me, holding a glass of Coke and a plate with what appeared to be a burger. His movements were confident, casual, but the tension in his jaw betrayed his composure.

"I'm sorry you had to see that," he said, his voice low enough that only I could hear.

I blinked, caught off guard by his directness. He stood there, the sunlight from the window glowing on the golden tan of his skin. His white shirt, the top button undone, clung to his frame in a way that was impossible to ignore.

I shook my head quickly, fumbling for words. "No, it's fine. I'm sorry if…if I had anything to do with it." I dropped my gaze briefly, before looking back at him.

Troy smiled—a warm, almost apologetic smile that sent a flutter through my chest. "You didn't," he said firmly. "Honestly, it's been a long time coming. I just…" He hesitated, and I looked up to see him staring back at me. "I just didn't handle it the way I should have." He gestured toward the empty chair across from me. "Do you mind if I sit?"

For a moment, I couldn't move or speak. Then I nodded quickly, trying to look casual. "Not at all."

He settled into the chair, close enough that I could feel the chemistry in the air between us. My appetite completely disappeared. The salad in front of me felt like a prop. I picked up my fork and stabbed at a prawn, more for something to do with my hands than because I intended to eat it.

Troy watched me for a moment, his gaze unwavering but not invasive. "You handled that well, though," he said suddenly, a faint smile tugging at his lips.

I frowned, confused. "What?"

"You know, the whole 'no speak English' thing." His grin widened, and the way he mimicked my terrible accent made me laugh despite myself.

"Oh god," I groaned, covering my face with my hands. "That was so bad."

"No, it was perfect," he said, chuckling. "You actually threw her off for a second."

We both laughed, the tension between us easing just slightly. I felt comfortable in his presence for the first time since I'd met him.

But as the laughter faded, his expression grew serious again. "I'm sorry you got caught in the middle," he said, his voice soft. "It's been over between Ashley and me for a while, but…I guess I didn't make that clear enough."

I hesitated, unsure how to respond. "Relationships are messy," I said finally, my voice quiet. "It's hard to…I don't know…let go, I guess."

Troy nodded, his gaze drifting to the window for a moment. "We've grown apart, but she has never wanted to admit it. I ended things with her months ago, but she still calls me all the time, and sometimes she tells me she's suicidal if she wants attention. I feel terrible—we were friends first, and I've known her since first grade." He sighed, looking out at the harbor. After a moment, he rubbed his chin and turned back to me.

My chest tightened at the sadness in his voice, the guilt that seemed to weigh on him. "I'm not sure what to say," I replied honestly. I had no experience with relationships.

He turned back to me, his blue eyes locking onto mine with an intensity that made my breath catch. "Yeah," he said softly. "Sometimes, you just have to let go. Even if it hurts."

For a moment, neither of us spoke. Then, in a lighter tone, Troy gestured toward my salad. "You're really giving those prawns a hard time. I'm pretty sure they're already dead."

I glanced down, realizing I'd been absently stabbing at the same prawn for the last minute. A laugh bubbled out of me. "I was just making sure this one's *really* dead," I said, holding up the prawn and pretending to inspect it.

He grinned, cutting his burger in half. "Here," he said, sliding half of it toward me. "If you're not into the salad, you can share with me."

I hesitated, glancing between the burger and his expectant face. "You don't have to—"

"It's fine," he interrupted, his grin widening. "I promise I'm not going to starve."

His lightheartedness was contagious. I picked up the burger and took a small bite and was immediately hit with the savory taste of cod and tartar sauce. "Okay," I said, smiling, "this is really good."

Troy leaned back in his chair, watching me with a relaxed, satisfied expression. He ran a hand through his tousled hair. "So," he said, his voice smooth, "what's your story, Jen?"

I swallowed, my heart singing at the way he'd said my name. He'd called me Jen before, but this time it felt different—more personal.

He continued, "I've been wondering about you ever since you walked into the lodge that first afternoon."

My cheeks flushed instantly, heat rising to my face. I shifted in my seat, suddenly self-conscious. "Seriously, you wouldn't believe me if I told you." I laughed anxiously. What was I going to say—that I had run away from home because my father wanted to marry me off? He'd think that was absurd. And I certainly couldn't tell him I'd picked Salem because I'd seen Rosalie and the guesthouse in my visions.

"I want to get to know you." His voice was lower this time, more husky. "Try me." He leaned forward slightly, holding my gaze.

I forced a small smile and said, "A friend recommended Salem, and I just…felt like I needed to be here. You know how you get those gut feelings sometimes?"

Troy nodded, his expression thoughtful as he leaned back in his chair. "Gut feelings are powerful. They can lead you to some unexpected places."

I smiled, but it was a fragile thing. My gut feelings had led me to Salem, yes—but they'd also led me to the knowledge of my sister's approaching death. What if me being here put everyone around me in danger, including Troy?

I glanced out the window again, watching the boats sway gently in the harbor. "What about you? What brought you to Salem?" I asked, hoping to shift the conversation away from myself.

Troy chuckled. "I didn't really have a choice. Born and raised here." He leaned forward, resting his elbows on the table. "My family owns the Bluebell Lodge—kind of a local landmark. I help out when I'm not at college. Keeps me busy."

"Ah, I remember now. You also said you worked at the lodge and go to college at the same time?" I asked, raising an eyebrow. "That sounds intense."

"It can be," he admitted, a flicker of exhaustion crossing his features. "But it's all part of the plan. I'm finishing my business degree, and if everything goes right, I'll land a job in New York—maybe even on Wall Street. That's the dream."

His face lit up as he spoke, and I couldn't help but smile. "Wall Street?" I asked, trying to picture him in a sleek suit, rushing through the chaos of the Financial District. It wasn't hard to imagine, though the thought felt strange—Troy seemed like he belonged in a place like Salem, with its quiet charm and slow rhythms.

"Yeah," he said, a grin tugging at his lips. "Don't get me wrong, I love Salem, but it's…small. You know? I want to see what I can do out there in the big leagues."

His passion was infectious, and for a moment, I forgot about the fear that was looming over me. "You sound determined," I said, meeting his gaze.

"I have to be," he replied. "Life doesn't hand you things—you have to go after what you want. Even if it means taking risks."

I thought about the risks I'd taken just to be here, about the life I'd left behind and the secrets I was carrying.

His eyes softened as he looked at me. "What about you? Do you have a dream you're chasing?"

I hesitated, my smile fading. "Honestly, I don't know," I said quietly. The only thing consuming me right now was catching the Salem Slayer. "I guess I'm still figuring things out."

"That's okay," he said, his tone reassuring. "Sometimes it takes a while to figure out what you want. But you've already taken the first step—coming here."

I looked at him, surprised by how genuine he sounded. He wasn't pushing, wasn't judging. He was just…listening.

Before I could respond, he leaned forward slightly, looking straight into my eyes. "Do you have plans for the rest of the afternoon?" he asked, his voice quiet but hopeful.

My stomach flipped in anticipation. "Not really," I said, trying to sound casual, though my pulse betrayed me.

"Then how about we take a walk?" he suggested. "The weather's too nice to stay inside, and there's this great little bar called the Hollow. We could grab a drink, maybe some dessert. No pressure, though," he added quickly with a crooked smile.

I hesitated for just a moment before nodding. "That sounds nice."

We paid and left the restaurant together, stepping into the crisp autumn air. Troy walked beside me, his hands casually tucked into his jeans pockets. I noticed how he slowed his pace to match mine, totally unhurried. The warmth of the afternoon sun filtered through the trees, casting dappled shadows on the cobblestone streets.

"Was it weird growing up in such a famous town?" I asked, glancing up at him.

Troy laughed. "You mean because of all the witch stuff?" He shook his head. "Not really. I mean, the tourists can get a little crazy around Halloween, but I've always liked the history of it. There's something…grounding about it, you know? Like, no matter what else changes, this place is always the same."

I nodded, understanding more than I expected. Salem had a sense of permanence, its mystique only adding to its timeless presence.

"And you?" he asked. "What do you think of Salem so far?"

I hesitated, unsure how to answer. "It's…different from what I'm used to," I said finally. "It's beautiful, but—" I stopped myself, biting my lip.

"But?" he prompted, his tone gentle.

I sighed. "I don't feel safe, what with the serial killer at large." I sighed heavily. "I don't think I will stay."

Troy stopped and turned to face me, his brow furrowed, concern etched across his features. "I hear you, but I'd be sorry to see you go," he said softly, his eyes searching mine. "These murders are unusual—nothing like this has ever happened here."

We continued walking. I hesitated, then added, "The police think it's Megan's boyfriend, Orion."

Troy's eyes widened in surprise. "I didn't know they already had a suspect." He rubbed his chin and looked over at me. "Surely that's reassuring enough that you can stay?"

I shrugged. Was it enough? Could they catch him before he killed my sister? No, I wasn't reassured.

Troy paused, then sighed softly, almost nervously. "Jen…I don't want you to leave." I stopped and looked up at his beautiful pleading eyes. The intensity of his gaze sent a warm flush up my neck, and my stomach danced like butterflies in a breeze.

He liked me. I could feel the attraction between us growing. It was undeniable.

I smiled shyly, biting my lip. Then I looked away, and we continued walking in warm silence.

We reached the Hollow, a cozy bar tucked into one of the quieter streets. The soft-lit interior was warm and inviting, with wooden beams overhead and twinkling fairy lights strung along the walls. A small stage in the corner was set up for live music, though it was empty now. Troy led me to a booth near the back, and we slid into the cushioned seats. The atmosphere was relaxed, the murmur of conversation and clinking glasses filling the space.

"I don't know about you, but I'm definitely getting dessert," he said, picking up the menu.

I laughed, grateful for the change of subject. "What do you recommend?"

"The apple crumble here is amazing," he said. "Trust me."

When the waitress came, Troy ordered two apple crumbles and a cider for himself. I stuck with sparkling water, too nervous to risk anything stronger.

"So," he said after the waitress left, leaning forward slightly, "how come you were a bit off the day you came into the lodge to ask for directions?"

I laughed awkwardly and covered my mouth. "I'm not sure why I was so rude to you." I looked away, embarrassed.

He chuckled softly. "I figured you'd just gotten into a fight and were looking for the next one."

I blinked, confused. "What do you mean?"

He gestured to his own lip. "The cut you had."

Flustered, I waved it off. "Oh, that's a story for another day."

Troy studied me for a moment, and I could see the curiosity in his eyes. But he didn't push. Instead, he smiled and leaned back in his seat. "Well, I'm glad you came in," he said.

His words sent warmth through me, and for the first time in days, I felt a flicker of hope. I also felt guilty for ruining his date with Ashley and that I was enjoying my day whilst the death of my sister loomed ahead. But maybe Salem wasn't just about danger and fear. Maybe, just maybe, it was also about finding something—someone—worth staying for.

EIGHTEEN

Elisa

Ava and I hadn't stopped moving all day. The café buzzed with the energy of the Halloween season—lines of customers spilling out the door, tables filling as soon as they were cleared, and the cheerful chatter of conversation mixing with the soft music in the background. The steady stream of regulars and tourists brought a flood of compliments on the warm atmosphere, the fast service, and more than once, on Ava's and my smiles. The flirty comments were plentiful, too: phone numbers scribbled on receipts, playful winks, and the inevitable question: "Are you two sisters?"

It was flattering and exhausting.

But as much as I appreciated the attention, none of it really mattered. The one person I wished would notice me barely gave me a second glance.

Officer Luca.

He ticked every box: he was handsome, confident, and had an air of quiet authority that made him impossible to ignore. But no matter how many times he stopped by the café for his morning double espresso, I couldn't seem to make him pay more than disinterested friendly attention.

I sighed, shaking the thought away. Lately, someone else had been occupying my mind, too.

Ed.

Every time the door chimed, my heart leaped, hoping it was him. There was something about his quiet charm and the way he cared for others that had crept under my skin. He wasn't as polished as Officer Luca, but there was a warmth about him that I couldn't resist.

I smiled at the thought of him as I arranged the thrift-store books I'd picked up earlier in the morning. Most were thrillers or books about ghosts and witches, perfect for the café's spooky vibe. Antonio had entrusted me with making a few changes, and I'd thrown myself into it. The tacky plastic spiders and broomsticks cluttering the display fridge were gone, and there was a simple vase of dried peonies on the counter—my favorite. I'd rearranged the tables to create more space for strollers and wheelchairs, and my proudest find was a secondhand bookshelf I'd painted a rich dark green. It looked like new.

The café felt cozier now, more personal. I stepped back to admire the little nook I'd created, where a sign on the shelf read: help yourself to a free book with your coffee, and bring in unwanted books for recycling.

My phone buzzed, snapping me out of my thoughts.

I can't go out tonight, Jenna's text read. *You go with the girls.*

I sighed, worry curling in my chest. Jenna hadn't been herself lately. She was distant, distracted, on edge in a way I couldn't put into words. Some nights, I woke to find her staring out the window, muttering under her breath. It was like she wasn't entirely here anymore, and it unnerved me. The whole Ouija board incident had scared me half to death, and I couldn't shake what she'd said about her vision—about Ava. Maybe I needed to give her some space.

I tapped out a quick reply: *If you change your mind, we'll be at the Mystic Flame at 6. x*

As I hit send, the door chimes tinkled, and when I looked up, the room seemed to brighten. Ed strolled in, his green eyes scanning the café before landing on me. He smiled, and for a moment, everything else faded.

"Hello, Elisa," he said warmly, walking up to the counter.

"Ed," I said, fighting the grin spreading across my face. "Lovely to see you." I grabbed a cup to make his coffee, grateful for something to do with my hands. In his black jeans and grey hoodie, he looked effortlessly handsome, the casual clothes only highlighting his muscular chest and easy confidence.

"Wow," he said, glancing around. "This place looks different."

"Do you like it?" I asked, tossing my hair over my shoulder.

"It's amazing," he replied, his gaze lingering on me. "You've done a great job."

Before I could respond, Ava sauntered in from the kitchen, carrying a tray of clean cups.

"Hey, Meg—" Ed started, then froze, doing a double-take. "Sorry," he said, blushing. "I thought you were Megan."

Ava giggled, setting the cups down. "Happens all the time."

I smiled. "This is my cousin Ava, Jenna's sister," I said. "And this is Ed—he's the nurse who took care of Jenna in the hospital."

Ed's face softened. "How's Jenna doing?"

"She's better," I lied, forcing a smile. I held up a mug. "Coffee on the house, like I promised?"

"Yes, please," he said, returning my smile. "And blueberry pancakes, if you have them."

"Coming right up."

When Ava slipped back into the kitchen, Ed said, "Hey, I haven't seen Megan around lately. Is she on vacation or something?"

I hesitated. "You haven't heard?" I lowered my voice. "She was found dead. The cops think her boyfriend killed her."

His face went pale. "What? When?"

Before I could answer, the kitchen bell rang loudly, making me jump. Antonio's voice boomed, "Elisa, food's getting cold! Let's go! No time for chitchat!"

I rolled my eyes and shouted back, "I'm coming!" I gave Ed an apologetic look. "I'll bring your coffee in a sec and fill you in on what I know."

When the pancakes were ready, I grabbed the plate and Ed's coffee. I strode toward him, balancing the tray as I swayed my hips subtly. I felt bad about leaving our conversation unfinished after blurting out such shocking news. But the café was busy, and Antonio's booming voice from the kitchen left little room for argument.

Ed was leaning forward in his booth, elbows on the table, his chin resting in his hand. His hoodie was folded neatly over his lap. I set the coffee and pancakes down gently, not wanting to startle him. "Here you go," I said softly.

He glanced up, his eyes clouded with emotion. "Thanks." He smiled.

I glanced back at the kitchen; Antonio could survive without me for a few minutes. I slid into the seat across from Ed, lowering my voice so no one else could hear.

"I'm sorry you had to hear about Megan like that," I said, folding my hands in my lap. "I should've found a better way to tell you."

He shook his head. "No, I'm glad you told me," he said, his voice strained. He picked up the coffee but didn't drink it, staring into the swirling steam as though it held answers. "I just…I can't believe it. Megan was such a good person. She didn't deserve that."

The raw emotion in his voice sent a pang of guilt through me. I thought of Megan's laughter, the way she'd lit up the café every time I'd come in to see her. Her absence was like a shadow over the town now, a constant reminder of the danger lurking in Salem.

Ed's brow furrowed as he put the cup back down. "Her boyfriend killed her?" he said slowly. "Did they catch him?"

I shook my head. "Not yet. The police think he skipped town. They're searching for him, but…" I hesitated, glancing around to make sure no one was listening. "It's scary. No one feels safe anymore."

His jaw clenched, and his hands tightened around the coffee cup. "I should've seen the signs," he said bitterly. "She came to the hospital once with a dislocated arm. I asked her about it, but she just laughed it off, said she tripped and fell at work. I didn't push her, but I should've. Maybe if I'd…" He trailed off, shaking his head.

"Ed, don't do that to yourself," I said, leaning forward. "You couldn't have known. None of us did."

He looked at me, and the anguish in his eyes pulled at my heartstrings. "I could've done more," he said softly.

"No one could've stopped him, I heard rumors he was too high on drugs," I said gently. "Don't blame yourself for something you couldn't control. There's a vigil for Megan on Friday at seven on the common. If you're free, come along. I think it might help. A lot of people will be there to remember her."

He nodded, his expression unreadable. "I'll check my work schedule," he said. "But I'll try to make it."

I glanced at the pancakes sitting untouched on his plate. "You should eat," I said with a small smile, trying to lighten the mood. "Antonio's going to kill me if he finds out his food is going to waste."

That earned a faint chuckle from Ed, and he picked up his fork and took a small bite. A group of customers walked in, their laughter filling the air. I glanced toward the counter, where Ava was trying to juggle two orders at once.

"I should get back," I said reluctantly, standing up. "But if you ever want to talk, you know where to find me."

Ed's lips curved into a small grateful smile. "Thanks, Elisa." He looked down shyly.

I nodded and turned to leave, and as I walked away, I felt his eyes lingering on me. A giddy rush engulfed me, and for a moment, I allowed myself to imagine what it might be like if this thing between us, whatever it was, grew into something more.

Between taking orders and running back and forth, I didn't get another chance to speak to Ed. By the time I glanced at his booth again, he was already gone, his coffee cup empty, and his plate clean. He had left a generous tip.

Later that evening, Ava and I made our way to the Hollow instead of the Mystic Flame after a last-minute change of plans. It was a short walk from Strega's, and live music was blaring through the speakers when we arrived. The warm glow of the twinkling fairy lights above, the buzz of conversations, and the faint scent of cinnamon cocktails lifted our spirits.

We met up with Salma, Roman, his friend Isaac, and Isaac's younger sister, Carmen Isaac and Carmen belonged on the pages of a glossy magazine, effortlessly charismatic and strikingly attractive. Isaac, who was twenty-two, stood just under six feet tall, toned chest and a square jaw that gave him a rugged, confident appeal. His easy laugh and the glint of mischief in his caramel-brown eyes made him instantly likable. Carmen, who was twenty, was his opposite in many ways—quiet, poised, and elegant. Her almond-shaped eyes were framed by dark lashes, and her sharp cheekbones gave her a delicate, ethereal beauty. Despite their polished appearance, both of them were refreshingly down-to-earth. I expected stories of private schools and weekend horse rides, but instead, they joked about struggling to parallel park and bickered over whose turn it was to clean the house. I liked them instantly, and it was easy to see why Ava and Salma spent so much time with them.

It didn't take long for the group to settle into an easy rhythm. Salma and Roman fell into a deep conversation, their heads tilted toward each other as they laughed. Isaac chatted animatedly with Ava, and Carmen sat back, her graceful presence adding a quiet calm to the lively table.

A grin spread across Isaac's face as he swirled the last bit of Jack and Coke in his glass. "All right, listen up," he said, his eyes glinting with excitement. "As soon as spring hits, we should all do the Appalachian Trail. Who's in?"

The table buzzed with energy; his enthusiasm was contagious. "Hell yeah!" Roman replied, slamming his empty glass onto the table, beaming.

Salma, sitting beside him, raised an eyebrow but smiled. "I'm in. I've never even been camping before, but why not?" She laughed, matching Roman's energy.

Carmen hesitated, her delicate features twisting into a skeptical expression. "I'm not a big fan of sleeping outside," she admitted, pushing her hair behind her ear. "But if you're all going, then okay. Why not?" She shrugged with mock reluctance, though the corners of her mouth tugged upward.

Isaac turned to me, his grin widening. "What about you, Elisa? You in?"

The Appalachian Trail. Just hearing the name sent a spark of excitement through me. Images of towering mountains, sun-dappled forests, and endless trails winding through the wild landscapes of the eastern United States whirred through my mind. I could almost feel the crisp air against my skin, the earthy scent of pine trees mingling with the distant rush of waterfalls.

"Count me in," I said, unable to hide my growing enthusiasm.

Isaac's grin turned triumphant as he clapped his hands together. "That's what I'm talking about! Picture it—miles and miles of pure wilderness. No work, no stress, just us and nature."

Roman laughed, nudging him. "And bears. Don't forget about the bears."

Isaac waved him off with a laugh. "Bears aren't going to bother us, man. As long as you don't put a steak dinner in your backpack, you'll be fine."

Salma tilted her head, her eyes narrowing. "You sound awfully confident. You've been reading up on how to survive a bear attack, haven't you?"

"Hey, knowledge is power," Isaac said with a playful wink.

Carmen groaned softly, leaning back in her chair. "Let me guess: we'll be sleeping in tents, no bathrooms for miles, living off granola bars and trail mix?"

"Come on, Carmen," Isaac said, leaning forward. "It's more than that, just imagine standing on a ridge at sunrise, watching the mist roll over the Blue Ridge Mountains. Or walking through the Smokies with wildflowers blooming all around you. It'll be like stepping into another world."

Even Carmen's skepticism seemed to waver as he spoke.

Roman added, "Picture the towering cliffs of Shenandoah National Park, the dense forests of the White Mountains, an endless expanse of rugged beauty stretching as far as the eye can see."

"And don't forget," Isaac continued, his voice rising animatedly, "at night, the sky is full of stars. No city lights, no noise—just the sound of crickets and the crackle of a campfire. It's magical."

"Okay, okay," Carmen said, holding up her hands in surrender. "You're starting to sell me on this whole hiking thing. But I'm not carrying my own backpack."

"We'll figure it out," Roman said, laughing. "I'll carry your makeup bag if it means you'll come."

Carmen smirked. "Deal."

Isaac turned back to me, his eyes sparkling. "Ever done anything like this before, Elisa?"

I shook my head, smiling. "No, but it sounds incredible. I've always wanted to see places like that—the kinds of landscapes you only see in movies or on postcards. I'm definitely in."

Isaac raised his glass, a wide grin on his face. "To adventure!" he said, his voice brimming with anticipation.

Carmen leaned toward Isaac and placed a delicate hand on his arm. "Let's tell them about the Halloween party," she said, her eyes sparkling. They were the same caramel brown as her brother's.

Isaac perked up. "Oh, right! I can't believe I forgot," he said. "Every year, we host a Halloween party at our place. Our parents always go out of town that weekend, so we have the whole house to ourselves. You guys are definitely coming—we won't take no for an answer."

Roman's eyes lit up, and he raised his glass. "Of course! Count me in. You know I love a good party."

Salma clapped her hands, excitement flashing across her face. "That sounds amazing! What's the vibe? Costumes? Drinks? Dancing?"

Isaac grinned. "Think dim lighting, spooky décor, a dance floor in the basement, and a fully stocked bar."

"And we're talking *serious* costumes," Carmen chimed in. "None of that 'sexy cat' nonsense. Get creative."

"We're definitely coming. Right, Els?" Ava said, nudging me playfully.

I hesitated, unsure how to respond. That was the day Jenna thought Ava would die. The memory of my cousin's warning flashed through my mind—the urgency in her voice, the haunted look in her eyes as she described her vision. I forced a small smile, trying to push the thought away.

"I'll have to check with Jenna," I said reluctantly.

Carmen tilted her head, her soft smile inviting. "Bring her, too," she said. "The more the merrier."

Ava gave me another nudge, her grin widening. "See? Problem solved. We'll drag Jenna out—she needs to loosen up. We'll all have an amazing time. You have to say yes."

My stomach twisted. I didn't want to dampen Ava's excitement, but the thought of attending a party on Halloween with the shadow of Jenna's warning hanging over us filled me with dread. I took a slow sip of my wine, buying time to compose myself.

"We'll see," I said finally, trying to sound casual. "I'll talk to her about it."

Isaac grinned, clearly satisfied. "Perfect. It's going to be the best party of the year, guaranteed. Do you guys have any costume ideas?"

As the conversation shifted, I leaned back in my chair, letting their laughter and chatter wash over me. But my mind kept drifting to Jenna.

Isaac's voice broke through my thoughts. "Elisa, what about you?"

I blinked, startled out of my reverie. "Uh, not yet," I said, forcing a small laugh. "I can get very creative with costumes, though."

I watched Ava closely throughout the evening. She laughed at Isaac's jokes and sipped her drink. She kept glancing at Roman, her smile fading whenever she saw him talking to Salma.

Concerned, I slipped my arm around her shoulders and moved her away from the group. "What's up?" I asked, taking a drag from my cigarette.

She hesitated, then muttered, "I think I'm just tired."

"Come on," I coaxed, handing her a cigarette. "Here, light one up. I know there's this weird love triangle between the three of you. How do you really feel about him?"

Ava lit the cigarette, taking a long drag before answering. "I like Roman," she admitted. "I think about him all the time. But he and Salma…I don't know. They spend so much time together. I feel like he's going to pick her."

I sighed, taking a sip of my wine. "I get it. You can't force love, Ava. And honestly, Roman's not all that. He talks so much that no one else can get a word in. Having said that, tonight it's his friend Isaac doing all the talking"

Ava let out a small laugh, her shoulders relaxing slightly. She gulped down her Coke, ordered another, and said, "You're not wrong."

Encouraged, I leaned in, trying to keep her spirits up. "But you never know. Maybe he likes you and is just trying to make you jealous. Guys love playing mind games. And if he doesn't like you, then screw him."

"If he picks Salma, I'll back off," she said with a sigh. "But he hasn't really said anything or made a move, so who knows?"

I hesitated for a second, then decided to share my own dilemma. "I've got a confession, too."

I blew out a long stream of smoke, and Ava's eyes lit up with curiosity. "Go on," she urged.

"I've got a crush on Officer Luca," I admitted. "But he hasn't shown any interest. What should I do?"

Ava shrugged, echoing my own uncertainty.

"I'm just trying to keep my options open," I continued with a grin. "You know Ed, the nurse who came in for the blueberry pancakes earlier?" Ava nodded, already smiling as if she knew what was coming next.

"Well, I think Ed's just as cute, and I felt a connection between us earlier. I asked him to come to Megan's vigil." I said loudly, and at that exact moment, the live music cut out. Everyone in the bar looked at me.

My phone buzzed in my pocket, saving me. I pulled it out, and my stomach tightened as I read Jenna's message: *He's outside the Hollow, watching you all. Be careful walking home tonight, and don't take your eyes off the girls. x*

I felt the hairs on the back of my neck rise. I glanced out the window, searching the foggy street for Jenna. She must be outside, but how did she know we'd changed our plan and come to the Hollow instead?

"Is everything okay?" Ava asked.

I forced a smile and began typing an angry text, *THANKS. YOU SURE KNOW HOW TO RUIN MY NIGHT!* I pressed send, stuffing my phone into my pocket.

"It's just Jenna," I said rubbing my temples. "She's…stressed. I think we should head back." As much as I wanted to dismiss her concerns, I knew she wasn't one to play pranks. I had seen enough to understand that she experienced things beyond my comprehension.

I gathered Salma and Ava, the stress of Jenna's words stirred up a sense of unease within me. "Let me give you all a ride," Roman offered, concern flickering across his face.

"No, it's fine," we replied in unison. "It's only a fifteen-minute walk," I added quickly.

As we stepped out into the chilly night air, Ava and Salma chattering behind me, I couldn't shake the feeling that we were being watched. A few drunk groups staggered past us, singing and stumbling. We ignored them and walked toward home. As we drew closer to the guesthouse, the streets got quieter, the laughter and music from the Hollow fading into the distance. The fog thickened with each step, swallowing the streetlights one by one.

Jenna's warning clung to me, whispering doubts. Three girls had already been murdered. What if the Slayer truly was out here, lurking in the darkest corners of Salem? Goose bumps crept across my skin, the chill in the air intensifying my sense of dread. *Thanks, Jen*, I thought bitterly, *for planting this fear in my head*. I knew my mind was likely playing tricks on me, but the nagging sensation wouldn't go away.

I glanced over my shoulder and caught a slight movement out of the corner of my eye. I turned my head just enough to peer down the side street to my right, and my breath caught in my throat. There, partially obscured by shadows and fog, stood a dark figure, staring directly at us. The streetlamp behind him flickered on and off a few times before dying completely.

"Come on," I muttered to the girls, quickening my pace. When I looked again, the figure seemed to blend into the night, the edges of its form blurring before it disappeared.

The lighthouse came into view, its distant glow a beacon of safety. But unseen eyes watched me all the way home.

NINETEEN

Was this what it felt like to be in love? A giddy sense of anticipation gripped me every time I thought of Troy. He was the only person who could chase away the oppressive cloud hanging over me—the inevitable loss of my sister. In his presence, the foreboding of the future faded, at least for a while.

The cool breeze rushed through the open window of Troy's car, brushing softly against my face as I leaned back against the seat. The faint scent of early autumn leaves filled the air as we drove, the sun flickering through the canopy of trees lining the road.

Troy was going to show me around Boston; I hadn't been back there since the day we'd arrived. The girls and I hadn't gotten a chance to make a day of it before we all got jobs. But I was secretly glad my first visit was with Troy. Butterflies fluttered in my stomach—not just because of the city, but because this was our first real date. *My* first real date ever.

Boston unfolded before us, its skyline dotted with historic brick buildings and gleaming modern towers. The streets were alive with energy: couples strolling hand in hand, runners jogging along the Charles River, and vendors selling roasted chestnuts on bustling street corners. The iconic Citgo sign glowed in the distance, a beacon that seemed to welcome us into the heart of the city.

Troy glanced over at me as he drove. He reached across the console to take my hand, his touch warm and steady. "I thought we could grab some lunch first," he said excitedly. "And then I want to show you Beacon Hill. It's a historic neighborhood, lots of old brick town houses and boutique shops. You'll love it."

"That sounds perfect," I replied, my hand still tingling from his touch.

"And after that," he continued, his grin widening mischievously, "I thought we could play paintball. Ever been?"

I laughed, shaking my head. "No, never. I saw it in a film once and wanted to go."

"You're in for a treat," he chuckled, giving my hand a playful squeeze. "But fair warning, you might end up with a few bruises."

I bit my lip, trying to shake the sudden memory that rose unbidden—the bruises I had collected from my father, the ones I had learned to hide beneath long sleeves and forced smiles. I pushed the memory away, refusing to dwell in the past.

"I can handle it," I said, forcing a playful smirk. And for the first time, I believed it. I wasn't that girl anymore—not in this moment, not with Troy.

As we passed Fenway Park, Troy pointed to the famous stadium, its green facade proudly bearing the words home of the boston red sox. The sidewalks around it were bustling with fans, some wearing jerseys and others snapping photos.

"You a baseball fan?" he asked, his eyes flicking toward me.

I shrugged, laughing. "Not really. I don't know the first thing about it."

He grinned. "Well, Fenway is iconic. Maybe I'll take you to a game sometime. Trust me, once you hear the roar of the crowd, you'll love it." The idea of spending an afternoon in a place so full of life, sitting beside Troy, felt thrilling.

We drove past more landmarks: the stately Boston Public Library with its grand arched windows; Copley Square, bustling with people; the gold-domed Massachusetts State House, gleamed in the sun. I'd not realized how charming this city was, with its mix of old-world history and modern vibrancy.

"Boston's beautiful," I admitted, glancing over at him. "I'd love to come back again."

Troy gave me a sidelong smile, his blue eyes catching the sunlight. "It is beautiful. Even more so with you here."

My cheeks blazed as I looked down at my feet.

We sat together in a quaint bakery tucked into the picturesque streets of Beacon Hill. The white tiles set off the rustic furniture, and the soft chatter of conversation and the aroma of freshly brewed coffee made the space feel warm and inviting.

Troy leaned forward, his eyes gleaming with curiosity as he took a bite of his toasted fried egg sandwich. "Tell me more about London," he said keenly. "What was it like growing up there?"

I hesitated, taking a small bite of my toasted sourdough salmon sandwich. I wanted to avoid the question. I mean, what could I tell him? The weather was grey, the people were cold, and home wasn't exactly a sanctuary. I swallowed, brushing toast crumbs from my lips. "It's not all it's cracked up to be," I finally said.

Troy chuckled, shaking his head. "That's the thing, Jenna. People always miss what's right in front of them. London has so much history—it's incredible. I want to see the Tower of London,

Parliament, and Buckingham Palace. I'd love to stay at the Ritz, shop at Harrods, hang out on Hampstead Heath, stroll through Primrose Hill and Regent's Park. Ride in one of those iconic black cabs, have lunch at Trafalgar Square…and don't even get me started on all the museums."

As I listened to him, I couldn't help but feel a little puzzled. Was he talking about the same London I'd grown up in? I thought about Stratford, the area where I'd been raised. There were no royal parks or historic landmarks, at least not the kind that made you feel like you were part of something grand. "Stratford doesn't have much going for it," I replied, my voice quiet. "It's pretty poor compared to other parts of London."

Troy's face softened, his expression shifting to one of concern. "I'm sensing home wasn't a happy place for you."

"What makes you say that?"

"You never talk about your family." He finished the last piece of his toast before he continued, "That first day you showed up at the lodge, you had a cut to your lip. I put two and two together."

I glanced away, not ready to share the full truth. "No, it wasn't a happy place," I admitted quietly. "But it's not something I like to talk about."

He nodded. "That's okay. You don't have to. Just…know I'm here to listen if you ever want to."

I thought about telling him more. But how could he possibly understand the struggle of growing up under strict rules, in a family bound by cultural expectations and the pressure to conform? How could I tell him I would have been married by now had I not escaped? His world was so free, so open—so different from mine.

"Maybe another time," I said with a faint smile, brushing the thought away.

Troy's excitement returned, undeterred. "That's fine," he said warmly. "But one day, I'll visit London. And when I do, you're going to show me around."

His enthusiasm was contagious, and I caught myself wondering what it would be like to see London through his eyes. Maybe exploring it with him wouldn't be so bad. But the idea of returning to London filled me with dread. I didn't intend to go back—ever!

The playful atmosphere of the paintball arena was a sharp contrast to the quiet streets of Beacon Hill. The goggles they gave us were oversize, reminding me of school science labs, and I couldn't help laughing as I tied my hair into a bun and loaded paintballs into the front pocket of the dungarees they provided. Troy had no idea how competitive I could get, but he was about to find out.

"I'll be gentle with you," he teased, flashing me a smile.

I smiled back, arching an eyebrow, feigning innocence. "We'll see about that."

Other groups were darting between barricades, laughing and shouting as they hid and chased each other.

While Troy was still picking out his paintballs, I saw my chance. I threw a blue paintball right at him, even though we weren't using guns, it splattered against his head with a satisfying burst of color, due to the thin, delicate outer shell, similar to a balloon.

His expression was priceless—shocked and amused all at once. "Oh, it's on," he said, his voice low and full of playful menace.

I took off running, laughing as I ducked behind a wooden barricade. The game was pure chaos—shouts and laughter echoed around us as paintballs splattered against walls and trees.

I peeked around the corner of a wall but couldn't see Troy anywhere…until I felt a sharp thump on my back. I let out a laugh mixed with a yelp. He had gotten me, and I hadn't even seen him coming. He must have known the layout of the space already.

Determined to even the score, I chased him down, and when he stumbled and fell, I seized my opportunity. Buckled over with laughter, I aimed a shot straight at his chest, red paint exploding across his dungarees like a wound. Before he could get up, I threw another one, hitting him on the side of the face.

"You're ruthless," he called out, shaking his head.

"And you underestimated me," I shot back, laughing as I darted behind cover again.

Despite the playful combat, I felt a growing connection with him. Every laugh, every glance we exchanged during the chase only deepened the fluttery feeling in my stomach.

I hid behind a tree, thinking I was safe, when suddenly I felt a paintball explode in my hair. I screamed and spun around, only to be scooped up by the waist, his arms strong around me, stopping me from running or launching another attack. For a brief moment, I forgot the paintball game, forgot everything except how close he was. But then I remembered myself. With a grin, I grabbed another ball, popping it right into his face. Green paint splattered everywhere, covering his goggles as I broke free, sprinting off with a laugh.

When we ran out of paintballs, we collapsed by a tree, watching the others continue to play. For the first time in a long while,

I felt truly happy. Even the looming dread of losing my sister had faded into the background.

Troy turned to me, his blue eyes softening as he leaned in. When his lips met mine, adrenaline surged through my entire body. His kiss was warm and soft, sending a spark through me that left me breathless.

My first kiss, and it couldn't have been more right.

TWENTY

Later that evening, after Troy dropped me off, I slipped around the side of the cottage, not wanting anyone to see the streaks of dried paint on my hair and face. The cool evening air nipped at my skin as I fumbled for my keys, glancing over my shoulder out of habit. The girls weren't back yet, and for once, I was relieved. I needed a moment of peace, a chance to shower without the usual chaos of shared living.

But the silence of the cottage was far from comforting. My sense of unease was growing stronger with each passing day. It wasn't just the strange noises in the attic or the fleeting shadows that I tried to convince myself weren't there; it was the oppressive sense of being watched. That feeling clung to me now, prickling the back of my neck.

I moved quickly through the cottage, flicking on lights as I went, checking the bedrooms, the kitchen, even the storage cupboards. My chest tightened as I opened each door, half expecting to find something—or someone—lurking there. Of course, there was nothing. Still, my heart didn't stop racing. Orion, the Salem Slayer, was coming for Ava, and I couldn't afford to let my guard down.

The silence pressed down on me, so I turned on the radio, cranking the volume until 'The Din Pedals' *"Waterfall"* spread through the house. The music was a buffer against the oppressive stillness, and I clung to it as I darted into the bathroom and locked the door behind me as if that would keep the fear at bay.

The warm spray of the shower was a welcome distraction, washing away both the paint and the tension in my shoulders. As I rinsed the conditioner from my hair, I started to relax, my thoughts drifting to Troy and the kiss we'd shared. "I'll meet you at the vigil tomorrow evening," he'd said as he waved goodbye. The memory made me smile, warmth blooming in my chest.

Then, suddenly, the music stopped.

The abrupt silence was jarring, startling me out of my thoughts. I turned off the water, grabbing a towel and wrapping it tightly around me. I strained to hear anything over the pounding in my chest, but the only sound was the faint creak of the house settling.

"Salma?" I called, my voice ringing out loudly.

No answer. I approached the bathroom door.

"Elisa?" I held my breath and pressed my ear against the door. A shadow shifted beneath the doorframe.

I checked the lock, my fingers trembling as they brushed the cold metal. "Sis?" I called softly, barely daring to breathe.

Nothing.

The cottage felt eerily silent, charged with an unnatural tension that seeped through the door and into my skin. For a long moment, I stood still, unsure whether to stay put or go investigate. Finally, summoning what courage I had left, I unlocked the door and crept into the hallway, looking left and then right.

The lights that had cast a warm glow were now dim and flickering. The air felt icy against my damp skin, and the sensation of being watched intensified. The radio in the living room was off. I walked toward it cautiously, glancing over my shoulder. I reached for the dial, but before I could touch it, the music crackled back to life, making me jump. "Enjoy the Silence" by Depeche Mode poured through the speakers, the irony chilling. I turned the volume down, but the unease didn't lift.

I turned toward the window, half expecting to see one of the girls outside, playing a trick on me. But the porch was empty, and the only sound was the light tinkling of the chimes as they swayed. I looked beyond the trees toward the maze. No one was there. The lighthouse lamp was off, which reduced my visibility, but a few bedroom lights were on in the guesthouse farther up the lawn, casting long ominous shadows.

I was about to step away from the window when the radio cut out again.

I froze.

The air shifted behind me, and I had the unmistakable feeling that someone was standing there. Every instinct screamed at me not to look, to run out of the room, but my legs felt rooted to the spot. Slowly, very slowly, I turned, catching a flicker of movement out of the corner of my eye. I inhaled sharply, goose bumps prickling all over my skin.

A figure hovered in the corner of the room. It was Megan.

Her translucent form shimmered faintly in the dim light, her eyes hollow and loaded with sorrow, locked onto mine. She didn't speak, but the air around her felt saturated with sadness. I stared at her, my breath shallow, my mind scrambling to make sense of what I was seeing. I sensed that she meant no harm, that she was here to help.

"Megan…" I breathed shakily. The figure floated swiftly toward me, and I took a nervous step back. This was real, not a vision. My mind reeled with questions.

"Why did Orion kill you and the other girls?"

She drifted closer still, her gaze distant and unblinking. My legs started to shake. I took a deep breath and tried again.

"Can you help me stop Orion from killing my sister?" My voice cracked with desperation.

When she finally spoke, her lips didn't move. Her voice came through warped, like a distorted recording. *It wasn't Orion.*

My heart sank to the bottom of my stomach. I stared at her, confused, my mind spinning. After a long pause, I finally gathered the courage to whisper, "Who was it?"

But Megan didn't answer. Instead, her form passed through me like a cold wind, sending a shock of ice through my core. My knees buckled, and I clutched the arm of the sofa for support. The radio crackled back to life behind me, the sound jarring after the oppressive silence, making me shudder.

And just like that, Megan was gone. But the terror lingered. If the Slayer wasn't Orion, then who was it? And where was he?

Keys jangled, and the lock clicked open on the front door. "Jen! *Jenna!* You home?" Elisa's voice joyfully called. She trailed off as she stepped into the living room and saw me standing there in my towel, and her expression shifted to bemusement. "Ah, there you are. What's wrong? You look like you've just seen a ghost."

"I just saw Megan," I whispered, trying to convince myself as much as her. My voice broke.

Elisa let out a laugh, shaking her head. "C'mon, Jen. Don't start with that again. I was just joking." She took her jacket off and draped it over the arm of the sofa. "I'm still shaken up about the text you sent the other night. Let's not do this now."

"I'm serious! Why else would I be standing here in a towel, soaking wet, too scared to move?" My words tumbled out in a rush. I started to shiver.

Her smile faltered as the radio started glitching, repeating the same word over and over: "Violence. Violence. Violence."

"What's wrong with this thing?" she muttered, flipping it off before yanking the plug from the wall. The silence that followed was uncomfortable. She glanced around the room, her eyes narrowing as she moved to the window, peering from left to right.

I joined her, my voice quieter now. "At first I thought it was you or the girls playing tricks on me. But then…she was here. *Right here*, Els. And then she disappeared just before you walked in."

Elisa stared at me for a moment, her expression softening. "All right, Jen. Put on some clothes before you freeze to death, and then tell me everything over dinner. I brought leftovers from the café." Her tone shifted. "And more importantly, I'm dying to hear about your date with Troy." She winked, clearly not wanting to dwell on the eerie.

I rolled my eyes at her attempt to lighten the mood, but I did feel a little better.

"You've got five minutes to get yourself decent and in the kitchen," she said, checking an invisible watch. "Your time starts… now! Four fifty-nine, fifty-eight, fifty-seven…"

"Okay, okay!" I shouted back, managing a smile despite the lingering chill. I darted into my room, the warmth returning to my limbs as I blow-dried my hair and pulled on some joggers and a sweater. I slapped on some face cream, already feeling more like myself. I didn't know what I'd do without Elisa.

When I returned to the kitchen, my cousin was singing along to radio. "Oh, kiss me, beneath the milky twilight. Lead me out on the moonlit floor…" I watched from the door until she called, "You've got thirty seconds! So, kiss me…"

"I'm here! Jeez." I slid into a chair, feeling more relaxed, though the memory of Megan and the shock of what she had said still played in my mind.

"Who sings this song?" I asked.

"It's called *'Kiss Me'* by Sixpence, or something like that," she replied with a grin. "It's even better when I sing along."

"To be fair, you do have a good voice," I admitted.

"Right, enough about my singing. Start eating, and start spilling." She leaned in, eyes gleaming with curiosity. "Did you kiss him?"

I nearly choked on my first bite of chicken salad, and her stare nearly burned a hole through me as I tried to keep a straight face. After swallowing, I sighed. "Well…" I began, but she cut me off.

"By the way, if you throw up any of this lovely food, I won't bring you anything next time."

I blushed, feeling guilty. "Of course I won't," I lied.

"Sorry, go on," she said, crunching on her salad and sipping her apple juice.

"I feel all gooey inside when I'm with him, Els. I know it's crazy, but I think I'm completely and utterly in love," I sighed, dreamy-eyed. "And yes," I added, looking up shyly and blushing. "We kissed. It was amazing."

"I KNEW IT!" Elisa squealed. "You so needed this, Jen. You deserve to feel all gooey and happy."

"He's coming to the vigil."

"Excellent, we can meet him properly. And he can meet Ed, and then we can all go on a double date!"

"Ed?" I asked. "The nurse?" I scratched my forehead, confused.

"Yes," Elisa replied. "Why are you looking at me like that?"

"No, I'm happy for you," I said quickly. "I just thought you were into the police officer."

"Yeah, but he hasn't made a move."

"Well, it wouldn't be very professional if he did," I said dryly.

Elisa shrugged, popping a piece of chicken into her mouth. "He's out of my league anyway."

I nearly choked on my juice. "Are you serious? You're gorgeous. You have long slim legs and big boobs, and your skin is so smooth and dewy all the time. If anything, he is out of *your* league."

Suddenly, my vision blurred, and in my mind's eye, I saw Elisa and Officer Luca kissing. It lasted only a few moments before it faded. I gulped the rest of my juice and smiled at her. "Just take things slow with Ed, okay? Maybe Officer Luca is just waiting for the right time."

Elisa opened her mouth to respond but then closed it, looking confused. Her eyes glazed over, and she stared right through me, lost in thought for a moment. Then she shot up from her seat. "Oh! I got you something. You're going to love it."

She dashed out of the room, returning a minute later. "*The Untold Secrets of the Salem Witch Trials*," Elisa said, sliding the book across the table with a grin. "I found it in a secondhand bookstore. It looked old and mysterious, so I figured it was perfect for you." She shrugged, clearly pleased with herself.

I reached for the book hesitantly, my fingers brushing against the worn leather cover. It was heavier than I expected, the dark green binding embossed with faded gold lettering that shimmered faintly in the light of the kitchen.

"Wow," I murmured, tracing the title with my fingertips.

"The guy at the store said it's rare," Elisa continued. "He said it's full of accounts of the trials, stuff they don't teach in history books. You know, the dark, juicy bits. I thought of you immediately."

I opened the book carefully, the scent of aged paper wafting up to meet me. The pages felt fragile, like they might crumble under too much pressure. The moment I touched them, a flood of images consumed my mind, fast and relentless, like a storm overtaking my thoughts. Frightened women and men, their mouths open in silent screams. Dark woods lit by flickering torches. A line of gallows silhouetted against a bloodred sky. The snap of a noose. A cauldron boiling over with something thick and black. The metallic scent of blood.

But it was the shadows that unsettled me the most. They were alive, twisting unnaturally, forming shapes that were almost human but not quite. I felt their presence as though they were reaching through the veil of time to meet my gaze, their hollow eyes turning bright green as they stared into my very soul.

I gasped and dropped the book onto the table. The images disappeared as quickly as they had come, leaving me breathless.

Elisa frowned. "Are you okay?"

"Y-yeah," I stuttered, though my hands shook as I picked the book up again. "It's just…intense. I wasn't expecting that." I looked up at Elisa and said, "This really is a special find. Thank you."

Elisa smirked. "It's a book, Jen. Why are you holding it like it's going to bite you?"

I gave her a weak smile, but my body stiffened fearfully. I couldn't shake the feeling that I'd seen something I wasn't meant to see.

I turned to the first page. The text was written in old-fashioned script that was hard to read. The introduction spoke of fear, hysteria, and the "poison of suspicion" that had spread like wildfire through Salem. Handwritten in the margins was a note in faded ink:

Fear feeds the fire. Shadows thrive where the truth is hidden.

What did that even mean? I flipped through the pages, finding more notes scribbled in the margins, some so faint they were barely legible.

They were not witches, but they were hunted like prey.

A pact was made in blood. Look to the evil shadow lurking in the woods.

Justice died on the gallows, but vengeance lingers. The judges were not acting alone—they were controlled by the shadows.

Each note felt like a message meant for me, though I couldn't explain why. The images I'd just seen lingered in my mind—the dark woods, the shadows, the screams.

"Elisa, this is more than just a book," I said quietly, my voice barely above a whisper.

My cousin raised an eyebrow. "What do you mean?"

I hesitated, unsure how to explain. "I don't know. It just… feels like it's trying to tell me something."

She laughed. "Okay, I have to confess, all the abracadabra stuff is growing on me. But now you're starting to get all creepy again."

I ignored her teasing and turned another page. This time, the words seemed to blur, the letters rearranging themselves into something new:

Beware the hands of betrayal. The innocent will be offered, and the guilty will wear a mask and hide amongst you, sometimes within you.

I blinked, and the words returned to normal. My stomach churned uneasily. What did it mean? Hands of betrayal? The guilty will hide amongst you?

The image of Megan's ghostly figure flashed into my mind again, and I heard her hollow voice saying, "It wasn't Orion." The Slayer wasn't who we thought. Someone was hiding in plain sight, just like the note said.

I shut the book abruptly, the sound making Elisa jump. "Whoa, what's with you?" she asked, setting her glass down.

"I need to do some research," I muttered, standing and grabbing the book.

"Jen, come on," Elisa said, her tone softening. "It's just a book."

But I wasn't so sure. *The Untold Secrets of the Salem Witch Trials* wasn't just recounting history—it was warning me. And if the messages in its pages were true, I didn't have much time to figure out who the real threat was before it was too late.

TWENTY ONE

The following morning, I walked out of my bedroom and into a full-blown argument between Salma and Ava.

"I can't believe you're doing this! You know how I feel about him." Ava's voice quivered with a mix of hurt and anger, her face flushed as she placed her hands on her hips.

"I have feelings for him, too, you know," Salma snapped back defensively. "And it's not like I planned this! We've just been spending time together, and…things happened." Her voice faltered, guilt creeping into her tone. She started pacing back and forth across the kitchen.

"You've known for weeks that I like him, Salma. Weeks!" Ava's eyes brimmed with tears, her voice cracking under the friction of her emotions. "And now you swoop in like this?"

Salma stopped pacing and turned toward Ava. "I didn't swoop in! He opened up to me last night—he said he likes me. What was I supposed to do? Ignore it?" Salma's voice cracked, and for a split second, her expression looked uncertain.

I sighed as I walked to the fridge, pulling out a carton of milk for my cereal. "Can you both lower your voices? You scared Luna—she literally bolted through the cat flap." I gestured toward the kitchen door, where the flap still swung back and forth. Rosalie's skittish white cat was long gone.

Neither of them answered. They stood on opposite sides of the kitchen, arms folded, glaring at each other. The tension between them was palpable, like a taut wire about to snap.

I poured milk over my chocolate-coated cereal and sat at the breakfast bar, the silence broken only by the clink of my spoon against the bowl. "Look, don't fight over a boy. It's not worth it. There are plenty of others out there," I said, trying to sound casual but firm.

Ava's voice cracked as she turned back to Salma, her eyes still glistening. "I thought I meant more to you than some guy. But clearly I don't. You'd rather hurt me than say no to him." She grabbed her cereal bowl and hurled it into the sink, the sharp sound making both Salma and me flinch. I was shocked it didn't shatter into pieces.

"Of course you mean a lot to me," Salma said, her voice softer now, guilt threaded through it. "But I can't deny how I feel about him. I'm sorry, Ava, but I can't just walk away from this." She looked down, her shoulders slumping under the strain of her confession.

Ava's face twisted with heartbreak. "Fine!" she shouted, grabbing her jacket from the back of a chair. She stormed out, slamming the kitchen door so hard the frame rattled. The sound echoed through the cottage like a gunshot.

Salma and I both shuddered, exchanging a glance. Her eyes were teeming with sadness as she said, "I hope you understand how I feel, Jen."

I put my spoon down and sighed. "Of course I do, Sal." I walked over and draped an arm around her shoulders. "You can't help how you feel. Roman picked you, and Ava will have to accept it. She'll be upset for a while, but she'll get over it. For now, just give her some space. But…" I hesitated, my voice dropping lower. "Can you please keep an eye on her?"

Salma's head snapped up, her brow furrowing. "Why? Is something wrong?"

I moved away and sat back down at the breakfast bar. "The Salem Slayer is still out there, and I don't want Ava coming home alone if you're out late with Roman. Just make sure someone's always with her, okay?"

Salma nodded, her face serious now. "Of course I will." She paused for a moment, then added, "Oh hey, I never showed you the photos we had developed."

I arched a brow, confused by the sudden change of subject. "I know. I've been meaning to ask about those ridiculous shots you took of me," I said with a laugh, trying to lighten the mood.

Salma disappeared for a moment and returned with a paper sleeve of photographs. I flipped through them one by one, smiling at the memories of the memorial and Ropes Mansion.

"Aw, I love this one of the four of us wearing witch hats, pulling faces. Let's put this one in a frame," I said, holding it up. "I'll buy one later."

Salma chuckled, but her expression remained clouded. "Most of these aren't too bad," I said, smirking at a candid shot of me laughing. "Hmm, actually, I don't like this one."

Then Salma handed me a photo, her demeanor shifting. "I haven't shown this to anyone yet. I don't know what to make of it, and I want you to see it." Her voice was quieter now, hesitant.

I took the picture. It was of Ava posing alone at the memorial, smiling at the camera. But in the background, hovering just above her, were three faint translucent figures. I held my breath as I squinted at the image, examining it in detail. The figures were female, their ghostly forms almost shimmering. One of them was unmistakably Megan. But how was this possible? Megan hadn't even died when we took the photo. I scratched my head, baffled.

My chest tightened. "Sal, please tell me that looks like Megan to you," I said, pointing at the figure on the right.

Salma nodded, her face pale. "Yes…that's what I thought, too. I thought I was imagining it at first, but it's definitely her. I don't remember noticing it when we first picked it up with Ava, but when I flipped through the photos again the other day, I saw all three ghostly figures hovering behind her. It really freaked me out."

My hands shook as I studied the other two figures. Recognition hit me in a flash: Melinda and Selena. The other two girls who had been murdered. The realization made my heart sink and fill with fear. This wasn't just a haunting. It was a warning.

Ava was going to be next, just like I'd seen in my vision during the séance.

"Don't show this to Ava," I said firmly, my voice sharper than I intended. "Promise me."

Salma nodded, rubbing her hands together uneasily. "I won't. I promise. It's very creepy. I've come across a lot of odd photos since I started working at Tricilla's shop, stuff with orbs and weird blurs, but I've never seen anything this weird or this clear."

I sat there, staring at the photo, my mind racing. What did the ghosts want me to do? Was there a way to stop what was coming?

I picked at my nails, torn between telling Salma everything and holding back to keep her from spiraling. She would definitely tell Ava, and I didn't want my sister panicking.

"Can I keep this?" I asked finally, my voice quieter now.

Salma nodded again, her movements slow. "Sure." She slipped on her sneakers, glancing at the clock on the wall. "I better go, I'm running a little late. I'll see you tonight at the vigil." She grabbed her jacket and headed for the kitchen door.

I sat alone at the breakfast bar, the photo clutched tightly in my hand. The figures in the image stared back at me, their presence hauntingly clear. Whatever message they were trying to send, I knew one thing for certain: I was running out of time to save my sister. I needed to speak to Rosalie and get her to tell me where she had hidden the Ouija board, I hadn't seen it since that night.

I walked into the reception area, catching her as she prepared to leave for a trip to visit a friend in Vermont. She stood by the desk, her scarf wrapped snugly around her neck, her expression a bit worried.

"Jenna, are you sure you'll be able to handle things here by yourself?" she asked, pausing to look me over. "I know you haven't been feeling well."

"I'll be fine," I lied, forcing a smile that I hoped looked more convincing than it felt.

"Maisie will take over for you after six p.m.," Rosalie added. "She can manage any inquiries remotely."

I nodded, watching as she gathered her bags, and I considered waiting until she returned to talk to her. But the ghosts in the photo were too distressing. I couldn't hold off that long. "Rosalie," I said hesitantly, "whilst you're gone, can I…can I use the Ouija board again, please?"

She froze and turned to face me, her brow creasing. "Jenna, I told you—I put it away somewhere safe after what happened last time. I don't think you can go through that again."

"But that séance…it was real. I saw the future, Rosalie. It might show me who the killer is and how I can stop him."

Her expression softened, but her tone was firm. "We've talked about this before, Jenna. The board is too strong, too unpredictable. It could do more harm than good."

I clenched my fists, my frustration and desperation bubbling to the surface. "My sister is going to die! The clock is ticking, and I'm scared I'm going to run out of time. No one is helping me." My voice broke, and my tears threatened to spill over.

Rosalie's eyes softened with sympathy. "You have the gift, Jenna. You don't need the Ouija board to see things others can't. Tune in to yourself—listen. You're stronger than you think."

I looked at her with pleading eyes, hoping for another answer.

After a moment's hesitation, she sighed, relenting just a little. "I do have a spell book in the greenhouse, along with some of the ingredients you'd need. The key for the locked drawer in the storage cupboard is under the large aloe vera plant. You can experiment with some of the simpler spells. But be careful—magic can be as dangerous as it is powerful."

A flicker of hope ignited in my chest. If Rosalie trusted me with her spell book, then maybe I could save Ava. Maybe I could stop the Slayer.

Rosalie smiled faintly, her faith in me steady. "I know you will, dear," she said, reading my thoughts, her voice saturated with quiet confidence.

I carried her small suitcase to the car, and she hugged me tightly before climbing into the driver's seat. For a moment, her warm embrace reminded me of Mum. I was surprised by how much I missed her.

I tapped on the window, and Rosalie rolled it down. "Do you mind if I use the reception phone to call my mum?" I asked quietly. "I want to let her know we're okay and check in on her. I've been putting it off for a while."

"Of course, my dear, you don't have to ask. She's been waiting to hear from you," Rosalie said with a knowing wink as she turned on the engine.

I smiled and waved goodbye, watching her car disappear down the gravel path.

The guesthouse felt eerily quiet when I went back inside. I swiftly cleaned up after the guests, wiping down the kitchen counters and putting away the last of the dishes. Once the kitchen was spotless, I moved through the communal spaces, fluffing pillows and ensuring that everything was in order. After a quick sweep, I sat down at the computer, double-checking the reservations system for any new bookings or special requests. Everything was under control.

I took a deep breath. The phone felt weighted in my hand as I dialed Mum's landline. My fingers trembled, my nerves making me jittery. It was nine thirty a.m. here, so it would be two thirty p.m. in London. Dad would already be at the café, which gave me the window of privacy I needed.

My knuckles turned white as I gripped the receiver tight. After three rings, I heard a click.

"Hello?" a familiar but strained voice rasped.

"Mum," I whispered, so breathless I was barely able to get the word out.

"Jenna? Jenna, is that you?" Her voice broke, desperate and raw.

"Yes, Mum. It's me."

"Oh, Jenna," she sobbed. "Honey, why…why did you leave? I haven't slept for weeks." She started coughing between sobs.

I remained silent. Her words gutted me, guilt pressing down on my chest. My legs gave out, and I crouched behind the desk, clutching the receiver like a lifeline. Warm tears rolled down my cheeks as I closed my eyes tight.

"Honey. Please tell me you and Ava are all right."

I took a shaky breath in. "Yes, Mum, we're fine." But we weren't fine. The image of Ava's lifeless face in the morgue flashed through my mind, and I had to cover my mouth to keep from sobbing into the receiver. Mum would never forgive me if something happened to Ava. She would die of a broken heart.

"Don't cry, Jenna," Mum said softly, her voice thick with regret. "I'm so sorry I couldn't protect you. I…I'm not strong like you."

"Mum, you can leave him, too. Come live with us," I said suddenly, my words rushing out. "You don't have to stay."

There was a long, silent pause on the other end.

"I can't," she finally whispered. "I just can't. He found me when I was completely lost. He gave me a life I wouldn't have had otherwise. Deep down, I know he loves you and Ava, even if…" Her voice trailed off.

"Mum," I pleaded, tears streaming down my face, "We're not coming back. You have to understand that." I struggled to breathe through the heartbreak that came in painful waves.

"Jenna, honey, please just tell me where you are. I won't tell your father. Or come home. Please," she begged.

"I love you, Mum. I'm sorry," I whispered, my voice breaking, and then I hung up the phone.

I sat on the floor behind the desk, sobbing uncontrollably into my hands for what felt like hours. Painful emotions pressed down on me, dark, intrusive thoughts of how I could kill myself flooded my mind. Suddenly, a rush of ghostly whispers made me flinch, snapping me out of my thoughts. I inhaled sharply, and listened.

You are strong, a fighter, a voice hissed in my ear. *You have the Varlett blood. You can save your sister.*

It was Julie.

I shot to my feet, the hairs on my neck prickling. The whispers swirled around me, echoing off the walls, then fading just as quickly as they'd come. I scanned the hallway, but it was silent now except for the distant whir of Roman's lawnmower and the soft ticking of the grandfather clock to my left.

I cautiously made my way into the living room, where I had heard the whispers previously. My eyes fell on Julie's portrait—well, Aurelia's. Her painted gaze seemed more piercing than before, almost alive.

"Julie," I whispered, my voice edgy. "I know it's you."

The room was silent, but the air around me felt electric. Strangely, the dark energy that had consumed my thoughts had disappeared, including thoughts about my mum, and my mood had shifted.

Suddenly, my phone buzzed. I jumped, putting a hand to my chest. It was a message from Troy: *Hey, how's your day been? Want to walk with me to the vigil? I'm about to finish up at the lodge. :)*

My hands still shook as I replied: *Hi! That sounds great. The girls are excited to meet you properly. :)*

His response was almost immediate: *I'm looking forward to meeting them too. I'll swing by the guesthouse at 6:30?*

A faint smile crept onto my face, the tension in my chest easing just a little. *Great. See you then! :)*

But as I sat down on the sofa, Aurelia's painted eyes locked onto mine again. The whispers had spoken of strength, of bloodlines, of saving Ava. What did it all mean? And more importantly, was I really strong enough to do what needed to be done?

TWENTY TWO

The vigil was held in Salem Common, the historic park transformed into a place of mourning. Under the deepening twilight, hundreds gathered in a solemn circle, each person clutched a flickering candle and murmured among themselves. The breeze tugged at the flames, threatening to extinguish them, but they danced stubbornly on.

At the center of the gathering stood a small makeshift shrine. A table draped in black held Megan's framed photo, her radiant smile a cruel reminder of the life stolen too soon. Around it were bouquets of flowers, cards, likely bearing heartfelt messages, and small stuffed animals left by mourners. The flickering light cast shifting shadows across her image, making it seem as though she were still alive, still smiling.

The grief in the air was tangible. Megan's mom stood by the shrine, her shoulders slumped as she dabbed her eyes with a crumpled handkerchief. A friend at her side offered quiet comfort, but nothing could mask the devastation on her face. A lump rose in my throat. Seeing her brought back thoughts of my own mom, the pain in her voice still echoing in my ear.

Nearby, a news reporter held a microphone toward Megan's grieving mother, she seemed to be giving an interview. The cameraman zooming in to capture the rawness of her tears. I clenched my jaw, anger bubbling inside me. This was her personal pain, her loss, and it was being turned into a spectacle.

Troy gently touched my arm, grounding me. "Is that your sister and your cousins over there," he said softly, nodding to the left.

Following his gaze, I spotted them near the edge of the crowd, whispering and waving in our direction. The sight of Ava's face gave me a pang of relief, though her posture was tense and her body was angled away from Salma.

Troy and I walked toward them, the golden leaves crunching beneath our feet. His hand was warm in mine, a respite from the chill of the evening. Around us, the autumn air smelled of damp earth and decaying leaves; even nature seemed to be mourning.

At the far end of the common, I spotted Officer Luca and Officer Mitchell standing near the rotunda their heads bent as they spoke with a priest. Officer Luca's sharp eyes occasionally scanned the crowd, as though he were trying to pick out the Salem Slayer among us.

Ava stepped forward as we approached. "Hey, sis. Hey, Troy," she said warmly, though the smile didn't quite reach her eyes.

Elisa extended her hand to Troy, her grin brimming with mischief. "I've seen you come in for your coffe, but it's nice to finally meet you properly. Jenna can't stop talking about you," she teased.

"Elisa!" I hissed, elbowing her gently, my cheeks flushing.

Troy only laughed. "Nice to finally meet you too. I love what you've done with the café," he said, and Elisa's smile widened with pride.

Before she could reply, Ed walked up and joined her, smiling at her shyly.

"Meet Ed," Elisa said, gesturing to him with a proud smile. "He's the nurse who looked after Jenna at the hospital."

Troy raised an eyebrow, glancing at me. "I'll explain later," I murmured quickly.

Salma stepped forward, tugging her long straight fringe behind her ear and offering Troy her hand. "Hey, I'm Salma. We haven't met before."

Troy shook her hand politely. "Nice to meet you," he said smiling.

Salma sidled up to me and whispered in my ear, "Oh wow, he is hot."

"Shhhh." I put my finger to my lips and giggled.

The priest's voice crackled through the speakers, drawing the crowd's attention. "Dear family and friends, thank you all for coming together to honor the memory of Megan Wiles," he began, his voice charged with solemnity. "Her light was stolen from this world, but it continues to shine brightly in our hearts. May we draw strength from the love she shared with us and unite in hope for justice."

As the priest spoke, I scanned the faces around me. The Slayer could easily be here, blending into the sea of mourners. I controlled my breathing as I closed my eyes, trying to quiet my mind and see something—anything—that could help me identify him. But my mind stayed blank, the images refusing to come.

"May we honor her memory by holding each other close, finding strength in our love for one another, and working toward a world where such violence is no longer tolerated. Lord we ask for your healing, your peace, and your light in this time of darkness. Though her physical presence may be gone," the priest continued, "Her essence remains with us. We trust God's love for us endures beyond the pain and sorrow."

I knew better. Megan's soul was trapped, tormented, unable to rest.

When the priest finished, the Mayor took the stand and apologized for arriving late, but made up for it by delivering an emotional speech. Following him, Megan's mother stood to speak from the rotunda, but the intensity of her grief left her unable to find words. People began to approach the shrine, laying down flowers and gifts as they whispered their condolences to her mother. Others lingered in small groups, their conversations hushed and laced with fear. As the song, '*Tears in Heaven*' played softly in the background, friends and strangers alike comforted one another.

After offering a small prayer for Megan, our group stood close together. "In all the years I've lived here, nothing like this has ever happened," Troy said, breaking the silence. "And now, three girls in three months…it's horrifying."

Ed nodded grimly. "I moved here because of the low crime rate. This…wasn't what I expected."

Salma crossed her arms thoughtfully. "Do you think Megan suspected that her boyfriend was the Slayer?"

I glanced at Ava, who was standing as far from Salma as possible. She hadn't said much all night. Roman wasn't here, and I couldn't help but wonder if something else had happened between the three of them. I opened my mouth to tell Troy about the first time we'd met Megan when a sudden sharp sensation prickled at the back of my neck.

Someone was watching me.

Before I could turn, a hard shove sent me stumbling forward. My candle fell from my hands, extinguishing on the ground. I barely managed to regain my balance.

"What the hell?" I gasped, whipping around.

Ashley stood there, her scowling face framed by blond waves. She crossed her arms, her cropped denim jacket exposing her pierced belly button. Her grey eyes narrowed at me, her lips curled into a sneer.

"I see you learned English fast, you lying bitch," she spat, her voice dripping with venom.

"Ashley, what are you doing here?" Troy snapped, stepping in front of me protectively.

Before I could respond, Ava stormed forward, shoving Ashley hard in the chest. "Don't touch my sister!"

Ashley staggered back, glaring daggers at Ava. "Get your hands off me!" she hissed.

Elisa was next, stepping forward until she was nose-to-nose with Ashley, her angry presence was intimidating. "You've got a problem with Jenna? Then you've got a problem with me."

Ashley's eyes darted between us, but she stood her ground and turned her anger on Troy. "Admit it! You've been cheating on me with her!"

Salma moved closer to me, looking concerned. "Are you okay?" she whispered.

"She's Troy's ex," I muttered.

Ashley scoffed loudly. "You *wish* I was his ex! We're still very much together. Right, Troy?"

Troy sighed wearily. "Ashley, we broke up. You know that."

Ashley's face crumpled, disbelief flashing across her features. "You didn't *mean* it! I thought that was why you texted me the other day, checking in and crawling back, like you always do!"

Troy turned to me, his expression pleading. He placed one hand on my shoulder. "I need to clear this up with her. I'll come find you afterward, okay?"

His words stung like a slap. He was going off with *her* to clear things up? I couldn't believe what I was hearing. He had been texting her? They hadn't really broken up? Had he been lying to me all this time? Anger coursed through my veins.

I gave him a long sharp look. "Don't bother. Just leave me alone." I snapped, shoving his hand away from my shoulder. Then I turned and locked eyes with Ashley, pointing at her threateningly. My voice was cold and unyielding. "Touch me again, and I'll snap your arm in half."

Ashley's bravado faltered, a flicker of fear crossing her face as she stepped back.

"Jenna, please," Troy called after me, but I didn't look back. My chest ached with anger and betrayal as I walked away, determined not to let him or anyone else see me break.

The girls hurried to catch up, their footsteps crunching against the path. "Jenna, wait!" Elisa called, breathless, catching hold of my arm. "Where are you going?"

I stopped and took a shaky breath, trying to compose myself. "Anywhere but here. They humiliated me in front of everyone," I muttered, staring at the ground as I shuffled my feet. "I thought he'd made it clear to her that things were over." I tried to shake off the sting. "Thanks for standing up for me back there." I forced a small, grateful smile, meeting their eyes in turn. Their quiet, unwavering support was all I needed—it spoke louder than anything they could have said.

Elisa slipped her arm through mine, her smile warm and comforting. "You know we've always got your back," she said. Ava and Salma followed suit, linking arms with us as well, setting their earlier tension aside for the moment. "Come on, let's get you to the Chocolate Coven," Elisa continued, her tone light and reassuring. "Nothing a little chocolate and some gossip can't fix."

Ava and Salma nodded, though they hadn't even been on speaking terms an hour ago. It hit me then how much we relied on one another—not just as family, but as each other's protectors. Our loyalty ran deeper than any argument. No disagreement could break the bond we shared.

Halfway down the street, Ava abruptly stopped, her brows knitting together as she turned to me. "Sis, are you wearing green contacts?"

I blinked, caught off guard. "No, why?"

"For a second," Ava said, studying me closely, "When you were glaring at Ashley, your eyes flashed lime green."

Elisa raised a brow, intrigued. "What? That's freaky. Maybe it's a witch thing?" she teased.

I laughed tensely, brushing it off. "It was probably just the reflection of a Halloween decoration or something."

We resumed walking. I glanced at my reflection in a shop window as we passed, and my dark eyes stared back at me, normal as ever. Still, the comment lingered in my mind, and I wondered what Ava had seen.

The streets were alive with the spirit of the season. Pumpkins of every shape and size lined the shopfronts, their carved faces ranging from spooky to intricate works of art. Ghosts and ghouls hung from doorways, swaying gently in the autumn breeze, their movements whimsical and eerie. The smell of roasted chestnuts mingled with the faint scent of cinnamon drifting from a nearby bakery.

As we turned onto Derby Street, we caught sight of Officer Luca and Officer Mitchell patrolling the area. Their stiff posture was a stark reminder of the danger still haunting the town. The Salem Slayer was still out there, watching, waiting.

"Good evening, everyone," Officer Luca said as we approached. His sharp gaze softened slightly when it landed on Elisa, who wasted no time fluttering her eyelashes. "It was good to see you all at the vigil," he added solemnly. "Very emotional. The three murders are drawing a lot of media attention."

Elisa unlinked her arm from mine and took a deliberate step closer to him, twirling a loose ringlet around her finger. "Any updates on Orion?" Though her voice tinged with sadness, there was a spark of flirtation in her eyes.

Officer Mitchell responded, "As a matter of fact, yes. We've tracked him to an address in Connecticut. Officers are on the way there with a warrant as we speak."

The girls relieved at the news, their shoulders easing as chatter broke out between them that they no longer needed to watch their backs. I stayed silent, biting my tongue. Megan had told me it wasn't Orion. But who would believe me?

Elisa, ever the charmer, changed the subject effortlessly. "We're on our way to the Chocolate Coven," she said with a grin. "Have you tried their chocolates before? Anything you'd recommend?"

Officer Luca broke into a rare smile. "I'm a fan of the pistachio truffle," he admitted. "But the tiramisu one is the real winner."

Elisa giggled, locking eyes with him. "We'll have to try both, then."

Before he could respond, his radio crackled to life. "Officer Luca, come in."

He reached for the radio. "Officer Luca receiving. Go ahead."

A static-filled voice replied, "Warrant relating to Orion Sterling in Connecticut successful. One arrested. Over."

Officer Luca's brows shot up, a flicker of triumph on his face. "Well, I'll be damned. We finally got him." He glanced at us briefly, then added, "I'm heading back to the station to prepare the file for interview."

"Yes, he's been caught," Officer Mitchell cheered.

Relief rippled through the rest of the group as we said goodbye, but I couldn't shake the unease gnawing at me. If Orion wasn't the Slayer, who was?

The warm, rich scent of cocoa enveloped me as I sat in the dimly lit Chocolate Coven, my hands wrapped around a steaming mug of hot chocolate. The soft chatter and the gentle clinking of teaspoons was comforting, but my thoughts were far from peaceful. I stirred my drink absently, lost in a whirlwind of emotions. Though the Slayer was obviously more important, I couldn't stop thinking about Troy and Ashley. What were they doing now? Had they made up, just like they apparently always did? What had he texted her? My stomach twisted, anger simmering beneath my disappointment. A darker idea crept into my mind, unbidden and unwelcome: Was there a spell I could use on her for revenge?

"I've decided not to see Roman for a while," Salma said suddenly, pulling me from my spiraling thoughts.

Ava glanced at her, her expression softening. "If he wants to be with you, I'll step aside," she said quietly, her tone surprisingly calm.

Salma remained silent, her eyes fixed on the table, as if weighing her feelings for Roman against her loyalty to Ava.

Elisa, sensing the awkwardness, shifted the conversation with ease. "Okay, girls, let's settle something: Officer Luca or Ed?"

"Officer Luca, obviously," Ava answered immediately, her lips curving into a small smile.

Salma giggled. "Agreed. Officer Luca's definitely the better-looking one."

I shrugged, finally cracking a smile, too. "Yeah, I'm with you on that. Officer Luca wins."

Elisa sighed dramatically. "He is gorgeous," she admitted. "But what if he doesn't think I'm on his level?"

I rolled my eyes. "We've talked about this a million times, Elisa. You're stunning. And since you've been here, your confidence has grown, which makes you even more attractive."

Elisa smiled faintly, though doubt lingered in her eyes.

"What about you, Jen?" Ava asked, her tone softening. "What are you going to do about Troy?"

I hesitated, swirling the last of my hot chocolate. "I don't know," I admitted finally. "I told him to leave me alone, but what if I was too harsh?"

Elisa reached over, squeezing my hand gently. "If he really cares about you, he'll find a way to make it up to you," she said. "You just have to wait and see what happens."

Salma nodded in agreement. "If you love him, you'll know what to do. But don't rush into anything. You deserve someone who makes you feel safe and loved no matter what."

As the conversation shifted to lighter topics, we passed around the chocolates, debating which flavor was best, sharing stories, and laughing until tears streamed down our faces. For a little while, all thoughts of the Salem Slayer faded, replaced by a warm glow. We didn't need anyone else to make us feel whole—boys or no boys, we were content and happy together.

In that moment, it was enough.

TWENTY THREE

Two weeks later, a text from Troy lit up my phone. *Hi, I really want to see you*, it read. I was in the middle of taking a booking at reception. Part of me was thrilled that he was still interested, but the more I reread the text, the more the message felt cold—detached, even. I sighed and ignored it, pushing it out of my mind.

After the vigil, when he hadn't followed up with me to explain or apologize, I had resigned myself to the truth: we wouldn't be seeing each other again. Troy had made his choice, and it wasn't me—it was Ashley. A wave of betrayal and sadness had left me feeling hollow. I had buried myself in work, research, and Rosalie's spell book since then, trying to fill the emptiness he'd left behind. But no matter how hard I tried, I couldn't stop thinking about him. Even so, my pride wouldn't let me reply to his text. I couldn't let him hurt me again.

By the end of my shift at six p.m., three more messages from Troy pinged on my phone. I didn't bother replying. If he needed two weeks to reach out, then I wasn't interested. I made my way to the greenhouse, hoping to distract myself from him. The air inside was warm and rich with the mingling scents of plants and herbs. I wandered through the rows, carefully selecting the ingredients I needed for the spell work I had planned.

Rosalie's book had a strong focus on aligning with the lunar cycle and clearing the mind through meditation. I had been meditating at night after Elisa fell asleep, calling on my spirit guides, slowly trying to unlock my abilities.

Tonight was clear, and the moon shone straight into the greenhouse. I wanted to enhance my psychic abilities, I had been focusing on the spell to open my third eye chakra.

I began gathering the ingredients: Marjoram, soil from the gum myrrh tree, dragon's blood resin, mugwort, and eyebright. I added a pinch of salt before grinding them together carefully. The rhythmic motion of the pestle calmed me, grounding me in the moment.

The candles danced as I cast a spell, chanting:

"Ancient forces, hear my plea,
guide the truth and set it free.
Through the veil of night and day,
keep the darkness far away.
By the moon and stars above,
protect the ones that I love.
With herbs and power intertwined,
open the path and clear my mind.
Spirit guides, I call to thee,
show what my third eye must see.
No harm may cross, no shadows stay,
guard us in your light, I pray."

As I began scooping the blend into the small fabric bag, a loud commotion suddenly came from reception. "Where is she? I'm not leaving until I see her!" said a familiar voice, loud and sharp, cutting through the stillness of the greenhouse. Even with the kitchen between the greenhouse and the reception hallway, his voice reached me clear as day, not through sound, but through the unseen thread that connected me to realms beyond the ordinary.

Troy.

I froze, my hands still hovering above the blended herbs. My heart lurched, each beat pounding in my chest like a drum. What was he doing here? The last thing I wanted was to see him. I finished scooping the blend into the small bag.

I quickly stuffed the herb bag into my back pocket, fumbling as Troy continued to shout. Taking a steadying breath, I hurried through the kitchen toward the reception area.

When I arrived, Troy's irritation was on full display. He was leaning aggressively over the desk, his face tight with annoyance, looming over Maisie.

"I know she's here, just call h—"

He cut off abruptly when he caught sight of me, his gaze locking onto mine with a mix of relief and desperation. He straightened up. Maisie, ever the protector, didn't back down. She glared at him fiercely, one hand on her hip and the other hand gesturing sharply in his direction.

"I don't know where you get your attitude from, but watch your tone with me, boy!" she barked, standing tall and unflinching behind the desk.

"Troy," I said quietly, positioning myself next to Maisie, my voice flat and emotionless.

Maisie turned to me, softening instantly. "You all right, baby girl?" she asked, placing a comforting hand on my arm.

I nodded, though my chest felt tight and my nerves frayed. My gaze shifted back to Troy. His shoulders had slumped slightly, as though Maisie's words had knocked some of the fight out of him. He exhaled heavily and ran a hand through his messy hair, the gesture making him look both desperate and exhausted.

"Look, I'm sorry for showing up like this," he said, his voice quieter now, though the edge of desperation remained. "But you ignored my messages. I didn't know what else to do."

I felt the eyes of a few guests descending the staircase behind me, their hushed murmurs carrying through the room as they observed the commotion. Heat rushed to my face, embarrassment and annoyance mingling as I turned and gave them an awkward smile and a small wave.

I turned back to Troy, keeping my voice measured. "Let's go somewhere else," I muttered. I grabbed my jacket from the closet, avoiding his gaze as I told Maisie, "I won't be long."

Maisie crossed her arms and kissed her teeth at him. "Call me if you need anything, baby girl," she said firmly, her tone leaving no room for argument.

Troy followed me out into the cool night air, the gravel crunching beneath our feet as we walked through the gate and toward the harbor. I kept my arms by my side, my shoulders tense.

The harbor was alive with quiet activity, underscored by the soft lapping of the water. A father and daughter darted across the pavement, the little girl laughing as she tugged a glowing pumpkin-shaped kite behind her. The father trailed her protectively, his eyes never leaving her. The sight made my chest ache. It was a fleeting moment of unconditional love, so different from the interactions I'd had with my father growing up.

Troy reached out to take my hand, but I flinched, pulling away and crossing my arms tightly across my chest. The rejection hung heavily in the air, the distance between us more than just physical.

We walked in silence for a few more moments before Troy finally spoke, his voice low. "Let's sit somewhere warm and get a drink," he said, his tone almost pleading. We were approaching the large red neon sign of the Moonlit Diner.

I hesitated, but the cold air was biting; it made my teeth chatter, and my fingers were starting to go numb. Reluctantly, I nodded, following him inside.

The diner was chaotic and busy—laughter and the clatter of dishes filled the room as servers weaved between tables, expertly balancing trays and dodging customers without missing a beat. A waitress led us to a booth tucked away at the far end, a quieter spot with a view of the harbor. I slid into the seat opposite Troy, keeping my gaze firmly on the wide window. Outside, I watched a fisherman tie up his boat, his movements methodical as he unloaded the day's catch. Beyond that, a couple climbed into their car and drove away, the headlights briefly cutting through the darkness. I focused on them, on anything that would keep me from meeting Troy's gaze.

"Are you going to look at me or stare out the window all night?" Troy's voice broke through the noise around us, quiet but weighted.

Reluctantly, I turned to him, my stomach knotting as I met his gaze. His usually bright blue eyes were dulled, shadowed by something I hadn't seen in him before—regret.

"I haven't stopped thinking about you, or that day," he began, his voice soft but earnest. I shifted uncomfortably, picking at my nails. "Ashley and I *had* broken up," he continued. "She just wanted to cause a scene. I'm sorry you had to go through that. I've fixed it now—it won't happen again. I promise."

His words should have soothed me, but they didn't. The memory of him leaving with Ashley that day was still raw, and I couldn't accept the fact that he had continued to text her while seeing me.

"What hurt more than being shoved," I finally said, my voice tremulous, "Was seeing you jump at the chance to go with her. Hearing that you'd been communicating with her…that cut deeper than anything she did."

Troy leaned forward, his hands clasped on the table. "I texted her once to check that she was okay, as she has mentioned having suicidal thoughts before. After you left the vigil, I just stayed with her until her friends arrived to take her home," he said earnestly. "The next day, she apologized for everything. She apparently had a freak accident—slipped and fell down the stairs. Her right arm's broken."

I looked up at him, my expression blank. "Good," I muttered flatly, a flicker of satisfaction bubbling to the surface. For a brief moment, it felt like things had balanced out. I had wanted revenge, and I hadn't needed to lay a finger on her. The spell I'd done had worked.

I took a slow sip of my hot chocolate, weighing my feelings. I liked Troy—I couldn't deny that. But my trust in him had been shattered, and the walls I had built to protect myself weren't easy to break down.

"Troy, can I be honest with you?" I finally said.

He nodded, leaning closer, his eyes filled with hope. "Of course."

"I don't trust you anymore."

Troy leaned back, his expression crumbling.

"How can I be sure you won't go running to her the next time something bad happens in her life? How do I know you won't keep texting her behind my back?"

"You don't mean that, Jen," he said softly, his voice tinged with hurt.

Suddenly, an overwhelming sensation swept over me. Everything else faded away—the hum of the diner, the clinking of dishes, Troy's voice. I was no longer in the booth.

I stood in the middle of the woods, surrounded by towering trees that loomed like silent, menacing sentinels. The darkness was thick, and I could barely see. The only sound I could hear was the rustling of leaves.

Ahead of me, a scene materialized, sharp and vivid like a terrible memory. The killer was there—an ominous, faceless figure, a black shadow clad in dark jeans, his hood pulled low over his face. He didn't move like a man; his presence was inhuman, unnatural, as though he were part of the darkness.

Melinda was on her hands and knees, her body jerking violently as a thick rope tightened around her neck. He gripped one end of the rope, pulling with monstrous strength from behind. Her gasps for air were faint and desperate, like a bird caught in a snare. Her fingers clawed uselessly at the rope, and her wide, terror-stricken eyes locked with mine for a fleeting moment, as if she could see me.

My hands felt sweaty. I tried to move, to look away, but I had no control over my body. The killer's strength was overwhelming, his shadowy form pulsating with pure evil energy. His malevolent presence wasn't just terrifying—it was *wrong*, like he didn't belong to this world.

Melinda's body convulsed, her legs kicking weakly as the rope bit deeper into her flesh. I wanted to scream, to rush forward, to stop him, but my feet wouldn't move. It was as if the darkness had wrapped itself around me, holding me still, forcing me to watch. My throat burned as I struggled to breathe, as though I could feel the rope's suffocating grip on my own neck.

And then the killer's head snapped toward me. Even though I couldn't see his features, I felt his gaze—bright green light, cold and cruel—pierce through me like a blade. A wave of nausea churned inside me as his shadow stretched toward me, entering my mind. My knees buckled. I clutched the amethyst in my pocket, the one that Julie gave me. I visualized a large white protective ball of light around me to stop the evil from entering my body.

It worked. Before I knew it, I was back in the diner, sitting across from Troy.

TWENTY FOUR

"Jenna?"

The voice broke through to me like a crack of thunder, pulling me back.

I gasped, my vision clearing. The bustling diner snapped back into focus, my heart pounding like a trapped animal's. It felt as though I'd physically been in the woods.

"Jen, I'm so sorry," Troy's voice was soft and full of regret as he slid into the booth beside me, wrapping his arm around my shoulders. His touch was warm, grounding, and for a brief moment, I let myself lean into him, craving the comfort of something real.

"I swear I didn't mean to hurt you," he murmured, his words meant to soothe an entirely different pain. "I promise I won't ever speak to her again."

But I couldn't focus on him. The panic still beat in my chest, and his embrace, though comforting, couldn't calm the fear the shadow had sparked within me.

Then Julie's voice echoed in my ears, clear and urgent: *The killer is close.*

Fear settled within me, the warning sinking into my bones. Roman's offhand comment resurfaced in my mind—he had mentioned that both Melinda and Selena had worked here, at this very diner. My gaze darted around the room, scanning the brightly lit booths, searching for a clue, a familiar face, anything. But everyone looked ordinary, chatting with their friends, their laughter filtering through my haze of dread.

The vision lingered in my mind, a bleak reminder that the danger wasn't distant—it was here. Watching. Waiting.

"I'm not in a good place right now. I…I can't do this," I said abruptly, my voice quivering as I stood. The walls of the diner felt like they were closing in on me; even the air was oppressive. "I'm sorry, I just need to be alone."

Troy shot up and moved out of the booth as I pushed past him. His hand reached out for me. "Jenna, *wait!*"

But I didn't stop. I pushed open the door, the cool night air slamming into me like a wave. The harbor stretched out in front of me, the moon casting its glow on the water, stars flickering like distant warnings. My head spun, my thoughts racing as I stumbled toward it.

Then the world blurred around me, and my legs gave out. I tumbled forward, the hard pavement rushing up to meet me—but just before I hit the ground, something steadied me. It was like an invisible hand had caught me, holding me upright just long enough for me to regain my balance.

I inhaled deeply, the sharp, salty air of the harbor filling my lungs and making my dizziness recede. The lighthouse lay just ahead, its warm light a beacon in the cold night, it stood behind a fence, closed off to the public. I had the key to the gate and eyed the maze entrance facing the seafront. I considered taking the shortcut through the maze, which would lead me straight to the entrance, across from the cottage, but I remembered when the image of my father had appeared. The maze wouldn't be kind to me in this state of mind; I couldn't put myself through that again. Instead, I rushed past it, keeping my eyes fixed on the path ahead.

When I reached the guesthouse, I paused outside the entrance, my hand hovering over the doorknob. I debated whether to find Maisie, tell her I was back, and offload the chaos swirling inside me. The person I really needed was Rosalie, but she wouldn't be back from Vermont for another few days.

Sighing, I moved past the door and into the garden. The faint rustle of the trees in the breeze was almost soothing, but then I stopped in my tracks.

A figure materialized before me, glowing faintly in the moonlight. She stood still, her translucent form flickering like a candle flame.

It was Megan.

Her eyes locked onto mine, sorrowful and desperate, and I could feel the gravity of her torment. She opened her mouth, her voice crackling like static: "He's watching your sister."

My stomach dropped. "Who?" I whispered, scared she would suddenly vanish. "Who is he? Tell me!"

Megan didn't answer right away. She tilted her head, her ghostly figure shifting closer to me. "Someone you know," she finally said, her voice soft but piercing.

"Megan, please!" I stepped toward her, reaching out, but her form dissolved like smoke, vanishing into the stillness of the night.

I spun around, searching for her, hoping she would reappear. "Megan! Come back! Megan!" I cried, my voice disappearing into the empty air. "Please! I need your help!"

There was only silence. She was gone, leaving me alone with her haunting words.

My legs shook as I hopelessly moved forward, collapsing onto the cool stone of the cottage porch. The large carved orange pumpkins on either side of me seemed to mock me with their hollow grins, their eerie smiles a cruel reminder of how little time I had left. I turned them to face the other way, unable to bear their gaze.

I looked up at the vast starry sky, silently searching for answers, for any sign of guidance. Space seemed so peaceful, watching over the chaos of the world below—the pain, the suffering, the despair. I sighed, giving up.

Someone you know…

Megan's frightening words replayed in my mind, the warning relentless. The killer wasn't some faceless shadow. He was here, close by, among the people I trusted. But who did I know who was capable of something like this? If I knew the killer, surely I would've seen him in a vision. Roman? Not a chance, not in a million years. Troy? I didn't know him all that well, and he had broken my trust, but could he really be a serial killer?

I closed my eyes tightly and lay my forehead on my knees, hugging them, I whispered a desperate prayer. "Please, God, angels, spirit guides, help me."

"Sis, what are you doing out here?" asked a voice from behind me, full of concern and curiosity.

I opened my eyes and looked over my right shoulder to find Ava standing on the porch, one hand resting on her hip. Her petite features, illuminated by the soft porch light, made her look even younger than she was.

"Just…seeking answers," I said, pointing up at the sky. As I did, the chimes started tinkling as they swayed in the wind.

Ava raised an eyebrow. "Move over," she said, plopping down beside me on the steps and linking her arm through mine. "Wanna talk about it?"

I hesitated, then sighed. "You know how I get those weird visions sometimes?"

Ava nodded. "What did you see?"

I hesitated again, debating how much to tell her. "I've been having these…weird flashes. They scare me."

"Funny you should say that," Ava replied. "I've been having nightmares lately. I keep seeing some faceless thing chasing me. Sometimes it catches me, but other times I escape."

I tried to keep my voice casual, wanting to hide the alarm building inside me. "Dreams can be weird like that," I said, forcing a small smile. But Ava's nightmares were too close to what I'd just seen. Too close to the truth, I feared.

I cleared my throat. "Sis, have you noticed anything strange lately? Anyone acting peculiar at work or when you're out with Roman and his friends?"

Ava shot me a sharp look. "Have you seen something in your visions?"

I quickly glanced away. "No, I'm just going by your dreams."

Ava hesitated for a moment before speaking. "Well, the other day on my way to work, I felt like someone was following me. I could hear footsteps so close behind me, but when I turned around, no one was there. And that same day, someone wearing one of those creepy Halloween masks stood outside Strega, just staring in the window for ages. I thought about going out to ask if he was okay, but I was so busy."

My heart ached—it was really happening. The thirty first was in a week, and I still didn't have a plan. But I couldn't let Ava sense my fear. "Maybe it was just one of Roman's friends messing around, playing tricks," I said, squeezing her hand tightly and kissing her head as she rested on my shoulder.

The garden stretched out before us under the moonlit sky. The lighthouse beam swept rhythmically across the yard, its cold light briefly illuminating the pumpkins beside us, then the trees opposite and the tall hedges of the maze behind.

I sighed and tried to focus on the warmth of Ava beside me. "I love you, Ava. I hope you know that."

"I love you too, sis," she replied, squeezing my hand.

The lighthouse beam passed again, and my stomach churned as I spotted movement near a tree—a faint silhouette ducked behind it just as the light swept by. My body tensed, and my eyes locked on the spot.

Had I imagined it?

Ava stirred beside me. "What's wrong?" she asked, her voice drowsy.

I didn't answer, my eyes still fixed on the tree. The lighthouse beam swung around again, and I saw it clearly—a shadowy figure standing partially obscured by the trunk. It wasn't moving, just watching.

A shiver slithered down my spine, and I instinctively pulled Ava closer. There was something unnatural about the way the figure stood—too still.

"What is it, Jen?" Ava asked, louder this time. She lifted her head off my shoulder and followed my gaze.

"Let's go inside, sis. It's cold out here," I said, my voice wavering slightly.

I scanned the garden over my shoulder as Ava went inside first, my eyes darting to every shadow, every corner. The lighthouse beam passed once more, revealing nothing but eerie stillness.

I moved through the house, shutting every curtain and double-checking every lock.

When I returned to the living room, Ava was curled up on the sofa, flipping through channels on the TV. I sat down next to her and pulled the blanket over us.

The spell in my pocket was working—slowly, the veil between worlds was lifting. I'd seen the vision in the diner and the shadow, heard Megan's haunting words: *someone you know*. But time was running out. I needed a plan. And I knew now that my strength and powers alone would be no match for what was coming.

Julie's image flashed in my mind, her voice soft and reassuring. She whispered, *Summon the dead.*

TWENTY FIVE

Elisa

The Hollow was buzzing, as it always did from six p.m. onward. I glanced around, taking in the familiar faces, mostly customers from Strega's. I waved at a couple who popped in daily on their way to work for takeaway coffees, but my gaze kept darting to the door. Where were they? I took a sip of my cocktail, the tangy mix of citrus and gin calming me a little. I checked my watch again and then started zipping and unzipping my bag just to do something with my hands. I was so excited I couldn't sit still.

This was my first double date—Salma and Roman, Ed and me. I'd invited Jenna and Troy to join us, too, but things had fallen apart between them, and now they weren't speaking. Troy had blown it, and I didn't blame Jenna for freezing him out. She didn't talk about it much, but I knew she was hurting a lot.

Ed had picked me up from work. He reached across the table, his hand warm and steady as it covered mine. "Elisa, that's distracting," he said gently, a teasing edge to his voice. "It's going to be a fantastic night."

His touch made me blush, and I gave him a small smile. I pulled away, unwrapped a fresh pack of cigarettes, and lit one up, taking a long drag. He leaned back slightly and raised an eyebrow. "Want one?" I offered, holding the pack out to him.

He shook his head, leaning farther back in his chair. "No, thanks. I'd rather not sign up for lung cancer."

I rolled my eyes, blowing out a thin stream of smoke. "Oh, come on. You've got to live a little. Besides, these days, you're more likely to get hit by a car than die of lung cancer—or, I don't know, get murdered."

"Very dramatic," Ed replied, shaking his head in mock disapproval. He took a swig of his beer, but I could see the faint smile tugging at the corners of his lips.

"All right," he said, sounding curious, "Tell me more about yourself. What made you decide to move to Salem?"

I hesitated, shifting my weight, avoiding his gaze. The question was unexpectedly difficult to answer. I decided to keep things vague and light. "Um, well…" I began awkwardly. "We saw this place in *Hocus Pocus*—the movie. It's one of our favorites, and, uh, we just thought, why not move there?"

Ed raised an eyebrow, a warm laugh escaping him. "Seriously? You're telling me a movie made you pack up and move across the ocean? That's got to be the most ridiculous thing I've ever heard." He shook his head, his disbelief tinged with amusement.

I forced a laugh, trying to match his energy, but his words sparked a flicker of unease in me. If only he knew the truth. "Our families were cool with it," I said, shrugging as if it were no big deal. "They even paid for our flights. Told us we could always come back if it didn't work out."

But my mind betrayed me, replaying memories of home—the shouting, the arguments. They hadn't been "cool" with anything I did. They had spewed insults at me when I'd refused an arranged marriage last year. Salem wasn't some whimsical choice inspired by a movie night—it was our escape.

Ed, oblivious, smiled as he took another sip of his drink. "Well, I guess Salem has its charms," he said, glancing around the crowded tavern. "Especially this time of year, it seems."

I nodded, flashing a big smile. Hoping to steer the conversation away from myself, I turned the question back on him. "What about you?"

"I grew up in Boston," Ed said. "I finished my Bachelor of Science in Nursing about six months ago. I didn't want to move too far, so I applied to Salem Hospital and got the job. I don't tell many people, but one of my ancestors, John Proctor, was hanged after being accused of witchcraft. Maybe subconsciously, that's another reason I chose to work in Salem."

"Jenna would love to hear the whole story." I smiled, nodding my head.

Ed's eyes glazed over before he continued, "On my days off, I usually visit my parents. They're getting older, and since I'm an only child, I try to help take care of them. You see, my mum suffers from heart disease, and my father has severe arthritis in his right hand."

Before I could respond, Salma rushed in, shrugging off her jacket. "Sorry we're late!" she said breathlessly. "I had to finish up the batch of invitations I designed, or I wouldn't have been able to relax tonight."

"I told her she could finish them tomorrow, but nope," Roman added, rolling his eyes affectionately.

"That's my sister," I said with a grin, giving her a playful wink. "She can't leave anything unfinished."

"Well, I'm here now, so let's enjoy the evening," Salma said, brushing a strand of hair from her face as she slid into the booth beside me.

"Hey, buddy, great to meet you," Roman said cheerfully, giving Ed a firm handshake. He glanced around the table. "You all set with drinks, or should I order you another round?" Both Ed and I shook our heads.

We flagged down the server to place our orders. The smell of sizzling food wafted through the air, making my stomach rumble in anticipation. Salma and Roman got burgers, I ordered a grilled chicken salad, and Ed got a steak sandwich.

The conversation flowed easily. Roman and Ed bonded over their love of cars and private number plates. Then they started asking us about moving back to London and suggesting that we should all take a trip there together someday. Salma and I nodded along, but I knew it wouldn't happen. Salem was home now, for better or worse.

Our food arrived, and the conversation shifted to Megan, as it so often did these days. "We met her the first day we got here," Salma told the boys. "She was so nice—she gave us tips on where to go, what to see. She made us feel so welcome that Elisa trusted her with a lot of money."

I winced at the memory, still embarrassed by what I'd done. "We hung out all the time, and I trusted her fully. She told me her boyfriend knew someone who could get us green cards," I admitted, taking a deep breath. "So I gave her four thousand dollars. And then…" My voice faltered, but thankfully Salma picked up the thread.

"And then the next thing we knew, she'd been murdered. Her boyfriend stole the money and ran off, but luckily he is in custody now."

Ed's eyebrows shot up. "Her boyfriend?"

Roman shifted in his seat, his face clouding over. "Wait. Which one?"

Salma frowned. "Orion. What do you mean, which one?"

Ed replied, "I remember her telling me she had broken up with her boyfriend, a guy named Steve. I thought he was the one who dislocated her arm."

"I don't think she had just one boyfriend," Roman said. "She went out with a lot of different guys. I didn't know she was officially dating Orion."

There was a long silence at the table as the implications of his words sank in. This wasn't looking good for us.

Ed cleared his throat. "I, uh…I went on a date with her once," he admitted, his voice quiet.

My head snapped up, and I leaned toward him, placing my elbows on the table. Jealousy flaring up inside me unexpectedly. "You went out with her? And?"

"It was just one date," Ed said quickly, avoiding my gaze. His face reddening as he wiped his mouth with a napkin. "We had lunch at the Moonlit Diner, but the conversation fizzled out pretty quickly. It was obvious we had nothing in common. I thought it might be awkward when I saw her at Strega's the next day, but she acted like nothing had happened."

Before I could stop myself, I blurted out, "Did you sleep with her?"

Ed's face turned crimson, his ears burning. He met my gaze. "No."

Roman, sensing the tension between us, leaned forward in his seat and jumped in. "You know, my friend Isaac went on a date with her, too. He said she was…well, kind of an attention-seeker. Always looking around, like she wanted to see who was watching her."

My appetite vanished. I pushed my plate away. If Megan had been dating multiple men, what if Orion wasn't the killer? What if the person who'd taken her life was still out there? I'd been feeling a lot safer since the police had arrested Orion, but what if they'd gotten it wrong? Jenna's premonition suddenly seemed like real cause for concern. I needed to tell her and Officer Luca what I had just learned.

Ed swallowed the piece of steak he was chewing. "Now that you mention it, she did wear those skirts," he said, his voice low. "The ones that barely covered anything. And she was overly friendly with the waitstaff when we went on that date. Like she wanted everyone' to lust after her."

I felt sad as I listened. Poor Megan. Her life with her mum and stepdad had been messy and complicated, and she'd come to Salem to start fresh. And now it was all over. She'd left behind so many unanswered questions.

Ed must have noticed the shift in my mood, because he reached over, his hand brushing my arm. "You okay? Don't you like the food? I can order you something else, if you like."

I shook my head. "The food's great," I lied. "I'm just not as hungry as I thought. My eyes were bigger than my stomach, I guess."

Ed nodded, but the concern in his eyes didn't fade. "All right, but if you change your mind, let me know. Another cocktail, maybe?"

"Sure," I replied, standing abruptly. "Could you order it for me? I need to pop to the ladies' room." I turned to Salma and asked her to let me out of the booth.

As soon as the door closed behind me, I pulled my phone from my bag and stared at the screen, debating. I checked my last call list until I found Jenna's name and hesitated. She might be in the greenhouse messing around with those herbs and she won't like being disturbed. But I couldn't keep this to myself any longer. I pressed the call button.

She picked up after two rings. Her voice sounded rushed and distracted. "Hey, Els, what's wrong? Is everything okay?"

"How do you know something is wrong?" I whispered, glancing around the restroom to make sure no one was listening.

"You're on a date," Jenna replied. "You wouldn't call me if everything was fine."

"Oh, right," I said with a sigh, she wasn't wrong.

"What happened?" Jenna pressed, sounding alarmed now.

"Okay, don't freak out, but Ed and Roman just told me that Megan had more than one boyfriend. And get this—Ed even went on a date with her once, he was shaming her for wearing short skirts. I don't know why, but hearing that put me off him a bit." I closed my eyes, leaning against the wall.

"*What? Ed*, like the one you're on a date with right now?" Jenna shouted, her voice shrill. "I can't see them together."

"Ouch, careful! You just blew out my eardrum," I winced, moving the phone to my other ear. "The point is, if she was seeing multiple guys, Orion might not be the killer after all."

There was silence on the other end for a moment, and then Jenna said, "I already know that Orion didn't kill her. Or the others girls."

I held my breath, waiting for her to continue.

"Apparently, the killer is someone we know. That's what Megan told me. But I haven't figured out who it is yet. Halloween is coming up fast, Els. Ava is still in danger. Whoever killed Megan…they're not done."

My grip on the phone tightened. The bathroom door creaked open, and a woman stepped in, her heels clicking against the tile. I didn't want to talk about ghosts anymore, especially not in front of a stranger. I lowered my voice. "I've got to go. I'm still at the Hollow with Ed and the others, but fill me in when I get home, okay?"

"Be careful, Els," Jenna warned before hanging up.

I took a look at myself in the mirror. My reflection was pale, and I swept pink blusher across my cheekbones and dabbed on some lip gloss to give myself a lift. My long curls were held back on each side with sparkly gold clips.

Straightening my shoulders, I pushed the bathroom door open. My gaze immediately landed on our group. Roman had moved to sit beside Salma, and Ed was sitting back in his chair, laughing at something Roman was saying, while Salma sipped her drink, her face glowing under the soft lighting.

I took a seat next to Ed, as he shuffled over. "You look beautiful tonight," he said softly, reaching out to take my hand.

I blushed under his gaze, feeling a flicker of affection for him return. His green eyes sparkled; he was incredibly handsome. "Thank you," I murmured, returning his smile. I was confused by my own emotions—did I like him or not?

He leaned closer, his breath warm against my ear. "Do you want to come back to my place when we're done here?"

The question caught me off guard. There was some chemistry between us, sure, but not enough to take things further. Sex had always been off-limits for me—one of the few strict rules from my upbringing that I still clung to. I was unlikely to wait until marriage, but I knew Ed wasn't the one I'd lose my virginity to.

Clutching my stomach, I feigned a pained expression and leaned over to whisper to Salma in Turkish, "I need to head home. Help me get out of this."

Salma's eyes widened in concern. "What's wrong, sis? You look pale all of a sudden."

"I have horrible cramps," I lied, pressing a hand to my abdomen. "I feel really sick. I should go home."

Ed's expression tightened for a moment before he forced a small smile. "Yeah, of course. I'll drive you."

"Shall I come with you?" Salma offered. I picked up my jacket and assured her I'd be fine, that I just needed to lie down.

The car ride was fraught with tension, the silence stretching between us. Ed kept his hands tight on the steering wheel, staring straight ahead. I fidgeted with my seat belt, wishing he would at least turn on the radio to break the awkwardness. The ten-minute drive felt like it dragged on forever.

When we finally pulled up outside the guesthouse, he cut the engine but didn't look at me. "Is it me?" he asked bluntly, staring out the window.

I felt bad. "No," I insisted. "No, it's not you." I forced a smile, hoping he wouldn't notice I was faking it. "I really did have a good time."

He nodded, his jaw tight. "Get some rest, then," he said quietly. He didn't look at me or attempt to give me a good-night kiss. It was clear he was upset and disappointed with me.

"Good night, Ed," I whispered, then slipped out of the car quickly. I turned around and watched him drive away, his tires screeching into the night. The thought struck me: he was after one thing and one thing only.

TWENTY SIX

Elisa

I punched in the code for the guesthouse, unlocking the door with a soft click. The familiar chimes tinkled as I stepped inside. The front desk in the hallway was empty, but the kitchen light glowed, so I figured Jenna must be in there. She mentioned she was helping Maisie due to influx of guests.

I approached quietly, calling out, "Jen?" There was only silence. Maybe she was upstairs helping a guest out with something.

I decided to make myself a tea, so I pulled out a cup and put the kettle on. I scanned the jars on the shelf, each label more ridiculous than the last. "What is this rubbish?" I mumbled.

moonlight elixir: brewed with the magic of the full moon
witch's brew chai: a bewitching blend of bark and yarrow
witching hour brew: the perfect blend for midnight magic

"Why is there no good old simple English Breakfast tea?" I shook my head. I really fancied one. I pulled out a jar labeled serpent's kiss. "A potion for clarity and insight?" I read aloud, raising an eyebrow. I unscrewed the lid and took a sniff; it smelt of elderflower mixed with something metallic. I wrinkled my nose, trying not to sneeze.

"I recommend that one." Rosalie's voice floated from the entrance to the greenhouse.

I spun around, nearly dropping the jar, my heart leaping into my throat. "Rosalie!" I gasped, clutching my chest. "You scared the shit out of me."

She stepped out of the shadows with that mysterious calm of hers, a faint smile playing on her lips. Without a word, she plucked the jar from my hand and studied the label. "This blend sharpens the mind and enhances intuition," she said, setting it down on the counter as though it were a sacred relic.

I let out a disbelieving laugh. "Are these labels just for show? You know, to fit the whole witchy vibe of Salem?"

Rosalie's smile faded, her gaze turning serious as it locked onto mine. "No. The teas do exactly what the labels say."

I bit back another sarcastic remark. It was obvious Rosalie just had tossed some leaves and seeds together and was trying to pass it off as something mystical. I bet she even sold them; anything to make a quick buck and fool people looking for a bit of magic. I'd always thought fortune-tellers were con artists who played on people's vulnerabilities, saying vague things that could apply to anyone.

"Don't knock it till you try it," Rosalie said, her eyes glinting as though she could hear my thoughts. "Do you want me to take a quick look at your tea leaves when you're done?"

I hesitated, then shrugged. "Fine. Go on, then, why not?" I could entertain this.

Rosalie poured the steaming water from the kettle into a teapot, scooped in two heaping spoonfuls of the blend, and set it aside to steep. The warm, earthy scent of herbs and flowers filled the room. As we waited, Rosalie told me Jenna wasn't needed, so she went back to the cottage.

I settled into a chair at the oak table. A few minutes later, she handed me a delicate china cup, its floral pattern intricate as lace. I took a cautious sip, expecting something bitter or medicinal, but the flavor surprised me. It was sweet with an almost electric fizz that danced across my tongue and warmed my throat. Before I knew it, I'd drained the cup. I liked it more than I wanted to admit.

"Turn it over on the saucer," Rosalie instructed.

I did as she said, tapping the cup to make sure my energy transferred to the leaves. Sliding it across the table to her, I watched as she picked it up with a strange reverence, her brow furrowing as she examined the patterns the leaves had formed. I tapped my fingers apprehensively on the edge of the table, a rhythm that echoed in the quiet kitchen. Why was I even doing this? Rosalie glanced up sharply, and I stopped tapping and folded my hands in my lap, feeling like a child who'd been caught misbehaving.

Her gaze darkened as she turned the cup in her hands, tilting it slightly to catch the light. She was taking forever, and I didn't have all night. "You have energy that's captivating," she began, her voice soft. "There are many people who admire you—more than you realize."

I rolled my eyes, leaning back in my chair. "Sounds like the usual fortune-teller fluff," I muttered under my breath, picking up my magazine next to me, and flipping through the pages absentmindedly.

Rosalie ignored me, her expression growing more serious. "I see you getting close to a man in uniform."

That caught my attention. I put the magazine down and leaned in closer. "Oh, is that so?" I asked, raising an eyebrow.

"It won't happen quickly," she continued, turning the cup again. "This relationship will take time to develop, but it will be worth it."

Officer Luca. I fought the urge to laugh. I hummed, playing along, though I wanted to roll my eyes. I was certain Jenna must have mentioned my crush on him.

But then Rosalie's face shifted, her expression tightening as though she were straining to see something in the leaves. "I see pain," she said. Her voice was quieter now.

The skepticism I'd been clinging to evaporated. "What do you mean?" I asked, my voice faltering slightly.

Rosalie looked up, her green eyes locking with mine. "You wear a brave face, but there's a lot you don't share. On the surface, you seem happy and lighthearted, but inside…" She trailed off, her gaze falling to my upper right arm.

Instinctively, my left hand shot up to cover the place where I had been cutting myself. How could she possibly know?

"You've been hurting yourself," she said gently. "Haven't you?"

My throat tightened, her words striking a nerve I didn't even know was exposed. My fingers pressed against my skin, feeling the faint ridges of the scars hidden beneath. No one knew about that. Not Salma, not Jenna.

"I don't know what you're talking about," I said, the words tumbling out in a rush. I lowered my gaze, staring at the floor, refusing to meet her gaze.

Rosalie didn't push. She simply nodded, her expression softening. "You've internalized the harsh criticism of your parents—words you shouldn't have believed. It's time to release them. To forgive not just them, but yourself. Only then will you begin to heal."

Tears burned at the corners of my eyes, but I blinked them back, refusing to let them fall. My thoughts drifted to my parents. Could we ever find peace? They had just been following years of tradition. Could I forgive them, or myself for thinking ill of them?

Rosalie's expression softened as she gazed back into the cup.

"I see success in your future," she said slowly. "You'll become a businesswoman—something to do with books and coffee. Maybe a café, or a bookstore, or both. But it's yours."

I didn't believe she could see that; Jenna had probably told her about my dream to own my own bookshop that served coffee.

"It's going to happen in the next two years," Rosalie added with a nod.

I shook my head, scoffing at the idea. "That's impossible. I don't have the money to start a business."

She smiled. "You'll get a helping hand when you least expect it."

I stifled the urge to roll my eyes. What a load of crap. I couldn't even get a green card, let alone start a business. What a waste of my time.

Rosalie turned the cup again, this time her expression darkened. "I see danger," she whispered.

The temperature seemed to drop a few degrees. I leaned forward, my pulse quickening. "What kind of danger?"

"I don't want to alarm you, but the person behind the recent murders…he's noticed you and Ava. He comes to the café—you've both spoken to him."

She couldn't be serious. "What do you mean, he's *noticed* us?"

"He's watching," Rosalie said, looking straight through me. "Trying to decide between you and Ava."

The blood drained from my face, and I shot up from my seat. "I've had enough of this crap. You're telling me the Salem Slayer is an ordinary person who comes to the café? That we can't tell when we're speaking to some sick psychopath? Is that what you're saying?" My voice rose higher. "You've got to be joking!"

Rosalie's eyes snapped back to mine with solemn intensity. "That's exactly what I am saying. He doesn't stand out. He looks ordinary on the outside, but inside…something darker controls him."

Anger boiled within me. I thought back to every man who had walked through the doors of Strega's: the smiling regulars, the men who left their numbers scribbled on napkins, the strangers who lingered a little too long. He could be any one of them.

"Go on, then, tell me: What does he look like? What's his name? How old is he?" I demanded.

Rosalie shook her head, regret flickering in her eyes. "I'm sorry. I can't see that. It's blurry."

"If you're a real psychic, then look harder!" I screamed, my voice breaking with fury. "What are we supposed to do? Wait around for him to decide which one of us he's going to kill? What good is your so-called 'gift' if it can't help stop him?"

Without thinking, I grabbed the cup from her hands and hurled it to the floor. The porcelain shattered, the sharp sound made Rosalie jump. Without waiting for her response, I stood and stormed out, my breath coming in ragged gasps, a hot rush of rage and disappointment coursing through my veins.

"Elisa, wait. There's something about Salma!" Rosalie called after me as I stormed toward the door.

But I didn't stop. I shoved the back garden door open and stepped into the cool night. My thoughts restless, Rosalie's warning looping in my mind. I screamed to stop her words from echoing in my ears. *He's watching you. Trying to decide between you and Ava.*

My legs shook as I walked to the cottage to find Jenna. What if it was me in the morgue instead of Ava? If we didn't stop him, one of us wouldn't make it past Halloween.

TWENTY SEVEN

Salma

After dinner, Roman and I strolled through town, our fingers intertwined as we wandered into the vibrant chaos of a Salem street parade. I'd never seen anything like it. The air buzzed with electric energy—laughter, music, adults and children with their faces painted in elaborate designs. Fireworks illuminated the towering church steeples and historic brick buildings.

As we turned onto Essex Street, my eyes landed on Ashley across the road. Her arm was in a cast, awkwardly secured to her side with a sling, as she was surrounded by a group of girls. Even from a distance, I could feel the sharpness of her gaze, her narrowed eyes cutting through the festive atmosphere. One of the girls whispered something in her ear, and I didn't need to hear it to know it was about me—no doubt they were discussing the incident with Jenna. I avoided eye contact and pretended not to notice.

Roman's hand tightened around mine. "Don't look at her," he murmured softly, steering me farther down the street.

We watched the colorful floats rolling past. A large haunted pirate ship went by, its crew of actors shouting, "Beware!" as fake cannons boomed. Behind it, a coven of witches cackled and twirled in a choreographed dance, their brooms trailing glittering sparks.

I pointed out a marching band dressed as Victorian-era ghosts playing a hauntingly beautiful melody, their drums and horns reverberating through the crowd. "I've never seen them before," said Roman.

The night air carried the scent of freshly baked pumpkin pies and caramel apples from nearby vendors, but I was too full to eat anything more.

We stopped outside a costume shop brimming with masks, props, and outfits. I still hadn't decided what to wear for Carmen and Isaac's Halloween party. Roman picked up a Hannibal Lecter mask and slipped it on, lowering his voice. "Hello, Clarice," he growled, shambling toward me like a zombie. "I think I'll eat your heart first…with some fava beans and a nice Chianti."

I couldn't help but laugh, covering my mouth as his muffled chuckles joined mine. "You look hilarious." I said, shaking my head. "That mask is too realistic for my liking."

He yanked it off, grimacing. "It smells awful. How do people wear these things without passing out?"

I pointed to a fisherman's outfit hanging nearby, complete with a hook. "Look, it's the costume from *I Know What You Did Last Summer*! That's one of my favorite horror movies."

Roman studied me for a second, then grinned. "You know, you kind of look like Sarah Michelle Gellar. Well, you would if you had blond hair."

I rubbed my chin, pretending to consider it. "Hmm, maybe I'll go full blond next time I go to the salon. But for now, my highlights will have to do."

"Actually, maybe you remind me more of the fisherman," Roman said, smirking.

I laughed, swatting his arm as he leaned in to kiss my cheek. My skin tingled at his touch, but guilt immediately followed. I couldn't share my happiness with Ava, not when I knew she still had feelings for him. As a matter of fact, I couldn't share any details with her, which was a shame. We had never kept anything from each other before.

"It's too bad Elisa had to leave so suddenly," Roman said, his brow furrowing as he slipped his hand back into mine. "Did she tell you the real reason?"

I shook my head. "She's always been unpredictable. I'll ask her when I get home tonight."

"She's great—funny and all—but I just didn't click with Ed," Roman admitted after a pause. "We don't have much in common."

"Honestly, I don't think she's all that into him either," I said. "She told me she's been making eyes at Officer Luca whenever he stops by the café." I giggled.

Roman raised an eyebrow. "Really? Officer Luca? That guy's so serious, but…I can see it. Maybe he is a better option."

I nodded in agreement.

We wandered deeper into the shop, pausing by a rack of long flowing dresses and cloaks. I picked out a sleek black dress and a dark wig, holding them up to my body. "What do you think? Morticia Addams?"

I could see the gears turning in Roman's head, imagining me in full costume. "You could pull it off perfectly. You'd be the most beautiful girl at the party," he murmured, his voice lower now.

Heat rose to my cheeks, and I found myself playing with my bracelets absentmindedly. Roman had a way of making me feel seen, like I was the only person in the room. But I couldn't stop wondering if he had a soft spot for Ava, too, or if his feelings for her were purely friendly. I tried to push down the thought as I placed the dress back on the rack. "If I don't find anything else, I will definitely get that," I decided.

"All right, let's get you home," Roman said, pulling his car keys from his pocket. He held the shop door open for me with one hand and let the other linger at the small of my back as I stepped outside. We walked a short distance to his car, which was parked one street up.

The parade had dispersed, making it easier to drive away from the town. The vendors were packing up their pop-up stalls and clearing away the rubbish.

Roman pulled up in front of the guesthouse and shifted the car into park. I turned to him, looking deep into his brown eyes. He was by far the most good-looking guy I had ever seen. "I loved tonight," I said, feeling fizzy inside.

"Me too," he replied, his tone full of warmth, but then he inhaled deeply and hesitated for a second before inching closer to me. A knot of anxiety twists in my chest. Did he wish he had picked Ava? I took a deep breath and pushed the thought away, I told myself to stop doubting his feelings for me. I was being paranoid.

He took my hand in his and held it tightly. "I'll see you for lunch tomorrow?"

I nodded, excitement bubbling in my chest. I didn't know why I had doubted him, even for a second. "How about the

Apothecary Café next to the print shop? They do great paninis," I suggested.

"Sounds like a plan." Roman said. He gazed deep into my eyes, then slowly leaned in closer, brushing his lips lightly against mine. The kiss was soft, gentle, but it sent heat rushing through me, leaving my insides in a state of chaos. I clung to his shirt, steadying myself as the world seemed to blur for a moment. How much longer could I keep holding back with him? We'd shared many kisses before, but he had never pushed things further, always respectful. I wasn't sure he would ever initiate the next step.

When he pulled away, his breathing was labored, like he also found it hard to stop. His eyes were brimmed with affection as he leaned back in his seat. "Good night," he said softly. "I'll text you as soon as I get home."

I pushed open the car door and stepped onto the pavement, and closed the door gently behind me. The sharp bite of the sea breeze hit me—it was much colder now that we were closer to the shore. I zipped up my jacket and crossed my arms over my chest.

I turned back and leaned into the car slightly. "Good night, and drive safely," I said.

Roman gave a quick wave before driving off, his taillights fading into the darkness.

I walked up the path and past the guesthouse, where the warm glow of the lights filtered through the curtained windows. The beauty of the house always took my breath away. As I rounded the corner, the greenhouse came into view, the soft glow of candlelight flickering inside. Through the glass, I caught a glimpse of Rosalie hunched over her worktable, grinding herbs with a mortar and pestle.

Rosalie stopped abruptly, fixing her gaze on the window. Her eyes seemed distant, glazed over, as if she were staring straight through me. I waved, but she didn't respond. I looked behind me to see if she saw something there, but nothing was amiss. She gave no sign that she had noticed me at all, though her features appeared stiff with apprehension.

My stomach clenched, not sure what to make of this, but I tried to dismiss it, chalking it up to her usual strangeness. She was always appearing out of nowhere and often seemed like she could read our minds.

I continued toward the cottage. It was half past ten, and I was surprised the girls hadn't texted me yet to ask where I was. I looked up at the moon and inhaled—what a beautiful night to be alive. My lips still tingled from Roman's kiss, and I touched them absently, unable to stop smiling as I replaying that moment over and over. I missed him already and eagerly anticipated his good-night message.

My high heels clicked sharply against the stone, my small toe started throbbing from wearing these shoes all night. I couldn't wait to take them off. I had changed out of my work clothes to get ready for the date and left them in the shop. I must remember to bring them back home with me tomorrow.

The shadowy outline of the maze loomed to my left, its creepy entrance teasing the edge of my vision. I had never liked walking past it alone in the dark, so I started walking faster despite my feet killing me. I stepped onto the cool, dewy grass, making my way through the cluster of trees toward the cottage. An owl hooted faintly in the distance, an eerie sound that made me walk even faster.

I dug through my bag for my keys, searching through a jumble of belongings—lipstick, compact mirror, nail polish, and the stack of invitations I'd designed earlier. My fingers finally brushed against the cool metal of the key. I pulled it out, making a mental note to start keeping it in the front pocket.

I pulled out my phone next, checking for missed calls. Nothing from Roman yet. He must still been driving.

As I looked up from the screen, I spotted something out of the corner of my eye. I flinched, sucking in a sharp breath, and my heart slammed against my ribs as I gripped my phone.

Just ahead, partially obscured by the shadows, stood a man's dark figure. It was still as a statue and dressed head to toe in black, his silhouette blending with the darkness. His head was turned toward the cottage, staring intently through the living room window. Whoever it was wasn't just standing there—he was watching.

Fear coursed through me as I ducked behind a thick tree trunk, crouching low. My tight minidress clung to my legs, making it difficult to move, and the heels pinched my toes painfully. I slipped them off, feeling the icy, damp earth against my bare feet.

What if he'd seen me? My mind spun, scrambling for a plan. I shoved the keys into the pocket of my denim jacket and set my bag quietly on the ground. Maybe he was just a lost guest from the guesthouse. But I feared this was something far more sinister.

I plucked up the courage to peek through the branches; the man hadn't moved, his gaze still fixed on the living room window. The faint flicker of light from the TV cast fleeting shadows across his face, but his features remained obscured.

The girls must be watching a movie. I remembered Ava saying something about renting one tonight.

With clammy fingers, I fumbled with my phone, desperate to silence it. The screen stayed lit, and the silent button wouldn't work. *Damn it!* I typed out a message to Elisa: *Turn the porch light on and lock the doors. There's someone outside.* I hit send, the slight whooshing sound deafening in the silence.

My breath came in shallow gasps as I squeezed my eyes shut. *Please don't see me. Please don't hear me.* Cold sweat beaded on my forehead, sliding down my temple as fear gripped me. My mouth felt dry as sand. He was still there, staring into the cottage. There was no sign of movement from inside. *C'mon, Elisa, hurry up and check your damn phone.* I fumbled to send the same message to Jenna, my hands shaking so badly I could barely type. Another whooshing sound.

This time, the lurking man must have heard something; his head snapped around, and he looked directly at me. Instinctively, I slapped my hand over my mouth to keep myself from screaming. My chest constricted. I was paralyzed with fear, unable to breathe. He had seen me.

I glanced frantically to my left, calculating my chances. If I ran that way, I'd hit the fence—a dead end. To my right was the path leading to the guesthouse, but he'd catch up to me before I got halfway, especially since I wasn't wearing shoes.

My only option was the maze entrance right behind me. My legs started to shake as I realized I'd have to dart into its dark, twisting corridors, hoping I could lose him inside.

I was still debating what to do when the lights in the cottage blazed on—first the living room, then the hallway, and finally the porch. The man hesitated for a split second, then started sprinting toward me.

I had no choice. I jumped to my feet and bolted into the maze.

The pitch-black corridor made my vision tunnel as I entered, panic pulsing through me. Leaves crunched under my bare feet, and sharp twigs jabbed into my soles, sending jolts of pain up my legs, but I didn't dare stop running. I veered left, then sharply right—the maze seemed endless, and I couldn't breathe properly.

Just ahead, I spotted a mound of fallen branches and leaves near a thick hedge. Without thinking, I dropped down and crawled beneath them. I lay flat on my back, the damp earth soaking through my dress as I frantically scooped the leaves over me, creating a makeshift cover, praying I wouldn't be seen and thanking my guardian angels that the lighthouse lamp wasn't on tonight.

I held my breath, listening intently.

The crunching of leaves grew closer. His footsteps were slow, deliberate. My heart pounded so loudly I was sure he could hear it.

Fear gripped my chest as my phone blared to life, shattering the silence with its piercing ring.

No. No. NO. What now?!

I shot up from my hiding spot, only to feel a searing pain as a twig gouged the tender flesh of my inner thigh. I clamped my hand over the cut, warm blood smearing against my fingers. I bit down on a scream, forcing myself to push through the agony. I sprinted blindly, ignoring the sting with every step. The phone continued ringing in my hand, relentless. It was Ava. I hit the answer button, breathless and shaking, but by the time I raised it to my ear, she had hung up.

As I rounded a sharp corner, I collided full force with something solid.

I stumbled back, gasping for air.

The man stood directly in my path. I looked up, my whole body shaking uncontrollably. It was him—the man who'd been watching the cottage. He was in front of me, blocking my path. There was a black nylon mask over his face, distorting his features. His eyes locked onto mine, cold and merciless.

I screamed, the sound piercing through the maze, but it was cut short as his hand shot out, wrapping around my neck. He squeezed hard, crushing my windpipe. I thrashed against him, trying to kick, but he was too strong—tall and broad, like a wall of muscle.

My phone blared again, I somehow managed to hit the answer button. Ava's voice came through, urgent and breathless: "Sal, Sal, can you hear me? Where are you?"

I opened my mouth to respond, but no sound came out—the man's gloved hand squeezed tighter around my throat, silencing me completely. Only a choked gasp escaped.

"Her bag and shoes are here!" said Ava's voice, faint and muffled, before he ripped the phone from my grasp and flung it into the hedge.

My vision blurred as he pushed me to the ground, squeezing tighter with both hands now. He spread my legs with his legs, positioning himself on top of me. I was completely trapped. Was he going to rape me? No, god, please, *no*.

I reached into my jacket pocket, my fingers closing around the key to the cottage. With all the strength I could muster, I drove it into the side of his face.

He let out a muffled grunt, pulling back slightly. But it wasn't enough. He yanked the key from my grasp and placed it in his back pocket.

I kicked and squirmed under his weight, but he was too heavy and too strong. My strength was fading fast. My limbs gave way, and my vision began to narrow.

This is it, I thought. This was the end. I was about to die.

Tears welled in my eyes and spilled down my cheeks. I wasn't ready—not yet. There was still so much I hadn't done, so much life left to live. I was only nineteen. My life was just starting to turn around. This wasn't fair—none of it was fair.

Fragments of my life whirred through my mind: my mum and dad's faces. My first day at school. Elisa's arms wrapped tightly around me in a warm embrace. The plane ride to Salem with Ava, full of nervous excitement. My first day at the print shop. And finally, Roman's sweet smile.

My body jerked desperately, trying one last time to gasp for air. I stared into his mask, feeling my soul slipping away from my physical form.

Just before everything went black, a beam of light swept across the maze from the lighthouse that had just turned on, illuminating his face behind the mask.

It was Ed.

My last feeling was dread for Elisa. He would kill her, too.

And then, there was nothing.

TWENTY EIGHT

The Salem Slayer

I slipped out of the maze with ease, climbed over the fence, and stomped the mud off my boots.

The night breeze carried the faint scent of saltwater from the sea, masking the metallic adrenaline taste in the back of my mouth. I had memorized every twist and turn of that maze, slipping through it countless times under the cloak of darkness, watching the girls through the cottage windows for hours on end.

I yanked the black tights from my face, stashed them in my coat pocket, and strolled across the road to the harbor, where I'd parked my car just out of sight near the side of the Moonlit Diner. I knew this area like the back of my hand—every blind spot, every CCTV—thanks to the countless nights I'd spent lurking, watching, and waiting for Melinda to finish shifts at the diner. She'd been my first kill.

I'd been carrying a small syringe of propofol that night, knowing it would act fast. With a practiced hand, I had slipped the needle into the soft spot at the base of her neck. She had barely flinched before her body had gone limp. It had been effortless.

I'd caught her before she hit the ground, then hoisted her into the back seat of my car.

I had driven to the secluded spot in Gallows Woods that I had already scouted. I'd parked and waited, watching her face for any sign of stirring. I had wanted her awake when I finished her—it would be more satisfying that way. When she'd awoken, I had let her run a little, just enough to have hope that she might escape in the woods before I caught her.

The memory sent a shiver of excitement through me, a dark thrill that I could still taste. I'd hidden Melinda's body so she wouldn't be found right away; that way the propofol wouldn't be detected. I hadn't wanted it traced back to me. Selena's death had been similar, but I hadn't needed propofol for Megan. She'd known me from the hospital and from Strega's, trusted me enough to invite me in for coffee after our date. She'd been a mess that night—her mascara smudged, her voice quivering as she'd told me about Orion stealing her money and deserting her. She'd been vulnerable, desperate, practically begging for comfort. So easy to manipulate.

I had listened, nodding sympathetically as she'd spilled her heartbreak. When I had finally wrapped my hands around her throat, she hadn't even fought back at first—she'd thought I was pulling her in for a hug. The best moment was when her body had gone limp as I'd squeezed the life out of her. I had undressed her afterward and touched myself; nothing compared to that familiar burst of dark pleasure as I climaxed. I had savored the rush. I was glad the shadow had chosen Megan.

Salma hadn't been part of the plan. She was never meant to replace Ava. But she had seen me, and I couldn't risk letting her walk away. Now the shadow was displeased, whispering its disapproval, urging me to stick to the original plan. It wanted precision, not chaos, and Salma's death was a complication, a messy deviation.

Ava was still the target, the one who'd been chosen for the offering on the thirty first. I had promised her blood to the shadow, and I had every intention of keeping that promise. The shadow never shared details with me; it told me who to kill, and I obliged.

If it were up to me, I would have chosen Elisa. Her rejection still stung, and I could picture her face twisted in fear, begging for mercy as I pulled the rope tighter and tighter around her neck. But I couldn't act on my impulses—not yet. The shadow's plan took precedence, and for now, I had to follow its desires. Ava would be the last offering this year. Elisa's time would come soon enough when I got to choose who to kill.

I slid into the driver's seat, the door locking behind me with a quiet click. I was adjusting the rearview mirror when I saw it—the shadow—sitting in the back seat, barely distinguishable in the darkness. He leaned forward, his lime-green eyes shining, his presence bearing down on me, his displeasure palpable. My pulse heightened, my carefully constructed facade cracking slightly.

"I had no choice," I murmured, gripping the steering wheel. "She saw me."

The shadow's voice slithered into my ears like smoke. "You've failed me. It will be harder for you now," he hissed, his tone sharp with rebuke. My vision blurred for a moment as the power of his anger pressed against my skull.

I swallowed hard, remembering the first time I'd seen him. It had been after a late shift at the hospital; I'd been leaving when he had materialized in the dark parking lot. At first, I had thought it was a hallucination, my exhausted brain playing tricks on me. But he hadn't disappeared. He had followed me home and never left.

Except when Jenna was near.

I had dared to question him once about why her presence seemed to drive him away. The memory of his response still chilled me to the bone. "Don't ask questions whose answers you are unable to comprehend," he'd whispered, his voice slicing through my thoughts like a blade.

Tonight, his tone was no less cutting. "Just get me my last offering," he hissed. "And do not falter. Your reward is eternity on Earth, but only if you succeed. If you fail me, you will feel my wrath."

I nodded silently, my jaw tightening. The promise of eternity burned in my mind, a temptation that consumed me. One last offering. Just one. Then I'd be free to kill at will for the rest of time.

I straightened my hair where the tights had messed it up and stuffed my makeshift mask back in the glove box. Then I examined the red mark on my cheek where Salma had jabbed me with her key. I let out a low snicker, fingering the cold metal shape tucked safely into my back pocket. Silly girl. As if she could ever get the better of me.

Suddenly, the flash of red-and-blue lights lit up the harbor, sirens blaring. My heart hammered for a moment, but I forced it back into a steady rhythm. I sank down low in my seat and watched as the patrol cars sped past, their wails stopping as they pulled up outside the Salem guesthouse.

That was a close call. I turned the engine on, put the car in gear, and sped off toward home, grinning at the shadow in the rearview mirror. His lime-green eyes shimmered back at me.

The following morning, I slipped on my scrubs, ready for another early shift at Salem hospital. I heard the usual chaos of beeping monitors and hushed voices as I entered the critical care unit, and the strong scent of antiseptic stung my nostrils, mingling with the faint metallic tang of blood. You'd think I would have been used to it by now, but it still made me nauseated first thing in the morning when I hadn't eaten. The ward looked busy today; all six rooms were full. It was always busier around here during the days leading up to Halloween.

As I went to get the handover from the night nurse, I noticed a police officer standing outside one of the rooms. Something serious must have happened. I turned my head just in time to see Ava stepping out of the room, her shoulders slumped. She looked up, and our eyes met. A ripple of excitement coursed through me, the usual dark pleasure that stirred in the pit of my stomach every time I saw her.

"Hi, Ed," she said, her voice splintery. Her wide nut-brown eyes were red and swollen from crying, and I couldn't help but enjoy her distress. "Are you working over here today?"

I plastered on a sympathetic smile, masking the thrill inside me. "Hi, Ava. Good to see you. Yes, I'm covering this ward, just starting my shift."

Her gaze shifted worriedly toward the room where the police officer stood. I was getting excited; I could tell she was weak and vulnerable, her usually silky brown hair knotted and unkempt. She was wearing an oversize sweater, sleeves pulled up to her elbows, and jeans that looked a couple of sizes too big.

"What brings you here?" I asked, injecting fake concern into my voice. Not waiting for an answer, I asked, "Is it Jenna again?"

I remembered the state she'd been in when she'd been admitted. I had enjoyed undressing her, but she didn't awaken the dark desire within me that the others did, especially Ava. Jenna had a fierceness to her; I'd had to restrain her several times. But recently, something seemed to be chipping away at her. The last time I'd seen her, she'd been a mess, running out of the Moonlit Diner with a horrified expression. I had gotten out of my car and followed her back to the cottage. I'd made sure she saw me that night as she'd sat on the porch steps with Ava. I knew I'd spooked her as intended.

Tears streamed down Ava's cheeks, and she lowered her eyes and wiped them away. "It's Salma—she's in a coma!" she heaved, covering her face with both hands. "She's dying."

Her words winded me like I had been punched in the chest. For a moment, the room tilted, and I clenched my fists, forcing my face to remain neutral as a flood of anger and disbelief roared through me. How could she still be alive? Yes, I had been disturbed when the lamp of the lighthouse had illuminated, but I had made sure she was dead. I knew what death looked like; I had killed three other people already. She'd been limp in my arms. I had watched the life drain from her eyes. I'd felt it.

Clearly, I should have held on to her neck for a few minutes longer.

But all was not lost. I glanced toward the hospital room; she was now on my turf, in *my* care. The stocky officer paced restlessly, cap in hand, clearly bored. A suffocating pressure squeezed my temples as the shadow slithered up next to me, warning me. I looked into his dark face so he could read my thoughts. I would finish her off the first chance I got. *She won't wake up from that coma*, I reassured him.

I looked down at Ava, my voice dripping with false sympathy as I said, "I'm so sorry to hear that." I wrapped my arms around her delicate frame, the scent of lavender shampoo and tears drifting up to my nostrils. She was fragile, so fragile, as her warm body pressed into me. Her breath hitched against my chest as she continued to cry.

"Ed!"

I forced myself to let go, startled as Elisa walked through the ward doors, her long curly hair tangled. She rushed over, her expression a mixture of fear and desperation. "Am I relieved to see you," she exclaimed, her voice rough. "Please, you have to do everything you can for my sister."

The grief on her face was very satisfying—watching her composure crack, the mask of superiority slipping away. She needed me now!

"Yes, of course I will," I said smoothly. I gave her a hug and felt her relax a little, then pulled away and searched her face. "What happened? Why is she here?"

Elisa's voice shook, her words coming in a rush. "We heard her phone ringing in the maze. Rosalie found her unconscious, just lying there. She'd been attacked. We don't know who did it." She paused, exhaling loudly, trying her best not to cry. "They're saying her brain was starved of oxygen, and…they're not sure if she's going to make it."

I beckoned the night nurse. "I'm about to take over for the day, and I'll see if there's anything I can expedite for you." I took the clipboard and scanned the notes.

The night nurse rubbed her eyes, yawning, and turned to Elisa. "Miss, you know the rules—one visitor at a time."

Elisa rolled her eyes and placed her hands on her hips, but before she could say anything, Ava touched her arm, "Els, I'm going anyway. I'll call you later for a swap if Roman can't make it. Call me if you need anything."

With a final glance at Salma's door, Ava walked out, her footsteps tapping faintly down the sterile hallway. I watched her leave, feeling hard down below, unable to contain my restless energy. I excused myself from Elisa and promised the night nurse I'd be back in a minute.

I hurried into the men's bathroom, locking the door behind me, desperate to find release from my throbbing ache. I closed my eyes and let the image of Ava naked while I twisted a rope tighter and tighter around her neck flood my mind. The image pushed me over the edge, and my body jerked as the dark pleasure spewed out into the toilet. I exhaled, satisfied. I waited a few minutes, composing myself, then flushed the toilet and rushed back to check in on Salma.

I pushed open the door and entered the sterile room where she lay. The fluorescent light overhead flickered faintly. The soft hum of machines beside her bed and the rhythmic beep of the heart monitor was maddening, a reminder she was still alive, if only barely. Tubes snaked from her slack mouth, and my fingers twitched by my sides, itching to pull them out and stop her breathing.

I leaned over her motionless form, and my lips curled into a slow smile as I examined her bruised neck, remembering how she'd squirmed and struggled beneath me last night before slipping into unconsciousness. A sharp pang of twisted satisfaction rippled through me.

But this wasn't over. I clenched my fists, the dark force pulsing within me. Between the girls swapping shifts and the police shuffling in and out, I would find a way to finish what I'd started. This time, there would be no mistakes. Salma would not be waking up.

TWENTY NINE

The icy fog wrapped around me as I stepped out of the cottage, weaving its tendrils through the dark trees as I headed toward the harbor. The cold air bit at my cheeks, so I buttoned my jacket and pulled the hood up over my head. Visibility was awful—just a blur of gray mist. I could barely even make out the faint red glow of the Moonlit Diner's neon sign cutting through the gloom just ahead. It was the only place open this early.

Coffee. I needed coffee.

The harbor was eerily quiet, save for the crunch of my boots on the frost-slicked pavement. My thoughts churned like a tornado, raw and chaotic, circling endlessly around Salma. She was in a coma, and the possibility of losing her ached deep in my chest. My legs felt weak at the thought. I should've acted sooner. I prayed it wasn't too late.

The Bewitched Cauldron would open in a few hours, and I could retrieve *The Witch's Black Book* of spells I'd found there. One of them would let me call back Salma's soul, as long as she hadn't passed over yet.

But that wasn't all I needed. I had to learn to summon the dead to fight the shadow I'd seen in my visions, the malevolent force that haunted my dreams. The serial killer terrorizing our town wasn't just one man, one murderer. It was a presence, a force. And it had chosen my sister as its next victim.

There were only two days until October thirty first. That was all the time I had. Two days to save her.

The bell above the door jingled softly as I stepped into the diner's warmth. The smell of stale coffee and sizzling grease hit me, comforting in its own way. A heater hummed in the corner, and I slid into a booth near it, shrugging off my coat and flexing my frozen fingers. The large clock on the wall read six a.m. A handful of early risers sat scattered around the tables—an old man sipping tea, a truck driver flipping through a paper and a fisherman eating eggs on toast. Perfect, not too busy. I needed time to think and plan without too much noise.

I rubbed my tired eyes. I hadn't been able to sleep, as was the norm these days.

I took the book Elisa had bought me out of my bag and unwrapped the fabric I'd used to protect it. *The Untold Secrets of the Salem Witch Trials*. This book wasn't just a relic—it was a weapon. Its brittle pages had already come alive on numerous occasions, revealing hidden truths. A dark shadow had manipulated the judges during the trials, forcing them to condemn innocent witches. That same shadow now haunted my visions and dreams, an ancient, hungry force I couldn't defeat alone.

The violent man who had put Salma in a coma was tied to the shadow, a pawn in its game. It was the same man who had killed those other girls. I knew it as surely as I knew my own name.

I gripped my mug tightly. Summoning the witches who had been unjustly killed during the trials was my only chance.

It was also dangerous and reckless; I feared some other dark entity could come through, and who knew what the witches would expect in return. But there was no other way. They were the only ones who might know how to stop the shadow. They, too, had been plagued by it right up until their untimely deaths.

I flipped to the same page I had read many times, the one with the margin note describing the shadows, just as the bell above the door jingled. I looked up, startled.

My stomach dropped. It was Troy.

What was he doing here? I didn't have the energy to deal with him right now. I quickly rewrapped the book and placed it back in my bag.

He spotted me instantly, his expression unreadable as he walked over to my booth and slid into the seat across from me. His jaw was tight, and his bright blue eyes scanned my face like he was trying to make sense of what he was seeing.

"Didn't think I'd find you here," he finally said. "Especially after you ran out of this place like you'd seen a ghost."

I forced myself to meet his gaze. "Didn't expect to see you here either." I took a sip of my coffee, trying to keep my voice steady. "Are you following me?"

Troy shook his head, exhaling softly and running his hands through his hair. "No, I was out for my morning run. This is the only place open, so I thought I'd grab a coffee."

My mouth twitched into a small, involuntary smile. I'd missed him, even if I wouldn't admit it.

"I heard about Salma," he said after a moment. "I can't believe it. I'm worried about you, Jen."

I looked away, avoiding his eyes. The waitress set a black coffee in front of him, but I stayed silent, turning my mug in slow, aimless circles.

His hand came down on my cup, stilling the motion. "Look at me, will you?"

I kept my gaze fixed on the mug.

"Jenna, please," he said, his voice softer now. "You're upsetting me. I'm trying my best to reconnect with you." He sighed, and when he spoke again, anguish edged his words. "My feelings for you haven't gone away."

His hand brushed against mine, and I didn't pull away. The warmth of his touch was reassuring in a way I hadn't realized I needed. For a moment, I let myself lean into it. I swallowed hard. My fingers tightened around the mug as I tried desperately to keep my emotions under control. If I spoke even a single word, I knew I might start crying, and I couldn't afford to fall apart here yet again.

He sighed again and pulled his hand back. The air between us felt awkward as he lifted the mug to his lips. "Where are you headed after this?" he asked, and I finally looked up. His eyes were full of concern he added, "I can walk you."

I flinched. How could I explain that I was on my way to learn to summon the dead? That I was trying to stop a nightmare that had begun the moment I had the vision of my sister's death. He could never know I was meddling with black magic.

"Jenna," Troy said again, leaning forward, his brow furrowed. "What's really going on?"

I met his gaze. Unable to hide it in any longer, I blurted out, "Troy, I see things." I took a deep breath and added, "Before they happen, I mean."

He blinked, confused. "What do you mean?"

"My sister…" My voice caught. I swallowed, forcing myself to go on, even though I felt uncomfortable. "She's next on the killer's list."

Troy's face paled, and his mouth opened slightly, searching for words. "I believe in the supernatural, but how can you be sure? Do you know who it is?"

"My visions always come true," I said, sharper this time. "The problem is, I can't see who it is. Not yet, anyway. But I'm going to find out."

I drained the last of my coffee, signaling for a refill. The tension between Troy and me was palpable, thick as the fog outside.

Troy leaned forward, determined. "You and I can watch your sister together—catch him before he gets anywhere near her."

I held up my hands, cutting him off. "Stop. When are you going to accept that there's no 'you and I,' Troy? You and I ended the night of the vigil. I don't need you; I'm doing this alone."

Hurt flashed in his eyes, and for a moment I thought he might argue. Instead, he pulled a ten-dollar bill from his joggers, placed it under his empty cup, and stood. Without another word or even a glance at me, he walked out, the bell jingling softly in his wake.

I stared after him, my heart breaking as an unexpected gush of emotion surged through me, catching in my throat. I leaned back in my chair and clutched my coffee mug in both hands, its warmth barely steadying my unraveling nerves. I closed my eyes tight, took a deep breath, and held it for several long seconds, forcing back the sting of tears. I hadn't thought I had any tears left in me after crying over Salma for hours on end.

I don't need him, I reminded myself. Letting him back into my heart would only reopen wounds that hadn't fully healed. I couldn't do that to myself, not with everything at stake.

The clock struck eight as I stepped into the Bewitched Cauldron. It was nice and warm inside. The ambient light spilled across the shelves, and the scent of incense encircled around me, thick and cloying, settling into my senses. Delicate music played softly, layering the air with a strange mystical energy.

I paused in the doorway, shivering, but it wasn't from the cold. It felt as if spirits inside the shop were watching me, waiting for me. Crystal balls glinted faintly on their stands, their surfaces catching the light of the flickering candles.

"Hello again," a smooth, melodic voice called out.

I turned sharply. The lady I'd met last time stepped out from behind the counter, moving with deliberate, almost feline grace. Her catlike blue eyes shimmered in the dim light, framed by perfect sweeps of makeup. Her long silver hair cascaded over her shoulders, and the soft clink of her jewelry punctuated her every movement. "I knew you'd come today. That's why I opened the shop an hour early." Her tone was airy but laced with curiosity, like a question left dangling.

I barely managed to whisper, "Hello," the word sticking in my throat.

She tilted her head slightly as she studied me. "So, have you discovered what kind of witch you are?"

Her question felt intrusive, sharp and probing. I averted my gaze, unwilling to let her pry too much. "I don't have time for that," I muttered, my voice low. "I need a spell to recall a soul. And one to summon the dead."

Her lips parted in a small gasp, and she stared at me. "Oh. I wasn't expecting that." Her voice was quieter now, her curiosity piqued. "So…a black witch?"

I shook my head impatiently, my impatience rising. "Look, I don't care what kind of witch I am—black, green, yellow. None of it matters. I just need the spells."

She stepped back, her brow furrowing. "Are you in trouble?"

I avoided her gaze, staring down at the floor as tension coiled in my chest.

"If you've never worked with black magic before," she continued carefully, "summoning the dead could be dangerous. It might have…unintended consequences."

"Listen," I snapped, my voice cutting through the air, sharper than I intended, "I don't care about the risks. I don't care about the consequences. Are you going to help me, or should I find someone else who will?"

The lady didn't flinch. Instead, she met my glare with a steady gaze, unshaken. Slowly, a faint smile curved her lips. "You're headstrong," she said, nodding. "And powerful. I can feel it. You'll handle the consequences, whatever they may be." Then her tone softened, as though she was extending an olive branch. "My name is Cassandra. Cass, if you like."

"Fine," I said curtly, brushing off the introduction.

"You must be related to Rosalie," she added, tilting her head thoughtfully. "We were close once, a long time ago."

I stiffened, overcome by curiosity, but I didn't respond. I didn't have time for stories. Cassandra seemed to understand my silence and sighed, gesturing for me to follow her.

"Come to the back," she said. "The books you're looking for aren't out here. I keep the occult and black magic tomes hidden, unless someone like you asks for them."

She led me down a narrow hallway that forced us to walk single file. At the end, she drew back a thick curtain, revealing what appeared to be a solid wall. With a swift, practiced motion, she slid it aside, revealing a hidden room.

Rows of shelves greeted me, stacked high with forbidden books. Their spines gleamed faintly in the faint light, each one radiating power and danger. To me, they looked like treasure.

A rush of energy swirled around me as I stepped inside, scanning the shelves. I reached out instinctively, touching one book after another. *Picatrix. Black Witchcraft and Shams al-Ma'arif. Dark Rituals. The Book of Forbidden Magic.* Each spine seemed to hum with potential. Some of the tomes were ancient, their pages yellow.

And then, as my fingers brushed over *The Book of the Dead*, I froze.

A faint whisper cut through the silence: *"Book of the Dead… Book of the Dead…"*

It was unmistakably Julie's voice. I flinched. Slowly, I turned to Cass. "Did you hear something?"

"No," she replied calmly, "I didn't hear anything." She sounded completely unbothered.

I shook my head, trying to brush off the unease, but the whisper persisted, growing louder. *"Book of the Dead…"*

A strange pull coursed through me, as I reached for the book.

Cassandra stepped closer, sensing my uncertainty. "Would you like some advice?"

"What kind of advice?" I asked warily.

"You'll need to perform the ritual under the full moon," she said, her voice soft but firm. "Only then will the spell work at full strength."

I exhaled, frustrated but resigned. "The thirty first of October—is that a full moon?"

Cass smiled knowingly. "Yes, it is. Halloween…Interesting." Her tone grew darker, more serious. "It is a powerful time for what you intend to do. You should know that there will be strong spirits out that night. Dark, evil ones. You'll need protection."

I could handle spirits, I thought bitterly. It was the living I was afraid of.

The realization came too late: I'd spoken the words aloud. Cass leaned closer, her blue eyes searching mine. "What was that?"

"Nothing," I said quickly, looking away. "I mean, I'll do whatever it takes. What do you recommend?"

She nodded thoughtfully. "The simplest protection is a salt circle, but you must wear a talisman, too. Something with protective energy."

I raised an eyebrow. "Do you have one that'll work?"

"Of course," she said. "They're out front. I can show you."

I followed her back to the shop front, *The Book of the Dead* heavy in my hands. In a glass display case, talismans and amulets sparkled faintly. The prices were steep, and I hesitated. But Cass's voice broke through my thoughts. "I know they're expensive, but they work. And with what you're planning to do, especially around Halloween, I wouldn't risk going without one or two."

I nodded, reluctantly picking out a silver amulet adorned with stars and cryptic sigils, along with an obsidian talisman etched with scriptural writing.

"Excellent choices," Cassandra said, her smile warm. "I'd have chosen those exact ones for you myself."

"I just went with what felt right," I murmured, my voice distant.

She raised an eyebrow, impressed. "Start wearing them now," she said as she rang me up. "And keep the book stored somewhere safe."

I nodded, clutching the items close. "Thank you for helping me."

She smiled, her expression softening. "I didn't charge you for the amulet. It's on me."

"I appreciate your generosity," I said quietly. "I'm sorry if I was a bit off when I first came in."

"No offense taken, dear," she said with a wave of her hand. "If you need anything, come back. There's nothing I haven't seen or done myself."

"My name is Jenna." I smiled.

Cass nodded. "Lovely to meet you, Jenna."

I turned to pull open the door but stopped in my tracks. Troy was casually crossing the street. He hadn't noticed me yet. Panicking, I ducked behind a poster advertising 20 percent off psychic readings for Halloween.

Cass's voice floated from behind me. "Is he your boyfriend?" she asked, a knowing edge to her tone. "You don't want him to see you here in case he figures out that you're a witch?"

"No, that's not the reason," I lied, glancing at her. "He's not my boyfriend."

She studied me for a moment, then shrugged. "You shouldn't hide your abilities. If he loves you, he'll understand."

"I—I need to go," I stammered, feeling the walls start to close in.

This time, I didn't hesitate. I sprinted out of the shop and didn't stop until I was safely home, my knuckles white from gripping the book.

Now came the hard part: getting Rosalie to help me. But she was away again, not returning until the thirty-first. Until then, I would delve into *The Book of the Dead.*

THIRTY

Rosalie

"Rosalie. Rosalie!" Jenna's panicked voice tore through the serene stillness I had cocooned myself in. Her desperation was a jagged blade, slicing through the thick protective wards around my sanctuary.

I opened my eyes slowly, letting the quiet haze of meditation slip away as I brought my focus back to the present, I checked the time, seven p.m. The room around me—the underground suite beneath the house—pulsed faintly with the ancestral energy that had been woven into its walls before I'd inherited the guesthouse from my mother. I had painted it a cream color to radiate warmth, as there were no windows to let in natural light, and placed several salt lamps in every corner. I'd also drawn intricate protection symbols on the ceiling in black ink, which guarded the room against unwanted energy.

There was a thick green rug on the floor, which matched the sofa nestled against the wall. Next to it was a tall bookshelf crammed with tomes, faded scrolls, and aged journals my ancestors had left behind, the spines worn and cracked from years of study. On the top shelf was a scrying mirror, its black surface faintly reflecting the salt lamps. I had used it many times to sharpen my visions. On the large wooden table lay my decks of tarot cards, their edges softened from use. Surrounding them were ancient ornaments: figurines, crystals, and talismans infused with the power of the Varlett bloodline, passed down through countless generations.

The suite was off-limits to guests for good reason. Here, the veil between worlds was thin, whispers and visions from the other side clearer and louder. The old magics resonated here, and I could draw upon the strength of my ancestors to sharpen my focus and fortify my spells. It was my refuge, a place where I was undisturbed.

I had shown Jenna my sanctuary once, and she knew not to disturb me.

Until now.

Jenna's footsteps thundered down the narrow staircase, and I stiffened as the oak doors burst open, the wards flickering faintly under the force of her unchecked urgency. She didn't wait for permission—she never did. But our connection through our visions before we'd met had given me a soft spot for her. Her fiery defiance mirrored the stubbornness I'd once had before grief wore me down. The girls turning up here that evening in August had been a blessing. Their energy had stirred feelings I hadn't dared to feel in decades. For so long, I'd been alone.

I rose from my chair slowly to meet her gaze. Her face was pale, her breathing shallow, and she shivered as though the fear streaming through her veins was too much for her body to contain. This was understandable, given what had happened to Salma. The sight of Jenna so raw and desperate tugged at something deep inside me.

I had no doubt who—or rather, what—had attacked Salma. He was the killer; of that, I was certain. He—or it—could not breach these walls. No harm would come to us here. Not directly, at least. But harm was his nature, and harm he would do.

The threads of destiny were tangled, twisted by some dark force that shrouded the killer's identity. I had tried everything: drawn on every ounce of my power, consulted every grimoire on my bookshelf, begged for guidance from spirits older than time itself. But it was no use. Whoever—whatever—was behind this wore a mask I couldn't pierce.

"Jenna," I said, keeping my voice calm, "What happened?"

She didn't answer immediately. Instead, she crossed the room, clutching a book in her unsteady hands. She slammed it onto my oak worktable with a sharp smack. "You're finally back! You have to help me call Salma's soul back," she said, her voice quavering. "She hasn't crossed over yet. There's still time, and she can tell us who did this to her."

I joined her at the table. My gaze drifted to the book, which she had flipped open—its pages were dense with glyphs and forbidden incantations. I didn't need to touch it to feel its power; the aura radiating from the text was palpable. My fingers hovered over it as I murmured, "Hmm. Powerful stuff." Then my brow arched slightly as I recognized it: *The Book of the Dead*.

Jenna's eyes were wide and pleading, her panic barely held in check. I inhaled deeply, steadying myself. I wanted to take her pain away, to shield her, but I had my limits. Carefully, I closed the grimoire and stepped back.

"I can't interfere," I said softly, almost to myself.

Jenna blinked, uncomprehending. "What? No!" She stepped closer, her voice rising. "You have to help me!" She was on the edge of hysteria, and her lips moved soundlessly for a moment as if she were searching for a more convincing argument.

I raised my hand to stop her. "Fate has to play out, Jenna. You know that."

Her eyes brimmed with indignation, her expression twisting into something sharp and defiant. She didn't understand—how could she?

Jenna crossed her arms tightly, her jaw clenched with defiance. "Then give me the Ouija board," she demanded. "I'll do this myself." Her voice cracked slightly at the end, but she stood firm, unyielding.

From the far corner of the room came a whisper. *Help her. Hand over the Ouija board.*

I sucked in a shallow breath. It was Aurelia.

I turned slightly, searching for the source of her voice. The shadows were still, yet I could feel her presence, as gentle and ephemeral as a sigh of wind.

I exhaled deeply, my emotions burdened by the depth of memories. The last time I had used the Ouija board, I had seen Aurelia's death foretold, a tragedy I'd been powerless to stop. And now here stood Jenna, shuddering with the same desperation I had once felt.

I considered the gravity of the situation. I couldn't deny that I, too, needed answers. The tea leaves had shown me something dark, something I couldn't yet make sense of. Perhaps this was the way forward.

"Fine," I said at last, meeting Jenna's fiery eyes. "I'll use the Ouija board with you. But we will do this my way."

Relief broke across her face, and she stepped forward, gripping my hands tightly. "Thank you, thank you," she said, her voice filled with gratitude. Before I could pull away, she hugged me fiercely and kissed my cheek.

I gently pulled away and crossed the room to the portrait of our revered ancestor, the woman who had started it all: Orenda Varlett, my great-great-grandmother. She'd been a healer, a midwife, and to some, a miracle-worker. Right here in this very house, she'd helped countless women through childbirth, their labors painless and swift, almost otherworldly.

But Orenda was known for more than her midwifery. Her skill with herbal medicines had been unmatched, and she'd crafted remedies that could mend wounds and cure illnesses. Some had even said she could heal broken hearts. People had traveled from far and wide to seek her help, but not everyone had welcomed her gifts. Whispers had spread through the town—accusations of black magic, dark rituals, and powers no one could explain. While some had continued to go to her in desperation, others had kept their distance, their fear outweighing their need.

Carefully, I moved the painting aside, revealing the hidden safe behind it. My fingers danced over the keypad, and the lock clicked faintly as it gave way. From within, I withdrew the Ouija board.

Carrying it to the center of the room, I gestured for Jenna to sit at the worktable. When I lit a few extra candles, the air shifted immediately. I moved the board gently in front of us. The candles flames leaned toward it as though drawn to its energy. Something was already waiting to speak to us.

"This isn't a game, Jenna," I said, my voice firm. I held her gaze, letting the seriousness of my words settle between us. "We're opening a door. Be ready for what might walk through it and what it might reveal."

Jenna nodded, tucking a loose strand of hair behind her ear.

"Place your fingers on the planchette," I instructed, "And close your eyes."

I inhaled deeply, grounding myself in the energy of the room before beginning: "Spirits of light and wisdom, we invite you to join us. We seek your guidance and truth. Only those with kind hearts and pure intentions may cross this threshold. Protect us as we open this door."

A sudden gush of energy swirled around the Ouija board, spiking a shot of adrenaline coursed through my veins. The air around us charged with an unseen force that pressed against us, thick and tangible. Jenna and I opened our eyes at the same moment, just as the planchette began to move.

"Welcome, spirit," I said softly, keeping my voice calm despite the intensity crackling around us. "Show us your name."

The planchette slid across the board with deliberate slowness, stopping at the letter A. Then it vibrated, hesitating for a moment before jerking erratically, as if uncertain or agitated. It stopped again at A.

"Why is it doing that?" Jenna's voice was tight with stress, her fingers pressing harder against the wooden piece.

"Stay calm," I said, then repeating the invitation. "Spirit, show us your name."

The planchette resumed its movement, sliding slowly, deliberately over each letter: A-U-R-E-L-I-A.

We both stared at the board, our breath catching. Excitement surged through me as the name settled between us, fragile and familiar. I glanced at Jenna, her wide eyes meeting mine with silent recognition.

I had heard my sister's whisper many times over the years, faint echoes from the other side, but this—this was different. I could feel her presence beside me, closer and more real than ever. Tears welled in my eyes, spilling over before I could stop them. I'd been twenty years old when she had left, and nothing had been the same since. Aurelia, ten years my senior, had always looked out for me like a mother. Losing her had shattered me. I missed her every single day.

The room seemed to pulse, vibrating with a dense, almost unbearable energy. Jenna and I pulled our fingers away from the planchette, leaning back slightly as the swirling force around the board condensed, coalescing into a flickering, ghostly portal.

Instinctively, I reached for Jenna's hand, gripping it tightly as the vision began to unfold.

Through the shifting energy, we saw her—Aurelia—leaving Salem. She wore a long cloak, the hood pulled low over her face, but there was no hiding the unmistakable swell of her belly. She was seven months pregnant.

Jenna inhaled sharply. "Julie!" she whispered, her voice rickety.

The vision shifted. A row of Victorian terrace houses stood tightly packed in neat rows, a tall bay window at the front of each. Black iron railings lined the narrow front gardens, many overgrown with weeds or scattered with old flower pots.

Jenna's voice broke through the silence, her eyes wide. "That's Romford Road in Stratford. I've seen those houses."

The vision shifted, and now Aurelia was in a dimly lit basement. All alone, she squatted on the cold floor, screaming in agony as she gave birth to a baby girl.

The image changed again. Aurelia, weak and pale with tears running down her cheeks, placed a tiny wailing bundle on the steps of a white church. The baby's cries cut through the night as Aurelia disappeared into the shadows, swallowed by her grief.

"I know that church," Jenna said, her voice barely above a whisper. "I walked past it every day on my way to school." She absently picked at her nails as if trying to anchor herself.

The portal shimmered, its swirling energy growing heavier with sorrow as the vision continued. We saw Aurelia again, her face etched with despair. She sat alone in the same room she'd given birth in, clutching a faded photograph of a man, her tears soaking into her dress.

The truth became painfully clear—Aurelia had died of a broken heart. The image we saw next was her pale, hollow face framed by an assortment of empty pill bottles. The father of her child had abandoned her. His rejection had been brutal, leaving her to carry the weight of her shame and heartbreak alone.

As the vision shifted again, we saw the child she had left behind. A tiny girl, shuffled through foster homes, her wide, innocent eyes growing colder with each rejection. She grew up feeling unwanted, cast aside by a world that should have cared for her. By sixteen, she was on the streets, lost and vulnerable, turning to drugs to numb the pain that consumed her life.

"Mum!" Jenna gasped, her shaky hand reaching toward the portal. Tears streamed down her cheeks as realization dawned, raw and undeniable, and she pressed her hand to her heart. "That's my mum," she whispered, her voice breaking with grief and disbelief.

The portal blurred, and the light dimmed as Aurelia's spirit whispered through the room, her words fractured like static. *You must reach out to Salma… You will have your answers.*

Jenna's tears didn't stop. She stared at the fading image, the pain of generations now crashing down on both of us. We embraced, our tears flowing freely, a bittersweet mix of grief and understanding. Jenna was Aurelia's granddaughter; that was why the visions had connected us. The missing pieces had fallen into place.

I had traveled to England not long after Aurelia's death began haunting my visions. The images were relentless—fragmented and unclear, but enough to push me to uncover the truth. My search had led me to East London Cemetery, where I'd stood beneath a gray, overcast sky, staring at the simple headstone that marked her resting place. Her name was etched into the stone, and beneath it, the dates that confirmed what I had dreaded. I'd had no idea until now that she'd been pregnant. When she had left home, I'd been traveling, consumed by my own pursuits, far removed from the life she had been forced to bear alone.

All this time, Aurelia had been guiding her granddaughter, leading her back here—to me.

"I'm your great-aunt," I whispered, my voice raspy with emotion. I held Jenna tighter, the warmth of having family near—a family I thought I had lost—beginning to heal the wounds of the past. For the first time in decades, I wasn't alone.

I pulled away and wiped Jenna's tears from her eyes. "We need to save Ava." I said. Jenna nodded, lost for words. "We'll start by guiding Salma's soul back into her body. Then we'll call upon our ancestors using *The Book of the Dead*."

Jenna shot up, grabbing *The Book of the Dead* and flipping to the right page with precise efficiency. "Let's do this, Auntie Rosalie."

I smiled, wiping a last tear from my cheek. I closed the Ouija board carefully, locking it back in the safe, then turned to watch Jenna as she prepared the table. She lit small candles at each point of a star representing spirit, earth, air, water, and fire. There was power within her—unrefined, untapped, but undeniable. One day, she would do remarkable things, healing others. But she wasn't yet ready for this kind magic. Still, we had no choice but to take the risk and do it anyway.

"I'm ready," Jenna said, her voice steady despite what we were about to do.

We joined hands. Together, we recited:

"By the light of the moon and the fire of the flame,

in the shadows where souls lie,

Athur'rah! Alathor's veen, awaken!

Sithara, cast thy chains of night!

Rha'karn tu, rennoth ee'sha, rise from the depths!

Salma Aslan! Thoth'ra ethalon nahr'veth!"

"Salma, come back to us, please," Jenna wept, her voice breaking as she clutched my hand tighter.

As the incantation ended, we sat in silence, the minutes stretching out endlessly. Then, a whisper, faint yet clear, drifted into our ears, echoing as though it were coming from the depths of a distant tunnel. The voice grew stronger, more recognizable—it was Salma.

We held our breath, waiting and watching, until the faintest hint of a familiar figure began to form beside us—a wavering ghostly apparition of Salma.

"Jenna, I heard you calling me," Salma said, her voice a mere breath. I shivered as she turned to me; I had never called upon a soul that hadn't crossed over yet, and I wasn't sure what to expect. "Rosalie, I don't have much time. I want to come back, but... he's stopping me from returning."

Jenna interrupted desperately. "Who is stopping you, Salma? *Tell me*."

Salma's ghostly gaze turned back to Jenna. Her voice was strained, and it sounded like she was using all her strength to speak. "He's also the killer. You must help me...before he switches off my machines."

My stomach lurched. "Tell us, Salma. Who is the killer?" I asked. "Who is stopping you, my dear?"

Salma's voice grew faint, splintering like static. "Ed...Ed did this to me."

The room fell silent, except the soft crackle of the candles. The color drained from Jenna's face, her eyes wide with shock upon hearing Ed's name. How had neither of us seen it?

"Salma, dear," I managed, forcing my voice to remain calm despite the shiver running down my neck, "We're waiting for you. Your body is here at Salem Hospital. You can come back. Your sister and Ava is with you now."

The apparition twisted, already fading, the faint light dissolved into the air, leaving only silence and the gravity of her disclosure.

Jenna and I stared at each other, trying to process what we had learned. Then, at the same moment, we both said it aloud:

"We need to call the hospital!"

THIRTY ONE

The phone slipped in my sweaty grip as I dialed the hospital. The line rang endlessly, but there was no answer. Frustrated, I tried Elisa, then Ava, and finally Roman. None of them picked up. My chest felt like it was caving in. I needed to go there right away.

I slipped the amulet and talisman around my neck for protection, tucking them beneath my shirt. I grabbed a small folding knife from the kitchen drawer, slid it into the back pocket of my jeans, and turned to Rosalie. "I can't get hold of anyone. We need to go. Now."

Rosalie was on the phone to Maisie, asking her to cover the desk remotely. She didn't hesitate, following me out to her car. I placed my rucksack in the back seat. As she started the engine, I called Officer Luca.

"Slow down, Jenna," he said, his tone infuriatingly calm. "I can't just storm into the hospital without a warrant or probable cause. I know you think it's Ed, but if you're wrong, it could undermine the case."

"*You have to trust me on this!*" I screamed into the phone, my desperation spilling over. I didn't trust the police to solve this, not after they'd mistaken Orion for the Salem Slayer. His alibis were airtight for the night of Megan's death, and he'd only been charged with stealing our money.

"Look, we are on our way to arrest another suspect." Officer Luca said. I couldn't believe what I was hearing. "This suspect was dating Melinda, and we have some evidence that puts him with her the night she died."

"You have it all wrong! Why won't you listen to me?" My grip tightened on the phone.

"I can meet you later and update you on the inv—"

"I don't have time," I snapped, cutting him off. I hung up, unwilling to waste another second.

My thoughts spun wildly. *Ava is safe*, I reassured myself. I had warned her not to go anywhere alone. Today was the day of my vision—October thirty first, *Halloween*. Today was the day Ava was supposed to die at Gallows Woods. But she was safe—at the hospital by Salma's bedside, with a police officer guarding their door.

But I couldn't shake my unease, which grew heavier with every passing second. Rosalie's knuckles were white as she gripped the wheel, weaving through traffic. The town center was alive with Halloween festivities; costumed partygoers paraded through the streets, and ghost tours crowded the sidewalks. Every road closure felt like another nail in the coffin, another minute stolen from us.

"We don't have time to summon any spirits," I muttered, thinking of our ancestors. "We'll have to handle this ourselves. I'll have to confront Ed directly."

Rosalie stayed silent, her gaze fixed on the road, her expression unreadable. As I watched her, a flare of love and gratitude swelled in my chest. The revelation from the Ouija board had blown my mind—Aurelia was my grandmother, Rosalie my great-aunt. It all made sense now: the whispers, the visions, the unexplainable bond I'd felt with Rosalie the moment we'd met. It wasn't just chance that I was here; it was something far deeper, rooted in blood and history.

I needed to tell my mum everything. She deserved to know where she came from, the truth about her past. Once this was over—once Ava was safe—I'd find the words to explain the legacy she was a part of.

Finally, Roman answered when I called. "Hey, Jen, you okay?"

"*No*, I'm not okay!" My voice came out sharp, my panic bubbling over.

"What's up?" Roman sounded concerned now. "Is it Salma?"

"Ed," I blurted, but he spoke over me before I could explain.

"I'm on my way to the hospital to relieve Ava. I think Elisa is wiped out, I'll tell her to go home too."

"Ed is the killer, and he is after Ava," I said, louder this time. "You need to get there fast. I can't get through to anyone else, not the hospital or the girls. I'm on my way, too."

"Shit." Roman muttered. His voice was broken by static and the sound of honking horns. "I'm stuck in traffic—it's so busy in town today—but I'll get there as soon as I can." He muttered something under his breath, a string of curses I couldn't quite make out. Then, clear as day, "I swear, I'll kill him myself." And with that, the line went dead.

Before I could make sense of that, my phone lit up with Elisa's name. I answered, gripping it tightly.

"Jen, I just saw your text…" She paused. "Are you sure about Ed?" Her voice shrieked.

"Yes," I said urgently. "Is he there?"

There was a long pause, filled only by Elisa's quick breathing. She cleared her throat, and then words tumbled out of her in a panicked rush. "Er, he…he finished his shift early, and—uh—when I swapped with Ava, he…he offered to drop her home. They left together about five minutes ago. They might even still be in the car park."

A sharp, icy pain pierced my chest. My pulse thundered in my ears. He had her. He had Ava. My worst nightmare was unfolding.

"Elisa, listen to me," I commanded. "Stay with Salma. Keep talking to her. She's trying to come back."

"I…okay," Elisa said, her fear palpable.

"And if Ed comes back," I continued, my tone growing sharper, "do whatever it takes to keep him away from Salma. Tell the police officer he sexually assaulted you or something. Don't let him near her. Got it?"

"I—I got it," she whispered.

"Good. Stay alert, Elisa."

I hung up, my hand shaking as I shoved the phone back into my pocket. The knot in my stomach tightened. Time was slipping away, and Ava was in grave danger.

"Rosalie, take us to Gallows Woods," I said, my voice steady despite the storm brewing inside me. "The top part, where the old headstones are tucked away on the hillside facing the harbor." I had no choice but to summon the dead witches from the trials. Legend says they always return around Halloween. They were my only hope. *'The Untold Secrets of the Salem Witch Trials'* revealed they were wronged by the same shadow that had controlled the judges to condemn them to hang. Maybe I could summon Megan too, she had helped me every step of the way.

"I know exactly where that is," Rosalie replied, determination hardening her tone. She spun the car around sharply despite the blare of horns. "I know a shortcut."

Ten nerve-wracking minutes later, after I had explained what Elisa had told me, the car wound up a dwindling road, and Rosalie parked the vehicle out of sight behind a cluster of dense trees. She turned to me as she killed the engine. "I'll keep a lookout for him," she said, her expression grim. "And if you get stuck with the spell or if it doesn't work, I'll come find you."

I hugged her tightly, overcome with gratitude for her steadfast support. "Thank you for being here," I whispered, clinging to her warmth for just a moment longer before stepping out into the cold.

Thoughts of failing and losing my sister consumed my mind as I walked along the path up the hill alone, twisting through dense fog. But as I neared the top, it got clearer. The air rising from the sea below felt damp and salty. At the very top, a massive oak tree loomed over the hillside, its gnarled branches stretching out like skeletal arms. This was it—the place I had seen in my vision, where Ava would be murdered. I will confront the Slayer here before he can go through with it.

I buttoned my coat tightly against the chill and crouched by the oak tree, placing my rucksack next to me. The harbor spread out below me, the ferry lights dotting the water. In the distance, I could just make out the small, steady beam of our lighthouse. For a moment, I felt a flicker of calm—until a bolt of lightning tore across the sky, momentarily illuminating the woods in stark, blinding white.

I thought I saw movement in the dancing shadows. My breath caught as I squinted, trying to make sense of what I was seeing. Several women in black dresses quivered into view, their shapes indistinct, but then I thought I saw Megan for a second before they all dissolved into mist.

"Keep it together, Jenna," I muttered, clutching the amulet at my chest. The cold metal reassured me, grounding me in the moment.

I had to wait, I needed to time it perfectly, ensuring the spirits of the witches come through when the Slayer brings my sister here. To distract myself, I pulled out my phone, praying for a signal. "Damn it, damn it," I cursed as the screen remained blank. No bars, no connection. "C'mon, please, please," I muttered, lifting the phone above my head, then out to the side, hoping for a miracle. Still nothing. I tried calling Ava, but the call wouldn't go through.

"It's fine. *It will be fine*," I said out loud, as if speaking it into existence would make it true.

Another bolt of lightning split the sky, followed by the deafening crack of thunder, a sound so sharp and violent it that felt like the Earth itself was splitting open.

I took a deep breath, trying to steady my fraying nerves. But deep down, I knew the thunderstorm gathering above me was nothing compared to the darkness that was coming.

The wind howled through the trees as I stood in the clearing in the biting cold, the mist of my breath mixing with the fog that had started to swirl around me. I pulled *The Book of the Dead* from my rucksack and laid it flat on the moss-covered stone before me. I sprinkled a circle of salt around me, the grains visible in the moonlight. It seemed as if it would offer little protection against the unknown.

When I opened the book, illuminating it with the beam of my small torch, a faint scent rose from its ancient pages, smoke and something earthy—decay, perhaps. The atmosphere grew heavier, the temperature dropping as though the woods themselves were recoiling from the book's power. Beneath the extraordinary curling script, pictures sprawled across the parchment—ritual circles, skeletal forms, and shadowy figures with glowing green eyes. In some corners were faint fingerprints, perhaps left behind by others who had dared to use this tome before me.

I knelt on the cold, damp ground and placed a small bundle of herbs before me in the center of the circle: rosemary for remembrance, yew for the dead, and a sprig of wormwood, a powerful bridge to the unseen. With a lighter, I set fire to the herbs and watched the thin spirals of smoke begin to curl up into the air. I then inscribed an ancient sigil into the dirt, carving each line with the deliberate precision of someone who didn't fully understand what they were summoning.

I decided to test it out to see if this would work so I took a deep breath, feeling the smoke twist and swirl before me, settling my mind.

My voice stammered as I read the ancient language, the words felt odd and foreign on my tongue. The space around me grew colder with each syllable, and the woods stilled unnaturally, as if holding their breath.

"Spirits wronged, your voices lost in darkened days: Sarah Good, Elizabeth Howe, and Rebecca Nurse, I call upon you,"

I said, my voice stronger now, projecting through the trees. "Witches silenced by injustice, hear my voice and rise! I summon you to this place—come through the veil!"

I took a deep breath, clutching the talisman around my neck as a chill spread across my skin. My hands shook as I turned the page and continued to chant:

"Salix seraiith, venaatis ka'lin,
Tor'eth sarah, elys'abeth, rebec'ah within,
Come forth, ye spirits, in light unbound,
by truth revealed, let justice resound.
Ka'shem rava, un'eth torai,
in shadows undone, let thee now rise.
To hear and to aid, to speak once more,
across the veil, through time's closed door.
I call upon your wisdom to help me protect my sister.
Together, we will put an end to the shadow."

The ground beneath my feet shuddered, and the wind exploded into a wild gale, whipping my hair into my face. The salt circle scattered as if torn apart by invisible hands.

Then the clearing went still. Deathly still.

I stood up, holding my breath. The woods seemed to lean inward, shadows thickening and shifting between the trees. A prickle ran down my spine as I scanned the darkness with wide eyes. I had been expecting spirits—I'd called for them—but this was something else.

"Jenna…"

The voice was low and guttural, vibrating through the air. It came from everywhere and nowhere at once.

I whipped my head around, my torchlight slicing through the darkness. A shadow emerged, its form shifting unnaturally before settling into something vaguely human. It floated above the ground, its feet never touching the earth. Its body writhed, composed of smoky black tendrils that twisted and curled, as though the figure couldn't fully hold itself together. Its head tilted slightly, its face distorted, but its eyes—lime green and shimmering like molten glass—glowed with an unnatural intensity. They pulsed faintly, unblinking, staring straight into my soul. It was the same shadow I had seen in my visions and in the book Elisa had given me.

"You dare call upon the dead witches?" the shadow snarled, its voice laced with disgust. "If you go further, there will be no turning back. You will open the door, and I will come through."

"I..." my voice faltered. Every instinct screamed at me to back down, to run, to turn away from the darkness curling around me. I hadn't been expecting this; I wasn't equipped for this. But Ava's face burned in my mind, her safety my only goal. I couldn't back down now. I had to save her.

The voice dropped lower still, grew even more menacing, and the shadow stretched out its thin pointed fingers, brushing against my arms like icy needles. "You seek what lies beyond the veil, but the veil does not part without cost. You have drawn me to you, and if you proceed, I will latch on to you. I will consume you."

My heart pounded violently. My knees felt weak, but I forced myself to stay upright. I couldn't control the words that tumbled out of my mouth: "I'm not afraid of you."

The shadow's fingers tightened around my shoulders, creeping toward my throat. I struggled to inhale. My breath coming in short, frantic bursts. My mind screamed at me to run, but instead I closed my eyes and started visualizing a protective white bubble around me as I held on to the talisman around my neck.

And with that, the shadow dissolved, sinking into the earth like oil. The wind roared to life again, the trees creaking and groaning as though crying out in protest.

My lungs ached as I gasped for air. The clearing was empty once more, but the oppressive energy of the shadow lingered, a dark promise hanging in the air. The shadow was on to me, but I had no choice but to continue. If it meant saving my sister, I would sacrifice my own soul.

I closed my eyes and reached for Ava through the bond we shared.

The vision hit me like a bolt of lightening, vivid and undeniable. I could feel the cold glass of the car window against Ava's temple and hear the low rumble of his engine on the road. I could even smell the faint tang of aftershave mingled with sweat. Ava was slumped in the passenger seat, unconscious. The dim glow of passing streetlights shimmered across her face. My stomach tightened as my focus shifted to the driver.

Ed.

His eyes glinted in the dark as he glanced at Ava with a sickening intensity. One hand gripped the steering wheel, steady and controlled, while the other hand hovered just below her waist, the faintest twitch in his finger revealing his lack of self-restraint.

Fear rippled through me as I felt his twisted intentions as silent menace radiated from him. Ava was completely unaware, vulnerable and in danger.

"AVA! WAKE UP!" My voice ripped through the vision, desperate to get through to her.

THIRTY TWO

Ava

AVA! WAKE UP!

Jenna's voice tore through the fog clouding my mind, yanking me back to consciousness. My eyes snapped open, but I closed them again when my head started spinning. Why did I feel like this? Goose bumps prickled down the back of my neck, warning me that danger was near. Where on earth was I? I seemed to be sitting in the passenger seat of a car, the seat belt securing me in place. I re-opened my eyes slowly, I scanned my surroundings and saw Ed sat in the driver's seat, his hands steady on the wheel, his face calm but unreadable.

Then it all came rushing back—he'd offered to give me a lift home after Elisa had taken over from me at the hospital. I remembered walking to his car, but I didn't remember falling asleep. I never fell asleep that easily. Something felt very wrong.

A flash of lightning lit up inside of the car, and suddenly my attention was drawn to something that glinted near the gear shift. My breath faltered as I realized what it was.

Salma's house key. I recognized it instantly—the sparkling silver S key ring I'd given her for her birthday last year. What the hell was it doing here?

Panic churned in my gut as I looked back at Ed, trying to make sense of it all. The look on his face was different from usual, somehow—almost animalistic. His eyes seemed darker and more hollow, and just looking at him flooded my chest with dread.

I glanced out the window—trees passed by on either side of us, one after the other. I didn't recognize the dark empty road stretching ahead of us. My mouth was dry as I swallowed a lump in my throat. I prayed there was an innocent explanation and tried to stay calm, but the question escaped anyway.

"Why do you have Salma's key?" I asked, my shaky voice betraying my fear.

Ed's response was a low, ghastly laugh that sent chills through me. He didn't answer, just looked at me with eyes that were wild and unhinged and possessive in a way that made me feel sick to my stomach, and for the first time, I realized he was dangerous.

My hands felt clammy as I bit my nails. "Where are you taking me?" Tears stung my eyes.

His lips curled into a cruel sneer. He reached out, touching my chest, and I flinched away, my skin crawling, my fight-or-flight instinct kicking in. I moved as far away from him as possible, pressing against the door.

"You can't escape me now, Ava," he hissed. "You have nowhere to run."

"Take me home, please," I begged, pulling my jacket tightly around me as if it could shield me.

Ed ignored me, his dead eyes locked straight ahead. Then, as if that wasn't horrifying enough, he tilted his head toward the back seat and shouted, *"You can have her once I'm done with her!"*

My blood turned to ice. I whipped around, but no one was there. My hands and legs started to shake uncontrollably. Who or what was he talking to?

Clearing my scratchy throat, I forced words out, trembling but steady enough. "Was it you? Did you hurt Salma?"

Ed's head tilted slowly, his cold, dead eyes meeting mine. I held my breath, dreading the answer. Then his mouth twisted into a wicked grin.

"Well done," he sneered, mockery dripping from his tone.

I had to get out of this car. I grabbed the door handle and yanked it, but it wouldn't budge—it was locked. My piercing screams reverberated in the car as I pounded on the window. "HELP! SOMEBODY HELP!" But it was no use. There was no one around.

I turned to Ed and started punching his arm frantically, my fists landing hard. His face darkened, and before I could react, his hand shot out, punching me in the side of the head. Pain exploded through my skull as I slammed into the window, thousands of stars bursting in my vision. Warm, sticky blood trickled down my forehead, and I pressed my shaking hand to the cut.

A few minutes later, the car jolted to a stop behind a cluster of trees just off the road. My heart sank. We were in the middle of nowhere, surrounded by darkness. No one could hear me or help me here; I was doomed. My palms started to sweat as Ed turned to me, his hand grazing my chin. I bit down on it as hard as I could, and he yanked his hand back with a curse, his rage boiling over. "You little bitch!"

Before he could strike again, headlights flooded the car. Ed cursed under his breath. "The hell is going on here?" he growled before shouting toward the empty back seat, "*I'll handle it, and you will have her before midnight, like I said!*"

Someone yanked Ed's door open from outside. "Get out of the car, you asshole!" shouted Roman's furious voice.

Jenna's voice resounded in my mind: *Be strong, sis. Get ready to run.*

Relief surged through me as Roman grabbed Ed by the front of his shirt and dragged him out of the car. I slid across the driver's seat, and Roman took my fumbling hands and pulled me out of the car. My legs buckled beneath me, and I doubled over, paralyzed with fear.

"*Run*, Ava!" Roman shouted.

I managed to take a few steps away from the car, then looked back at Roman. He had his back turned to Ed and didn't have time to react as Ed grabbed a metal pole from the back seat and swung it with brutal force, striking Roman across the back of his head. The sickening crack echoed through the air, sending a shiver through my chest.

"*Roman!*" I screamed, dropping to my knees as I watched him collapse to the ground, his face pale and still. "Noooooo! Roman, get up! ROMAN!"

My feet wouldn't move as terror took hold of me. Then Jenna's voice cut through the chaos in my mind. *Run up the hill, sis. Aim for the large oak tree. Go!*

I hesitated for a moment, torn between escaping and helping Roman, who was lying motionless before me. There was no way I could leave him like this. I cradled his limp head in my trembling arms. The wet warmth of his blood seeped through my fingers, slick and sticky, sending a fresh wave of panic through me. My breaths came in short, rapid gasps. "God, no. No. No. Roman, talk to me, say something," I begged, my voice cracking.

When I looked up, Ed was gone.

I reached into my pocket, frantically searching for my phone, but it wasn't there. My stomach twisted—he must have taken it. I shrugged off my jacket, placing it carefully under Roman's head. Then, shivering, I pulled off my small cardigan. I rolled it up and wrapped it tightly around Roman's head, using the sleeves to knot it in place. Blood immediately seeped through the makeshift bandage. Hot tears flooded down my cheeks, dripping onto Roman's pale face as I clung to him. "Please, Roman, I need you to wake up," I whispered through sobs, my heart aching. I leaned in and kissed his cheek, my lips quivering against his cold skin. "Open your eyes, Roman. Please."

A sudden noise jolted me—a car boot slamming shut. My head snapped up, and my body froze. Ed took a slow step forward, a noose dangling from his hand, his eyes locked on me with a hunger that chilled me to the bone. I screamed, scrambling backward on my hands, my palms scraping against the ground. Ed took another step forward, his gaze never leaving me.

Jenna's voice rang through my mind again, sharp and urgent. *Sis, I'm waiting for you. If you don't run now, he will kill you.*

Adrenaline surged through me. My body reacted before my mind could catch up. I shot to my feet and bolted toward the woods, my vision blurred with tears for Roman. The dark trees loomed ahead, shrouded in fog and shadow, but I didn't care. I had to get away. Thunder cracked, splitting the night. I ran uphill, as Jenna's voice had told me to, branches tearing at my arms, scratching my face and pulling at my hair.

My god, it was so dark, and the fog was getting thicker. Brittle twigs snapped under my feet as I ran, every step harder than the last. Lightning illuminated my path in brief flashes, and I made the mistake of glancing back. Ed was there, barreling toward me, the rope still clutched in his hands as he shouted after me, his words slurred with anger. "YOU CAN'T RUN FROM ME, AVA!"

My breath came in sharp bursts, the air burning my lungs. Fear coursed through me, spiking with every sound. Another deafening crack of thunder shattered the sky, and I let out the loudest scream of my life, pain slicing through my throat as if my vocal cords had exploded. *I'm going to die*, I thought. My legs threatened to give out from exhaustion.

The woods stretched endlessly before me, an impenetrable maze of darkness. I wasn't sure where I was going—I just needed to keep running. My chest burned as I pushed myself harder, faster. Jenna was here. I could feel her. The pounding of Ed's feet behind me was relentless, his powerful strides closing the distance between us with terrifying certainty. Warm blood continued to ooze down into my eye as I ran.

Keep going straight ahead, Jenna's voice whispered in my mind. *You can do this. See the big oak tree? I'm there.*

A flash of lightning illuminated a clearing, and there it was—the massive oak tree standing sentinel at the top of the hill. Relief surged through me, giving me the strength to push forward.

"Jenna! Jenna!" I screamed as I stumbled breathlessly into the clearing.

"Ava!" Jenna's voice cut through the storm, sharp and commanding. She stepped out from behind the oak tree, her eyes glowing with an unnatural green light. I collapsed into her outstretched arms, terrified, and clung to her like a lifeline. Though the storm raged around us, for a fleeting moment, her embrace felt safe. But we weren't out of danger yet.

Jenna pulled back, her hands gripping my shoulders. "Ava, listen to me. You need to run downhill on this side, past those headstones. Rosalie is there, waiting for you in her car." Through gritted teeth, she commanded, "Get out of here. *Now!*"

"I can't leave you with that monster!" I screamed, shaking my head as tears streamed down my face.

"Yes, you can, and you will." Her voice broke, but her grip on me tightened. "Please, just go. I'll handle him. *Go!*"

Before I could argue, a hand grabbed my hair, yanking me backward. "You're not going anywhere," Ed snarled, dragging me to the ground.

Jenna screamed, her voice piercing through the storm. "GET OFF MY SISTER."

A flash of silver caught my eye as she lunged at him fiercely, a knife gleaming in her hand. She plunged the blade into his chest, and Ed staggered back, growling in pain.

But he didn't fall. He ripped the knife from his flesh as though it was nothing, his sinister grin widening. He clenched his fist and swung, catching Jenna in the mouth with a brutal punch and knocking her to the ground.

My heart roared in my ears as I scrambled to my feet, adrenaline rushing through my body. I couldn't let him hurt her.

In one swift movement, Ed wrapped the rope around Jenna's neck from behind, pulling it tight with a feral snarl. Her face twisted in pain as she clawed at the rope, gasping for air. Ed pulled tighter, baring his teeth like a wild bear, choking her.

Without thinking, I jumped onto his back, digging my sharp nails into his eyes like daggers. His roar was primal, a sound of pure rage. He released the rope and threw me off, sending me crashing to the ground. My body erupted in pain, and I twisted and screamed out in agony.

In a strained and desperate voice, Jenna began to chant. Her eyes were closed like she was in a trance, her hands stretched out to the sky. Some of the words slipping out of her mouth were foreign, an ancient language I couldn't understand, but they carried a power that made the wind swirl fiercely.

"Tor'eth Sarah, Elys'abeth, Rebec'ah, et Megan,
come forth ye spirits, in light unbound.
By truth revealed, let justice resound.
Ka'shem rava, un'eth torai,
in shadows undone, let thee now rise.
To hear and to aid, to speak once more,
across the veil, through time's closed door."

The ground beneath us shuddered as a chilling wind tore through the clearing. My breath caught; right before my eyes, four glowing apparitions emerged from the fog, their black dresses rippling as if caught in an invisible current. Their faces were solemn yet unyielding, their eyes burning with purpose. They floated past Jenna toward Ed. One of them was Megan, her face illuminated by a soft, otherworldly glow.

"Megan…" Ed's voice wavered for the first time, his bravado crumbling. He stumbled backward, pointing at her with a shaking hand. "No…no, it can't be. I killed you!"

The apparitions didn't answer. They joined hands, forming a circle around Ed, their glow intensifying until it bathed the clearing in ethereal light.

I watched, mesmerized, and then Rosalie was suddenly there, pulled me into an embrace. Jenna reached for my hand and Rosalie's and drew us into the circle. The energy was overwhelming, coursing through me like a wildfire. The heavens opened, and rain poured down in sheets, soaking us to the bone, but I barely noticed.

Megan broke the circle, floating toward Ed with terrifying grace. She pressed her ghostly hand against his chest, and his screams reverberated through the woods as he clutched his chest. "Help me!" Ed doubled over, dropping to the wet earth on his knees. I couldn't explain how I was able to see what was going on inside his body, but I watched as Megan's hand wrapped around his heart. Her grip tightened until it exploded into a thousand pieces, and with one final earsplitting cry, Ed crumpled to the ground. Suddenly, a shadow with green eyes peeled away from his body, swirling around Jenna as it hissed, *"I'll be back for you."* Jenna watched in horror as the shadow spiraled upward and vanished into the stormy sky.

Ed lay still, his arms limp by his sides. His lifeless eyes stared up at the night sky, rainwater filling them and spilling down the sides of his face like tears.

I stared at him in stunned silence. "He's…dead," I mumbled, the words barely audible over the pounding rain.

Jenna collapsed to her knees with relief and exhaustion, her sobs mixing with the sound of the storm. "Megan…thank you," she whispered, her voice shaking. "Thank you for helping me." Then she turned to the other three ghostly figures. "Sarah Good, Elizabeth Howe, Rebecca Nurse—I'm so sorry you were wronged and that no one saved you, but thank you for saving my sister and me."

Had I just heard Jenna say the names of the witches from the memorial, the ones who'd been executed?

The apparitions turned to her, their solemn expressions softening. One by one, they began to fade, their glow retreating into the fog. Megan lingered for a moment longer, her gaze fixed on me. She nodded once, then disappeared into the shadows of the woods. Their departure left the air empty and still, the rain washing away the chaos.

I stared at the spot where she'd stood. "She's gone," I whispered.

Rosalie pulled me into her arms, her embrace warm despite the rain. Jenna rose shakily to her feet, a cut on her lip bleeding but her eyes steady. Rosalie held an arm out to her, too, and the three of us stood there, drenched and freezing, clinging to each other in stunned silence. The shock of everything that had just happened pressed down on us. My breath stalled as it finally dawned on me—Jenna wasn't just my sister. She was also a witch.

"Sis…" I whispered, my teeth chattering. "How…how did you do that?"

Jenna's eyes met mine, dark with exhaustion. "Ancient spell books," she said simply. "It worked. It really worked. It's over." Her voice was tinged with disbelief, and she sounded as if she was trying to convince herself more than me.

A voice rang out through the clearing, desperate and familiar—a voice I thought I might never hear again. "Ava! Ava, are you all right?"

"Roman!" I turned, my heart leaping as he stumbled toward us, clutching his head. Breaking away from my sister and Rosalie, I ran to him, splashing through muddy puddles. I threw my arms around his neck, clinging to him as though he might vanish. Tears streamed down my face. He squeezed me to him just as tightly. "You're alive," I sobbed. Thank god you're alive! How… how did you find me?"

He released me, wiping the blood and rainwater from my brow and looked deep into my eyes. He still had my cardigan wrapped around his head, now completely soaked through.

"When I got off the phone with Jenna, I started driving like a maniac, weaving through side streets, desperate to escape the traffic," Roman said, his voice tight with emotion. "Then I saw it—Ed's car. I almost missed it, but the personalized plates…I knew it was him. I stayed back with my lights off, keeping my distance so he wouldn't notice. But when he pulled off onto that dirt track, I knew I had to act." He swallowed hard, his gaze dropping to meet mine. "I pulled in behind him and turned on my high beams. I thought it might throw him off, buy some time…" His voice cracked, and he trailed off, shaking his head.

Tears streamed freely down my face as I threw my arms around his neck again, holding him as tightly as I could. His heartbeat thudded against my chest, fast and strong, steadying me in a way nothing else could. He pulled me closer, and I buried my face in his shoulder, inhaling the faint, familiar scent of his aquatic cologne mixed with rain. In that moment, it hit me how much I loved him. Even if I couldn't be with him, I loved him with everything in me.

"Roman," I whispered, my voice laced with gratitude, "I owe you my life."

He squeezed me, his voice soft but fierce. "You don't owe me anything, Ava."

Jenna approached, limping slightly, her lip swollen and bleeding. She slipped her arm around Roman and leaned into him briefly. "Roman, what you did…" Her voice choked, thick with emotion. "That was incredible. Thank you."

He looked at her, his expression unreadable for a moment before his lips curled into the faintest smile. "I didn't do much. I mean, he knocked me out almost immediately."

Rosalie joined us, rain dripping from her hair. She reached out, pulling Roman into a warm, lingering hug. "I've watched you grow into such a good man," she said softly, her voice teeming with pride. "I've always seen you as family, Roman. Thank you for everything."

For a long moment, we stood there in the rain, the four of us huddled together beneath the oak tree. The storm raged around us, but the nightmare felt far away now, its shadow lifting as we held on to each other. We were drenched, battered, and bruised, but alive.

Together.

THIRTY THREE

Christmas lights twinkled outside shop windows, casting a warm glow on the bustling streets. Children ran through the snow, building snowmen and hurling snowballs at each other, their laughter echoing in the crisp winter air. Christmas trees stood proudly, adorned with glittering ornaments and delicate tinsel, filling the town with magic as Salma and I wandered through the snow, shopping for all things sparkly—glittery makeup, shimmering tops, and dazzling accessories to celebrate the new millennium.

I couldn't help marvel at how much had changed. Last year at this time, I'd been dreading the future, the prospect of being married to a stranger. And yet this had turned out to be a year filled with revelations about my family and myself. I had discovered my true heritage, my place in the Varlett bloodline. Julie—or rather, Aurelia—was my grandmother, her spirit a guiding light that had led me to this place. Through her, I'd begun to understand who I was: a variety witch. I also understood and accepted my mother's choices, including why she couldn't leave my father. I had even made a fragile peace with my father's actions, though I wasn't yet ready to confront him. That time would come.

Rosalie was my anchor, her love and kindness felt like a protective shield. She had opened her home and her heart to me without hesitation, and in her presence, I'd found a sense of belonging I hadn't known I was missing. Fate hadn't just brought me here—it had tethered me to this place, to her, with purpose.

For the first time in weeks, I felt steady. Ready. Whatever lay ahead, I knew I could face it.

Even the shadow's parting words didn't rattle me anymore. "I'll be back for you," it had hissed, revenge dripping from its voice as Ed clutched his chest and collapsed into death's cold grip. My amulets stayed with me always, constant reminders of the shadow. I felt its presence sometimes. Late at night, when the house was silent and sleep just out of reach, I'd sense it—a flicker of movement at the end of the bed. Molten green eyes glowing in the darkness, watching. Waiting.

The first time it had happened, fear had paralyzed me. My breath had caught in my throat as I'd stared at those unblinking eyes, shimmering with malice. But as soon as I had acknowledged it, the shadow had vanished, melting into the darkness like smoke dissipating into the air.

It was still there, lurking at the edges of my world. But not even its presence could strip away what I'd gained here: freedom, purpose, and the resolve to fight back when I needed to. I chose to live fully, embracing the present and the promise of brighter days ahead.

Without Megan, I never would have found the strength to defeat Ed or the shadow. Looking back, her funeral in Oregon was a day loaded with emotion. But as she was laid to rest, a sense of peace settled over me, and I felt her soul finally pass on. We stayed a few extra days after, accepting Mary's invitation for dinner as she took us through Megan's childhood home, showing us her room and sharing stories from her past. On our last day, Elisa insisted we visit Cannon Beach—Megan's favorite place and the filming location of *The Goonies*. It was a chilly day, but we promised to return in the summer, once we'd saved up a bit more, with plans to explore Seattle too.

After our shopping spree, Salma and I ducked into Strega's to meet Elisa and Ava, the warm glow of the café, the air scented with coffee and cinnamon. Ava and Elisa stood behind the counter, dressed in matching Christmas outfits—Santa earrings swinging and tiny Christmas tree clips sparkling in their hair. They were dancing to "Rockin' Around the Christmas Tree," their laughter infectious.

When "Last Christmas" by Wham! followed, even some of the elderly customers joined in, swaying and clapping along. The whole café felt warm and magical, alive with the spirit of the season. Thanks to Ava and Elisa, the place was busier than ever, buzzing with joy and energy.

When the afternoon rush of Christmas shoppers finally died down, they shut the café early and sat with us. As Ava brushed a strand of hair from her forehead, I caught a glimpse of her scar, a stark reminder of how close I'd come to losing her. It still haunted me.

Elisa, always the spark of the group, leaned in, her red glitter eye shadow catching the light as she gushed, "Officer Luca is taking me out for a drink after work!" Her excitement was contagious, and I couldn't help but smile. They'd make a sweet couple.

As Elisa talked, my attention shifted to Ava. She was smiling, nodding along and asking questions, but I knew her well enough to notice the slight tightness in her expression. Salma and Roman were still seeing each other, and I knew it stung Ava, even if she never said it out loud. But she was trying to be supportive, trying to move on.

Salma leaned forward, her eyes sparkling with excitement. "All right, so how are we ringing in the new millennium?"

The giddy energy at the table was catching. "New York City," I said, unable to keep the grin off my face. "I booked the hotel and flights weeks ago, I wanted to surprise you all. We'll stay in Times Square so we can count down to midnight in the heart of it all."

"Times Square?" Ava repeated, her eyebrows lifting. "You know it's going to be chaos, right?"

"Exactly," I said, laughing. "That's the fun of it! Picture it—ice skating under the Rockefeller Center Christmas tree, shopping at Bloomingdale's on Fifth Avenue, taking photos on the Brooklyn Bridge with the city skyline behind us, and—"

"—visiting the Twin Towers." Elisa finished, her voice saturated with awe. "That's going to be incredible."

"It's going to be unforgettable," I said, my excitement bubbling over. I could so clearly imagine us bundled up in scarves and gloves, skating on the ice, sipping hot chocolate, snapping photos, watching the world come alive around us.

Elisa clapped her hands together, practically bouncing in her seat. "I can't wait!"

Neither could I. For the first time in what felt like forever, we had something to look forward to, a fresh start. We would step into the new millennium, surrounded by the magic of New York City. And in this moment, surrounded by twinkling lights, holiday music, and the people I loved, I couldn't help but feel grateful. Despite everything, we were still here. Together.

After double checking the itinerary with the girls, confirming times and details, I finished off my second cup of coffee, Sal and Ava decided to head on home.

"Girls, I'll meet you back at the guesthouse," I called over my shoulder, stepping out onto the snow-covered path. The cold bit at my cheeks as I slipped on my gloves and tucked my hands into my pockets for extra warmth.

My fingers brushed against something smooth in my pocket. I pulled out the crystal that Julie—my grandmother's ghost—had given me back in London, and for a moment, its surface felt warm, almost alive. A wave of emotion engulfed me, tightening my throat. The sadness of her death was a weight I couldn't yet bear. And the unanswered questions she'd left behind…I wasn't ready to confront those either. Not the mystery of what had driven her away or the truth about who my grandfather was.

Not yet.

"Sure," Salma said, reaching out with a warm smile, her eyes twinkling. "Give me your bags—I'll take them back with me. Just promise you won't be late for Christmas Eve dinner."

"I promise," I said, handing over the bags. "I'll be there."

"You'd better. Rosalie's been planning this for weeks—you don't want to face her wrath." Ava said with a giggle.

I laughed softly, watching them head off down the snowy path, the colorful shopping bags swinging by their sides.

There was one more thing I needed to do.

The Bluebell Lodge stood opposite the café, its front door adorned with an exquisite Christmas wreath, the pine needles dusted lightly with snow. As I pushed open the door, the bell above it jingled softly. The warmth of the lodge enveloped me, and I stamped my boots on the mat, shaking off the snow.

Approaching the reception desk, I cleared my throat nervously. "Um, could you tell me how to get to the Salem Guesthouse, please?"

Troy glanced up from the computer, his eyes widening. "Hey," he said, standing so quickly his chair scraped against the floor. His eyes locked with mine, and for a moment, the space between us seemed to buzz, charged with the strain of everything we'd left unsaid. His cheeks flushed as he ran a hand through his messy hair, that self-confidence I remembered so well breaking through the tension. "You know," he said, his lips curving into a teasing smile, "We could offer you a much better rate here."

A soft laugh escaped me, and I felt heat creep to my cheeks as I dropped my gaze. I gripped the strap of my bag tightly, my pulse quickening. My boots scuffed lightly against the floor as I shifted anxiously.

"I'm sorry," I said finally, my voice barely above a whisper. I forced myself to look back up at him. "I'm sorry I kept pushing you away."

His expression softened, his teasing smile fading as he studied me. Encouraged by the warmth I saw in his eyes, I tucked a strand of hair behind my ear and pushed forward. "I thought…" My voice faltered, but I swallowed the lump in my throat and finished, "I thought maybe we could start again?"

The silence stretched just long enough for me to wonder if I'd said too much. Then, without a word, Troy stepped around the desk and closed the distance between us. His arms enveloped me, pulling me close, and before I knew it, he was lifting me off the ground.

"Troy!" I gasped, laughing as he spun me in a circle. "You're going to drop me!"

"Never," he murmured, his voice low and steady. "I've got you, and I'm not letting go."

When he set me back down, his hands lingered at my waist, holding me steady as our eyes met. The world seemed to blur and fade; the only thing I could focus on was him. Then, slowly, his lips brushed mine. The kiss was tender, warm, and sweet, like the promise of something new.

When I opened my eyes, I saw the sprig of mistletoe above us, dangling from the doorway, swaying slightly in the draft. My lips curved into a smile, and I couldn't help but laugh softly.

Perfect.

THE END

Printed in Great Britain
by Amazon